Praise for *Anumpa Warrior*

WITHDRAWN

"*Anumpa Warrior* tells the history of the Choctaw Code Talkers in an exciting and new way—through the eyes and emotions of fictional characters we have come to know and love through Sarah Elisabeth Sawyer. As a three-decade collector and student of Code Talker information, I was delighted to see that Sarah has woven accurate details of history into an exciting and memorable book. Her dedication to research is apparent on every page. Thank you, Sarah!"

Judy Allen, Historic Projects Officer
Choctaw Nation of Oklahoma

"A deeply moving book that explores events of several men in WWI who became known as CODE TALKERS. The book takes the reader on a journey of emotions and touches on what is real."

Nuchi Nashoba, President
Choctaw Code Talkers Association

"Well written and very accurate historically. I was captivated by B.B.'s experiences that made him who he was. The human experiences brought the facts to life."

Erin Fehr (Yup'ik), Archivist
University of Arkansas at Little Rock
Sequoyah National Research Center

"Sarah is a truly a gifted storyteller and author and I say *châpeau*, hats off to you! This is such a great story that needed to be told and shared with the world. Her eloquent style and words give it so much life and spirit. Your book left me with a very strong, uplifting message."

Jeffrey Aarnio, former superintendent
American Battle Monuments Commission

"In *Anumpa Warrior*, Sarah Elisabeth Sawyer has produced a fine work, capturing the savagery and waste of the Great War, while making a subtle comparison with the historical sufferings of the Choctaw Nation. Her vivid description of attempts to suppress the use of the Choctaw language mirrors similar moves in my own homeland to outlaw the use of Welsh, the most ancient of all the European dialects. Welsh is today flourishing again, thanks partly to combat on the rugby field, where thousands of voices sing the Welsh national anthem to overawe their opponents. Sarah's narrative describes the seminal moment when the Choctaw Nation also regained pride in their native tongue through combat, but on the bloody battlefields of Northern France."

**Roger Branfill-Cook, Meuse-Argonne,
historian, author, translator and tour guide**

ANUMPA

WARRIOR

CHOCTAW CODE TALKERS OF WORLD WAR I

A Novel

SARAH ELISABETH SAWYER

ANUMPA WARRIOR

RockHaven Publishing
P.O. Box 1103
Canton, Texas 75103

Editors: Lynda Kay Sawyer, Mollie Reeder, Catherine Frappier

Interior Design: Sarah Elisabeth Sawyer

Cover Design: Kirk DouPonce (www.DogEaredDesign.com)

Author Photo by Lynda Kay Sawyer

Title page illustration by Paul King

ISBN-13: 978-0-9910259-5-4
LCCN: 2018910860

To the heroic
Choctaw Code Talkers of WWI
and their descendants

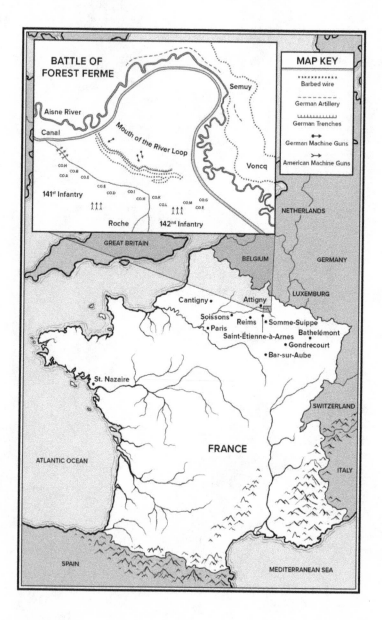

Be strong and of a good courage; be not afraid, neither be thou dismayed: for the Lord thy God is with thee whithersoever thou goest. Joshua 1:9

THE GREAT WAR BEGINS

Western Front, France
November 1914

Matthew Teller ducked as another shell whistled overhead. Listening, he was able to calculate its trajectory: the chortling whistle, a mournful moan of a locomotive, *swish swish* of blowing into an empty bottle. Then a fierce screech, like a wildcat in the Ouachita Mountains, and finally, the earth-shaking boom as the shell exploded in front of the trench where he huddled.

Shrapnel sprayed over him. German soldiers shouted urgent words he couldn't understand. Despite the trench being reinforced with dirt-filled wicker cylinder gabions, corrugated metal, and concrete, casualties added up from that shell.

Tom Alders, camera gripped in one hand, crouched at Matthew's side, observing the chaos and smoking a cigarette he'd plucked from a dead soldier's mouth. The German he swiped it from had slumped low after the previous shell burst and put the cigarette between his lips. Lighting it was the last thing the soldier did in this life.

Alders, who bore honest eyes with a set of crows feet slanted down toward his earlobes and his nose long and narrow, nodded toward stretchers being carried out of the trench.

"That one there is talking to his mother. He says he wished he'd been a good boy and not smacked his little sister that time. The medic is going to leave him alone a few minutes to die." Alders paused, listening to the German language. "Sounds like the French are over the top. They should be—"

Machine gun fire shattered the momentary calm.

Rat-a-tat-tat.

Matthew tucked his writing tablet close to his chest. The paper he held was smudged, hard to tell where the gray-penciled words and the smears of gray chalk from the French soil began and ended. He'd sort it out later.

German soldiers clambered onto the fire step, a second level shelf built on the west side of the trench, and aimed their rifles. Matthew scribbled the time, his position, and the number of men in his sight. The live ones. The dead ones. The dying. Fairly equal amounts.

Matthew had been a war correspondent since the first shots rang out in August. He understood a decent amount of the soldiers' words and phrases, but not enough to save his life if he ended up in the wrong place at the wrong time. When he had decided to get the other side of the war's story—the Central Powers—he partnered with Tom Alders, an American photographer of British parentage who spoke French and German. Despite his intelligence, Alders had no more common sense than Matthew.

After German troops leveled and then occupied neutral Belgium, France and Britain met them at the Marne River to the east of Paris. The countries raced to dig trenches that plowed through French farmland and villages, trying to reach the North Sea first. The result was a stalemate. The Germans dug in on one side, the French and British on the other. Neither side wanted war correspondents on the front lines. Reporters weren't allowed to write anything other than what the military gave them, which wasn't truth.

Alders and Matthew were both fools for going to Belgium and then slipping back across the border into France. They happened upon a German captain so proud of his recent achievements, he welcomed the renegade war correspondent and photographer when they landed in the braggadocio man's concrete bunker.

From the bunker, they slipped through the elaborate German trench system, which included reserve and support, to reach the front line trench. If anyone caught them snooping too much, they'd be shot as spies.

Movement from the rim above caused Matthew to shift to the east side of the trench.

A young soldier's face appeared over the top. He pulled forward with his elbows, dragging his limp comrade. They slid over the sandbags and down corrugated metal to land hard on the wood duckboards. A medic hurried through, checked the unconscious man, and left him to die. He then turned to the rescuer and rolled him onto a stretcher to await transportation to the dressing station.

Matthew knelt next to the stretcher that held the German soldier, who looked so young beneath his bushy but trimmed black mustache. His legs shook violently beneath his field gray trousers. One leg bounced off the stretcher and his feet trembled, blood leaking from the soles where machine gun bullets had torn through, scraping his heels.

"What is your name?" Matthew turned to Alders, whose cigarette was down to a nub. Alders knelt next to the man and translated the question.

"Ernst Gustav Hubschmann."

"Mr. Hubschmann, why did you go out there?"

"To save my fellow soldier. We are proud soldiers."

His legs shook harder. The soldier was on the verge of hysteria.

Matthew tucked his tablet in his inner coat pocket—the

only safe place unless a bullet hit there—and rested a hand on the man's leg as the sound of rapid machine gun fire filled the air. And shells. Always exploding shells.

"Tell me about your family."

"Brothers. A house full of brothers. My girl, she waits for me. We will have many children. We will be happy after the war."

Two stretcher-bearers came and roughed Matthew aside. As they lifted the soldier and took him away, Matthew wondered if Ernst Gustav Hubschmann would live to see his girl again.

The comrade that Hubschmann had dragged back regained consciousness and screamed for his mother. He was half on the fire step, half off. Matthew crouched to stay low as German soldiers raced up and down the trench, shouting.

His back ached like never before. When he was a young reporter roaming Indian Territory in the 1890s, he had never doubted his physical abilities or his purpose. But now, midforties, his body complained and the lines in life blurred.

This war, the fuse lit by the assassinations of Archduke Franz Ferdinand and his wife, was poised to change the whole world. Matthew's world had been turned over a time or two.

When the war broke out, he had shut down his newspaper—the *Choctaw Tribune*—and left the controversies he'd tried to untangle all his life. He crossed an ocean to experience another kind of struggle, hoping this war and the individuals in it would help him understand his own battles among mankind.

Straightening but head still below the top of the trench, Matthew stumbled over bodies in the bloody, knee-deep water toward the fire step. Alders followed and took a photograph of the dying soldier.

Matthew lifted the man fully onto the fire step and leaned over him.

"May I pray for you?" He glanced up at the photographer and waited for him to translate.

Alders' mud-crusted lips turned down. He spit the cigarette stub out. "I stopped praying when my son died."

The wounded man flailed and grabbed onto Matthew's arm. Matthew's gaze was still on Alders. He had not known about the man's son. "I'm sorry for your loss. But you're not praying. You're translating."

"Same thing, Yank."

Alder's British roots ran deep. But being from the South, Matthew resented being called a Yank even though it was the common term for someone from America.

Alders turned away and hopped through the sludge, mud, and human limbs to find an open spot on the fire step to capture the oncoming assault.

The dying soldier's grip on Matthew's arm grew weak. Matthew placed the man's spiked pickelhaube helmet to the side and bowed his head.

There, on that foreign continent among a hostile force that might kill him at any time, Matthew spoke words in his native tongue over the dying man, a prayer his grandmother would have prayed.

Piki vba ish bininili ma
Tvshka ilvppvt chimmi.
Ish ibafoiyoka ho hvshi kanvlli yvt olasi.
Nuktanla chi ka e chim asilhha.
Nana moma ka yakoke e chi yakoke.

Our Father in heaven above
This warrior belongs to you.
You have remained with him until time is near.
We ask for peace upon him.
We thank you for all things.

Amen.

The German soldier did not understand the Choctaw language, but his eyes fluttered and his expression calmed before he died.

Anumpa. Language. There was power in words.

OKLAHOMA

"When I told him of that chamber in the British Museum wherein are preserved household memorials of a race that ceased to be, thousands of years ago, he was very attentive, and it was not hard to see that he had a reference in his mind to the gradual fading away of his own people."

Charles Dickens' conversation with
Chief Peter Pitchlynn

CHAPTER ONE

It started off as a good day. Sun shined through tree branches overhead on the outer edge of the Armstrong Academy grounds. The branches waved at me as I settled in bare tree roots with my friend, Isaac Hotinlubbi.

We were two ordinary nine-year-old boys, dripping wet from having snuck down to Bokchito Creek for a Saturday swim. I normally went home on weekends, but Daddy, a tribal lawyer, was in Washington, D.C. and Mama had too many little ones at home to come and fetch me.

I felt sorry for the other boys, mostly orphans like Isaac, who had to stay at Armstrong Academy all the time, even in the summer and on holidays. I had it good, they told me.

Isaac was one of the skinniest boys at the academy. He was already underfed when he arrived, and he didn't care for the food they dished up. Sometimes the older boys went hunting and shared their meat with us, but Isaac didn't grow much, except in his dark brown eyes. They showed defiance, along with a jaw he'd learned to hold firm when his mouth was washed out with soap for speaking Choctaw. Isaac, a full-blood, was ignorant in ways of the white world and he wanted to keep it that way.

I was pretty little myself, but more like a shadow, always where I was supposed to be, doing what I was supposed to do without creating any funny shapes. My ruddy skin was lighter than Isaac's, but we had the same dark brown hair and eyes. I got an oval face from my mama, and a sharp jawline from my daddy.

Water dripped from Isaac's long bangs that he got away with by keeping them combed back. He kicked my leg.

"Onnakma, anonti kil okshinilla chike." Let's swim again tomorrow.

"Keyu. Aiitvnaha il ia chi." No. We have church tomorrow.

I curled up in the roots, the bark scraping my skin as it tore at my shirtless back. Swimming wore me out.

I'd never snuck off from school before. Isaac had, but he wasn't any smarter than me about not getting caught. We talked awhile, feeling the lazy Saturday and not paying attention to the gliding sun.

A long shadow fell across the lawn like it was a stern finger of God, bouncing and condemning and coming straight for us.

One of the strictest teachers at the academy, Mr. Watson, marched toward where we lounged at the edge of the woods. He looked right at me and I froze. I knew we'd be in trouble for swimming at the creek—shirtless, soaking wet—but what if he heard us speaking Choctaw?

Isaac was oblivious of Mr. Watson coming up behind him. I tried to stammer a warning, but before I could, Mr. Watson loomed over us. We scrambled to our bare feet.

The sun struck the shiny skin of Mr. Watson's receding hairline made worse by his raised eyebrows. I hadn't thought he was tall when he was seated at the front of my first class. Then he stood, and when I left the classroom, my neck ached from looking up at him so long.

Towering over us now, he used his disciplinary voice. "Were you speaking that Indian language?"

I couldn't move. Isaac had no trouble answering.

"*Chahta sia hoke!*"

Mr. Watson took him by the arm and turned to me.

"Were you speaking it, Bertram?"

I couldn't move, thinking of the green hickory stick Principal C.E. Fair wielded "for our own good," and the shame of it being used. They would tell my parents. Everyone in our community would hear I'd caused trouble at school.

I slowly shook my head.

No.

Mr. Watson ordered me to come with him and Isaac. We marched back to the two-story brick building with arches above the balconies and entered the principal's office. Principal C.E. Fair was gone that weekend, leaving Mr. Watson to administer punishments. The only kind of punishment they found Choctaw boys responded to was whippings. But I'd never gotten one at school.

At the academy, it wasn't uncommon for Principal C.E. Fair to whip 15 boys a day, no matter their size or age. He wasn't mean about it; whippings were what we understood in our culture. There were only two kinds of punishments the Choctaw Lighthorsemen had ever given for crimes—you were either whipped or shot.

Mr. Watson took up the dreaded green hickory stick and turned to look down at Isaac. I felt how very, very small we were.

"I am doing this for your own good. You will not survive in the world as an Indian. Do you understand?"

Isaac lifted his chin. "*Chahta sia hoke!*"

Mr. Watson sighed heavily. I started to bolt, but he caught my arm.

"Bertram, you will remain and learn why you must never speak your language. Do you understand?"

I nodded.

Mr. Watson had Isaac bend over, facing me, hands on his

knees. He raised the hickory stick and waited a few moments.

Then the whack came. Hard.

Isaac glared at me. *Strong.*

Another whack.

Bold.

Again.

Fearless.

And again.

Isaac never whimpered, but his head shook with the pain and resistance building inside him. I saw anger in his eyes. It was for me.

Another whack. Big tears rolled down my cheeks. So many whacks! More than students got for sneaking off to the creek, more than being late for class, more than anything. If only Isaac would cry. He needed to cry! Then Mr. Watson would stop.

I cried for both of us. I cried for my ancestors. I cried because I knew I could never, ever, let a white man see me being Choctaw again.

Isaac dropped to his knees, but he looked up at me. "*Holabi. Vlla nukshopa.*"

Liar. Cowardly child.

Then he slumped on the floor, face red and sweating but not one tear escaped.

Mr. Watson stopped, breathing heavy. He set the green hickory stick against the wall and observed Isaac.

"English only."

Isaac whispered, "*Chahta anumpa.*" Soft but clear: *Choctaw language.*

Mr. Watson lifted Isaac from the floor and took him to the hall closet where mops and buckets were kept.

"You must learn, for your own good."

Mr. Watson put Isaac inside the dark, windowless room, closed the door, and turned the key.

Isaac pounded and kicked the door from the other side, yelling in Choctaw and clawing the wood. I cried hard. Mr. Watson turned to me.

"I will forgo punishment for your running off this afternoon, but never do it again."

He bent eye level with me. I could barely see his solemn face through my tears as Isaac screamed from the closet. He was scared of the dark.

Mr. Watson made sure I gave him my full attention before saying, "Never speak that heathen language again. Do you understand?"

I nodded. Never again, not in front of a white man.

For the first time in my life, I wondered if being Choctaw was something to be ashamed of.

◆◆◆

The day after he was whipped, Isaac ran away from Armstrong Academy. They caught him and brought him back. After several more months of whippings and him calling me a liar and a coward every day—in English because he refused to speak to me in Choctaw—Isaac ran away again. They didn't catch him that time.

The only thing I had left of my friendship with Isaac was a drawing he'd given me not long after we met, when we vowed we'd be brothers for life. The drawing was a map of the Ouachita Mountains where he was born, so fine and detailed I thought a grown man had drawn it. He gave me the map, telling me that when we grew up, we'd strike out into those mountains and no civilization would grieve us again.

I never told anyone what happened that bad day that had started off good. Mr. Watson didn't write my parents a letter that I'd caused trouble at school, and they were still proud of me. Their oldest son was going to be a respectable, educated Choctaw who would do worthy work for the tribe like my ancestors before me.

Daddy was a lawyer who continued to fight for tribal sovereignty though it was all but gone. Mama and her brother, my uncle Matthew Teller, had run a newspaper in the old Choctaw Nation, Indian Territory. Now we lived in the state of Oklahoma, and they were helping write a new chapter in history.

I likely wasn't smart enough to be a lawyer. And I didn't like writing much. But I'd have to do something when the time came. I couldn't stay a cowardly, lying nine-year-old forever.

The morning after Isaac ran away for good, I woke up, put on my school uniform, and marched downstairs with dozens of other ruddy-skinned Choctaws. We ate breakfast, then headed for the barn to milk cows.

At 8 a.m. sharp, we lined up on the drill field for thirty minutes of military exercises. Peru Farver was leading us. At twenty, he had almost finished his studies and would graduate next spring.

Peru was good at the drill exercises, and even better at football. I was still too little to play, but I loved watching the older boys make Armstrong proud. That was what I looked forward to most during this, my second year at the boarding school.

"Attention! Forward, march!"

We moved over the grounds in perfect time from the oldest student to the youngest. I stepped proudly, thinking about one thing: at the end of the school year, the academy drilled down to the best student and that student got a $5 gold piece. I was determined to get it one year, my first real medal to join our family's legacy.

Daddy wanted me to keep in mind the history of Armstrong Academy and how it had once served as the capitol of the Choctaw Nation when a community, Chahta Tamaha, had grown up around it. The building had been used for a Confederate hospital during the Civil War.

The academy had been reestablished as a school in the 1880s. The Presbyterian Church ran it for a time, and then the Choctaws supervised it. When the tribe faded into Oklahoma statehood, the federal government continued the school.

We finished the drill exercises. Peru had paid special attention to me once or twice, which was a good sign.

Before afternoon classes, I had work duty all morning. It was between these two parts of the day that I met the newest student at Armstrong.

I recognized Samson Coxwell from church. His family had just moved to the area. Turned out, his folks and mine knew one another from way back, but I didn't talk to him. I hadn't talked much to anyone since Isaac had been whipped and locked in the closet. I wasn't looking for a new friend.

Finishing up chores in the school cornfield, I saw Samson being led off by one of the boys, older than me, toward the cemetery a quarter of a mile west of the main building. I knew what would happen. Same thing had happened to me when I first arrived. I wished Isaac had heeded the lesson the older boys tried to teach us, and wondered if this new boy would be just as stubborn.

Shaped like a dumpling, Samson looked slow, but there were advantages to his size on a football field. He was a head taller than me though we were the same age.

I had finished my chores early so I trotted to the cemetery where a dozen boys had already started the kangaroo court—as Daddy would have called it—with the unsuspecting Samson in the middle. These boys took it on themselves to make sure new students learned the rules in an unforgettable way.

I stayed back and no one paid me any mind as the solemn-faced twelve-year-old "judge" asked Samson where he was from and how old he was. But he stopped when Samson answered in Choctaw.

"Silence!" the judge howled. "That is not allowed here. You are guilty and will face punishment. What is the desire of the committee members?"

"Send him home!"

"Give him a permanent job emptying the slop jars!"

"No! Make him wrestle!"

The last shout won the day.

Samson lived up to his biblical name in size. Still, he didn't outsize a twelve year old. The first match began.

After some tugging and kicking, Samson slung the older boy to the ground. He didn't have time to catch his breath before the next one was on him.

When I'd been caught speaking Choctaw by the other boys, I'd been made to carry slop because I didn't want to get in trouble for fighting. But when the third challenger came at Samson, I knew he was about to be handled. He was tired.

Mama had spoke fondly of Samson's mother, telling me that they used to help each other when one faced trouble. She'd be proud if I stood up for her friend's son.

I pushed my way to the new student's side and waited, fervently hoping the court would adjourn.

Another boy stepped up to face me, making it two on two. I didn't back down.

The boys looked at one another and chuckled. Samson had been accepted, and in a strange way, so had I. The court dispersed and everyone scampered back to their chores.

I headed straight for the showers. We showered twice a week whether we needed it or not, and I didn't want to be tardy for classes that afternoon.

"Hey!"

I ignored the high-pitched call of the new student. I didn't want a friend.

In the shower, I stripped and turned on the faucet. Samson talked to me over the wooden stall door.

"Saw you in church. My mama is old friends with your mama."

I grabbed the bar of lye soap.

"This your second year at school, ain't it? You could teach me the rules and I'll fight anybody that gives you trouble. Deal?"

I scrubbed my scalp.

"Aw, now. Sometimes ya gotta fight. My daddy says good fellers shouldn't start fights, but they should finish them."

I stuck my head under the gushing water, hoping it would plug my ears.

The water was good and hot. Then it was just hot. Boiling hot!

"Yow!"

I jumped and crashed into the stall door, slinging my head to clear water from my eyes and hearing laughter. Samson had turned the faucet all the way to the hot side.

"So you *can* talk!"

Yanking my trousers on, I darted out of the stall to chase Samson across the drill field. He was big and lumbering and easy to catch. I tackled him, or rather, tried to. He carried me a ways then gave in. We hit the dirt together, rolling, and then I was laughing too.

We came up chuckling and best friends.

◆ ◆ ◆

Having Samson at Armstrong Academy and around home in Durant helped me transition through those difficult years of navigating being Indian with my family and being white at boarding school. Samson was good at it. He had no trouble singing Choctaw hymns on Sunday and speaking perfect English to the Armstrong principal on Monday morning.

My folks knew boarding school could be hard, but it was critical for me to learn new skills our people needed in the coming years.

I could have gone to Jones Academy—that was where Mama had wanted me to attend—but Daddy wanted me to go to Armstrong because it was closer to Durant and I could come home on weekends and holidays. I suspected the real reason, though, was because Armstrong had a better football team.

When 1912 rolled around after my fourteenth birthday and Jim Thorpe of the Sac and Fox tribe won gold medals in the pentathlon and decathlon at the Summer Olympics in Stockholm, I was like most boys—in awe of the great Indian athlete. Thorpe was also a football player. Every boy at the academy wanted to be the next champion. I continued to admire Peru Farver, who was an excellent athlete in college. He was appointed superintendent of Armstrong Academy in 1913 at the age of 25.

A year later, I played my first game on the Armstrong team, tasting what it meant to have a real chance to prove I wasn't a coward, to fight with the pride of my ancestors, and show my worth since the miserable failure to stand with Isaac when we'd been caught speaking our language.

I was a good running back. Though I'd never be a champion, I dreamed of playing sports after high school graduation.

And I spent those years between boyhood and manhood trying to figure out what it meant to be Choctaw; what it meant to me. But I never talked about it. Even when my cousin Victoria, who loved me like a little brother, rebelled against her upbringing and took off for the white world at a prim Eastern boarding school, I kept it all inside.

That was about the time other countries in the world went crazy and declared war on one another.

CHAPTER TWO

"Help me, Father, to learn self-discipline and self-control in my studies and my work. Use my fighting spirit, oh, Lord, not for evil or for myself but for my people and all mankind. Help me learn good qualities and have understanding in every task you put before me. In Jesus' blessed name. Amen." —Charles McGilberry, Choctaw student, Mercersburg Academy, Ivy League preparatory school

Grant, Oklahoma
November 1914

Uncle Matthew came out of the house and onto the porch where I sat alone on the steps. Daddy was behind him, carrying a burlap sack. I tried to stop my heels from bouncing up and down, making my legs jittery. They'd think I was just excited. They didn't know the confession I had to make before the blessing ceremony, if I had the courage to make it.

Thanksgiving dinner was long over and evening was coming on, but there was something we still had left to do before the sun set over my great-uncle Preston's lake. Loaded with pine trees, cattle, and circled with love, his ranch was the gathering place for all the family and that Thanksgiving was no different. Except for what was about to happen.

The three of us headed to the woods and down a well-worn path in silence.

When should I speak up? What should I say?

Daddy, there's something you don't know I did seven years ago. I shamed the family, shamed our people. I hurt my friend.

Uncle Matthew, tell me how to have the courage to be Choctaw. What does that even mean for our people now?

Nothing sounded right.

We came to the natural lake, one of the largest in the state, and halted by the shore. My fondest childhood memories came from that lake. And now, a new memory was about to be made.

In traditional ways, it was the mother's brother who bore the duty of training and discipline for her children. My family had continued this way with my uncle teaching me alongside my father. Our family also had a tradition of blessing a boy when the father and uncle deemed him a man.

I had just passed my sixteenth birthday.

Uncle Matthew faced me, his back to the lake where the sun cast soft glows for the mild November evening. My uncle was a distinct mix of the old and new ways of our people, even in how he looked and dressed. At home, time spent in the sun and wearing a work shirt, hair growing a little long over his ears, he looked like any Choctaw farmer who'd grown up on the land and in the woods, hunting with a rabbit stick and telling stories over a pot of *tanchi labona*—hominy mixed with pork roast.

Then there was Matthew Teller, the newspaperman—hair trimmed, suit and tie, polished shoes, and going nose to nose with government officials around the world. Yet Uncle Matthew never failed to be true to himself and what he believed no matter how he dressed or what he did.

He looked tired but strong that day by the lake.

"Bertram Robert Dunn. B.B. You are a fine young man.

You work hard at school, you're respectful to your family, honest and generous. Your good character honors God and your ancestors. I'm proud of you."

I swallowed hard and prepared to confess what I'd done on that good, bad day. But nothing came out.

Daddy opened the burlap sack he carried and withdrew a finely carved rabbit stick. He dropped the sack on the ground and held onto the stick at each end. He didn't have to say he was proud of his oldest son. That was in his eyes and his smile. He held the rabbit stick out to me.

It represented more than an ancient hunting weapon. It was a symbol that I was to carry the old ways of our people into an uncertain future. To take it was to cross a threshold, to accept my role in our family and our tribe, to walk proudly into the future as if I knew where I was going.

I didn't.

But I took the weapon in honor of the men who had helped shape my character. That was the importance of the moment. It wasn't about the long-ago lie that had altered my being.

The rabbit stick balanced perfectly in my hand. I grinned as I swung it to test the weight. Uncle Matthew told how my father had carved it from hickory and then my uncle smoothed it with a piece of broken glass. It wasn't my first rabbit stick, but it was now my most special possession.

Uncle Matthew held up a hand to still me. He was tired, his energy depleted after just arriving home the day before. He'd been in Europe for five months as a war correspondent in the deadly trenches of France. He didn't talk about all he'd seen, but I'd read enough stories from over there to know this great war was like nothing the world had ever seen.

He had come home for the holidays, but the way he greeted me with a hearty handshake and hug when he arrived said he had also come for me.

He looked me in the eyes, and I managed to hold his strong gaze as he said, "*When I was a child, I spake as a child, I understood as a child, I thought as a child: but when I became a man, I put away childish things. For now we see through a glass, darkly; but then face to face: now I know in part; but then shall I know even as also I am known.*"

I gripped the rabbit stick. Did he know the truth? Did he see my fear about the challenges ahead in life while I tried to walk in two worlds?

"B.B., you've always been conscious that everything you did reflected on your family, your people, and your faith," Uncle Matthew said. "You are now building your own reputation as a man. You are responsible for your actions. Keep this in the forefront of your mind and you will live a life based on truth and strength."

I dropped my gaze and stared at the rabbit stick, hoping he wouldn't see the doubt in my eyes.

Daddy stepped to my side and placed a hand on my shoulder. Uncle Matthew gripped my other shoulder as Daddy prayed over me in his quiet way. The lyrical cadence of our language carried me to a peaceful place as he asked *Chihowa*—God—to give me wisdom, a life of blessings and love, and good fruit coming to bear.

And for me to be strong and courageous in facing my future.

CHAPTER THREE

Armstrong Academy, Oklahoma
May 1915

The woods were alive with God's creatures, and I planned to take one of them home for supper. I felt the balance of my rabbit stick in one hand and eased my way through the woods around Bokchito Creek. A whole slew of my Armstrong Academy buddies were hunting that Saturday, but I went further upstream to get game. Though I normally went home on Fridays, we'd planned a special hunt.

The other boys stayed together to show how they could knock a squirrel out of a tree at twenty yards, but I wasn't there to show off. It was the first time I'd taken my special rabbit stick on a hunt. Uncle Matthew had set sail for the war in Europe again last weekend with hundreds of European and American passengers on a commercial British ocean liner, the Lusitania. I didn't know when he'd be home again.

That special day meant as much to him as me. It was good for his soul. He was especially hurt by his daughter, Victoria, leaving our Choctaw ways behind, striking out into a life away from our family to live at a boarding school in the east. He had tried to talk to her many times, but she refused to accept his words. She'd written me long letters about the conflict, encouraging me not to remain trapped in Oklahoma.

Victoria was in Europe now, serving as a volunteer with the Red Cross, but she and Uncle Matthew hadn't tried to see one another. I missed her, though she wrote me regularly. She hadn't come home for Thanksgiving.

The stick felt heavy in my hand as I scouted the creek. I planned to cook the game in a stew and tell a story about my uncle while I shared the pot with my friends.

On the other side of the creek, green ferns twitched. I stilled, holding the club-shaped weapon loosely in one hand. The rabbit was hidden beneath the ferns.

I could sneak closer and take a random shot. But I didn't want to chance losing it. Though striking a rabbit on the run was far more challenging, I was bold and daring when I was by myself.

I bent and picked up a smooth stone with my left hand, then flicked my wrist to send the stone on the other side of the fern.

A gray rabbit streaked out. I tilted and flung the rabbit stick. It arched gracefully in a rapid sideways spin before striking the rabbit in the head, an instant kill.

There would be rabbit stew and a story to honor my uncle tonight.

Back at Armstrong, there was no shortage of stories as we gathered around the woodpile to collect pieces and build an open fire to cook on. The cooks didn't want us messing up the detached kitchen.

But our hunting stories were interrupted by a scream at the door of the main building.

I was trampled on the way. Samson, still my best buddy after seven years and his dumpling shape twice as big, steadied me as we ran into the main building through a side door. Running indoors was not allowed at Armstrong, but even the professors and the superintendent dashed into the hall to find a matron in the doorway, her face blanched as she clenched a handful of telegrams.

Superintendent Peru Farver slowly took the papers from her. The matron's lips moved and words finally emerged in the deathly silence as we waited.

"The Lusitania…Germans…a U-boat sank it. Over a thousand dead…my sister…" She slumped as another matron supported her.

Superintendent Farver's gaze swept over the shocked expressions. The Lusitania wasn't—hadn't been—a warship. It was carrying civilians!

Including Uncle Matthew.

My attention fell to the stack of telegrams. Superintendent Farver thumbed slowly through them and raised his eyes. He offered a creased telegram to me without looking at it. I grabbed it and backed away until I bumped the banister of the stairs.

The telegram was from my mama.

Germans sank Lusitania. Hundreds dead. Received wire from Matt. He is well. Requests prayer.

That moment, Europe's horrible war became my horrible war. American civilians were dead. My uncle could have been killed.

I was just sixteen, but I was ready to enlist right then. Someone had to stop those barbarians.

Americans were ready for war.

CHAPTER FOUR

"When you see only dark clouds, be patient. When all you hear is thunder, do not fear, be patient. The rainbow will soon appear." —*Charles McGilberry*

Newkirk, Oklahoma
October 1916

The truck lurched and the fellows around me groaned. Sweat and mud covered the smelly uniformed players in the wood sidewall truck bed where we sprawled on top of one another, agonizing over our cuts and bruises. Football games were fiercer than ever since the sinking of the Lusitania over a year ago. America hadn't gone to war, so we battled on football fields.

Samson had his leg stretched over my head where I lay at the bottom of the pile. One hundred and fifteen pounds wringing wet with sweat like I was now, I could ride on Samson's shoulders and everyone thought I was still a kid.

The truck hit another pothole as it chugged along the

dark road out of Newkirk, Oklahoma. I stared up at the sky—the inky black, the stars like a blanket of diamonds that belonged to me.

When I was little, Mama told me each star was a miracle waiting to shoot from the sky and explode, showering blessings on mankind. She'd say, "Miracles are plentiful, but they don't always look as we think they will."

When I asked her why there were still so many stars in the sky, she said God kept packaging miracles because we humans needed them.

Samson's leg drifted over my forehead. I shoved it back and heard a shout. But it wasn't from my dozing friend.

The truck made a hard swerve to the left then the right. My teammates sat up, fingers curled into fists as they strained to look through the sidewall panels holding us in the farm truck that belonged to Armstrong Academy. Samson scraped my forehead with the back of his football cleat as he sat up sharply and grabbed one of the panels to steady himself. He peered between the two slats.

We were used to this sort of thing with Oklahoma still a young state and Indian Territory fresh in our people's memory.

The shouts were taunting. Those Newkirk boys were whipped pups that wanted to yip and yap and make out like they were the victors.

"Yellow Indians!"

"Just try and come back here next season."

"This ain't your land no more!"

I squatted beside Samson as the truck slowed and dodged the Newkirk football players, still in muddy crimson uniforms from the game we'd just bested them in, 36-0. Not only were we undefeated with Superintendent Peru Farver as our coach, no team had scored against us yet.

Our coach gassed the truck clear of the antagonizers. We turned in unison to watch the boys throw mud clods at us, so big and brave from where they'd run up from the ditches outside of town to fling their insults.

My fingers curled around a wood panel as the truck turned around sharply on the narrow road. I strained to see the headlights land on the surprised faces of the Newkirk team. They backpedaled and stumbled over one another in their haste to clear the road. Coach Farver slammed on the brakes and we piled out. The fight of the day wasn't over yet.

Samson and I ran together. As it turned out, town was too far away for those boys. We'd seen one of them dive deep into the woods, but he was clumsy in his escape, panicked at being chased by what he thought were wild Indians.

I outpaced Samson, maneuvering the uneven Oklahoma terrain like I was going out for a deep pass. Fifty yards. Over a fallen tree. Thirty yards. Sailing over a shallow ravine. Ten yards.

The player in the crimson uniform looked back one too many times. He stumbled. I hooked him around the waist and slung him for a hard tackle on the edge of a steep ravine.

Samson caught up and landed on top of us. I was sure he cracked half my ribs. The three of us rolled down a carpet of leaves and sticks to land in a shallow creek bed with just enough water to chill our sweaty bodies. The Newkirk player lay at the bottom of the pile, but Samson was crushing my skull with his linebacker frame.

"Get off!"

Samson scrambled up. I stood, my head spinning. The boy we'd captured still cowered in the creek.

I tightened one fist. This was a chance to prove I wasn't a coward. We could beat this boy to a pulp. I could take revenge for what had been done to Isaac, to all our people, to our tribal sovereignty with Statehood.

But two against one didn't take much bravery. Besides, my daddy and uncle taught me there were better ways of changing people's minds other than beating sense into them.

I looked at Samson. He shrugged. We turned and slipped and slid our way up the bank. I glanced back at the boy's moonlit face. I'd never forget his look of sheer amazement.

He'd never call us names again. Not because we'd

whipped him good.
　　But because we didn't.

CHAPTER FIVE

Durant, Oklahoma
March 1917

"Move one hair closer and I'll shoot you stone dead."
I froze.

Samson didn't. He snatched a cookie from the end of the sawhorse picnic table and gave a whoop as he ran away.

Ida Claire Jessop let loose with the slingshot she'd trained on him and missed by a mile. I knew that was because she secretly liked Samson. But it was hard for me to take a gangly fourteen-year-old, freckle-faced, slingshot wielding girl seriously.

I was tempted to snag a cookie before the dessert tables were uncovered, but we were in the churchyard and didn't need to be causing trouble. Besides, Ida Claire was loading her slingshot and eyeing me. I hurried away and found Samson willing to share his cookie where he was hiding behind his folks' wagon.

He slugged me in the shoulder. "You gotta get some gumption, B.B."

Few people called me Bertram anymore, though nicknames weren't allowed at Armstrong. It was so easy for Samson to shift between worlds.

He smirked. "Show some warrior spirit like when we chased down that Newkirk fellow."

That had been five months ago, and the first wild onion dinner of the spring didn't seem a good time to pick a fight with a girl. Especially in the churchyard.

Our buddy from Armstrong Academy, James Edwards, bumped into me from behind, thinking I might shield him while he teased Samson.

"You only stole that because you're sweet on her."

Samson grinned. "Don't cry when you have no one to write you love letters after we join up."

They bantered a few more rounds, but I didn't want to think about the war in Europe and how America might jump in soon. I was eighteen, old enough to enlist. I would do what I had to do for my family and country, especially after the sinking of the Lusitania. Remembering the women and children who had died got my blood boiling and I was ready to fight, but I didn't want to think about it sooner than I had to.

My folks were mostly thinking about college for me. I wasn't ready to decide about that.

The war had been going on for over three years, and the British gave us a hard time about not joining in. They wanted to know, how long could we stay neutral with the atrocities the German troops had committed against the Belgians, French, and Americans? The Central Powers attacked neutral ships and even killed American civilians.

But President Woodrow Wilson held firm. America would remain neutral. He'd been re-elected on that platform.

The war hollered at us every day, and folks around Durant hollered at one another over whether or not America should be in the thick of things.

My uncle hadn't been home since the sinking of the Lusitania to tell us about what happened. But he did write about it, how the Germans had warned Americans not to set sail on the ship. Then he told the story of his personal experience and of the 1,198 passengers and crew, including 128 Americans, who died from drowning and hypothermia even though it had been a sunshiny afternoon in May just off the coast of Ireland.

When I was home a few weeks later, I watched Mama read the story in the Washington Times. She went straight to bed afterward. She and her brother had always been close.

Today, though, I was enjoying church and the wild onion dinner with home folks and my fellow students from Armstrong.

Singing and preaching had started Saturday night, and Sunday afternoon was a wild onion spread, a Choctaw tradition. Onion gatherers began in February, hunting the woods for small-sized onion tops before the bulbs formed. Cleaned and then boiled until tender, with salt pork chunked in for flavor, the onions were served up in scrambled eggs alongside *tanchi labona*, pinto beans, and *walakshi*, grape dumplings. And more desserts. *And* more singing and preaching.

Pastor Turner was a fiery preacher. He preached in two languages, Choctaw and English, overlapping and firing off words like I imagined a machine gun sounded.

Rat-a-tat-tat.

Sometimes I wished he would preach softer, the way Daddy talked about Jesus. Folks said I was growing into a good man like my daddy. My classmates teased me about being too good sometimes.

It took gallons and gallons of onions to feed a crowd this size, but the hard work was always worth it. It brought our people and friends together for stories and singing.

The gathering usually lasted all day, but we needed to leave early for Armstrong. They had strict rules about us being back on Sunday before dinner.

A whole gang from the academy had come to my church that weekend, which didn't happen often. Orphaned, most of the boys went to church in Bokchito which was closer to the academy than Durant. Along with James Edwards, two of my friends, Mitchell Bobb and Solomon Bond Louis had come to my church. "Bond" was his father's name and I suppose keeping it with his own kept them close.

I interrupted James—we called him Jim—and Samson's war talk. I spoke in Choctaw since we were at church. Few other places felt safe to use my native tongue. "Where's Solomon? We need to get going."

"Look for Mary Patterson and you'll find him quick."

Jim was ruddy, handsome, and as the oldest, knew just about everything.

He was right about how to find our buddy. Solomon had been seen a whole lot with Mary Patterson since they met at a football game a few years back. They were both orphans, so I guessed they shared an understanding of things in life I would never experience.

I was happy for Solomon. Mary was a sweet girl who gave flesh to all that was good and beautiful in the old Choctaw Nation without the sorrow and hurt.

We snuck up on them where they sat on the tailgate of a wagon, sharing a piece of pie. Ida Claire Jessop stood there with a full plate of cookies, talking and giggling with Solomon and Mary.

Ida Claire flushed red when Samson, Jim, and I popped up. But she wasn't angry, and the slingshot was nowhere in sight. She offered the cookies to Samson first.

CHAPTER SIX

Bokchito, Oklahoma
April 1917

I wasn't thinking much about the war that spring. But April 6, 1917, I did more thinking than ever before.

Something big was happening, and I got the kind of feeling our ancestors must have had when they were about to become a part of history. Or maybe they didn't realize it. But the way Superintendent Peru Farver loaded us older boys into the truck and drove to Bokchito, four miles southwest of Armstrong, had me wondering if this was a page of history I wanted to get written into.

The Zimmerman telegram had changed everything. Some German official sent a message to Mexico saying that if they attacked the United States, Germany would ally with them. We heard about it through British intelligence, who was certain this would force America into the war at last.

But the Zimmerman telegram was so preposterous, President Wilson sent a memo to Germany, demanding they denounce it before things got out of hand. Except Germany didn't. With the Mexican border crisis and Pancho Villa, that little telegram was all it took to start an uproar, and a special session of the U.S. Congress was called. They'd make an announcement today through all the newspapers, and Superintendent Farver wanted us there for it.

Folks crowded around the newspaper office at Bokchito. The moment built to the point I thought I would bust. Then a hush settled among the crowd of hundreds. The announcement was coming. My scalp tingled.

The newspaper door banged into the quiet and the publisher ran out, shouting and waving a piece of paper.

"President Wilson petitioned Congress for a declaration of war! We are going to war!"

A cheer went up from half the crowd. The other half set about shutting them up. It was war, all right.

Superintendent Farver whistled for us boys and marched away from the fight. But we didn't all go with him. Even though I made a point to stay out of trouble, I couldn't help hanging back with my buddies—Samson, Jim, and Solomon—as we slipped to the outskirts of the brawl to watch.

Samson rubbed his meaty hands together. "I'm joining up right now!"

"Me, too," Jim said. "We'll scare the old Jerry out of their wits with our whoops."

He cupped his lips and gave a couple of short, low bursts to emphasize. We chuckled, except Solomon. He was looking off, that longing in his eyes I'd gotten used to since he met a certain gal at a football game. He had another look too, and I knew he was thinking like I was, about what it meant to be a soldier. Solomon had a problem I didn't, though. I was eighteen; he was still seventeen. But if he didn't join with the others who would head straight to the nearest recruiting station, he'd be left behind.

Solomon, full-blood Choctaw with a round face, high forehead, and sober eyes, looked older than his age. He was bold, confident, and ready to do his duty.

Jim must have seen the look too, because he slapped

Solomon on the back and lowered his voice. "We all go in together, they'll never know."

Jim turned to me. "How about it, B.B.?"

I hesitated. It was a serious decision.

He frowned. "Aren't you ready to fight? We're warriors!"

"Come on, B.B." Samson shook my shoulder. "Let's show everyone we're one hundred percent Americans! Our country needs us."

Jim poked Solomon again. "They'll take us all together, as men."

Not a one of us looked like a man, but I decided not to argue.

The ruckus between the pro-war and pacifist factions settled down and a man jumped onto the bed of a pickup truck. "All those who aren't German-loving, anti-patriots, follow me! We're gonna practice drilling and get ready for war!"

We might have joined them, but Superintendent Farver found us first. He wasn't upset that we had slipped off to watch the ruckus. I think the reason he brought us older boys out was to get us thinking about enlisting.

I didn't imagine being in the army was much different than boarding school. Drill exercises were nothing new to us.

The year before, I had finally earned that $5 gold piece for being the best student in drilling. My folks were proud.

I didn't know what I was supposed to do when I graduated Armstrong Academy that spring. Everyone assumed I would do what was expected of me, and that made me think it must be what the good Lord wanted me to do, but I couldn't bring myself to go to college yet. If I joined up, it would give me time to figure things out. Maybe fighting a battle on foreign soil would help me win my own battles back home. I suspected that was why my uncle went over there.

Truth was, war couldn't have come at a better time.

◆ ◆ ◆

Captain Walter Veach visited Armstrong Academy the

day after the United States Congress declared war on Germany. He had just returned from chasing Pancho Villa down in Mexico and was making a trek through the former Choctaw Nation, recruiting for the massive war effort our country had gotten into.

A mid-thirties Choctaw, Captain Veach was a large man with the shadow of a double chin. He was well-respected, and his opinion highly valued. He talked to ordinary folks in the communities, and business owners, and even went to the Choctaw legislature about the grave task ahead. With people like him promoting the war effort, it wasn't long before most everyone in Choctaw country was full-steam behind it. We were Americans, and the world—especially Germany—would know that soon.

All the boys at Armstrong Academy looked up to Captain Veach. After hearing him, I was anxious to join up.

That same day, I received a letter from Mama. She'd heard the news the day before, too. She didn't say anything directly, which said a lot. No mother wanted to see her son go off to war, and my mama had grown up in violent times. Outlaws had killed her father when she was a teenager.

I'd have to ask for my folk's blessing on becoming a soldier. That would be harder than anything I'd done in my life.

◆◆◆

"You'll have to ask your mama."

Daddy's face was grave, aged by the significance of the moment. I thought wrestling with the decision on my own was tough. Seeing the pain in his expression, I knew I'd never be able to face Mama.

My daddy was proud of me. I saw that. But I also saw years of loss in his eyes, of battling a government that now wanted his son to fight for them.

Then the pain was gone, and I saw pride and love that would carry me across an ocean and back, in body and in spirit, because it was deep, deeper than either of us understood, the kind men don't talk about, but it's there. That kind of love would be there behind Mama's tears and terror.

When I asked for her blessing to enlist alongside my schoolmates from Armstrong, she nodded.

Somehow, I knew Chihowa would give me miracles, all the way to the time I returned home. The love of family and the long-ago prayers of my ancestors would be my miracles.

CHAPTER SEVEN

"It was a foregone conclusion that when America entered the war, she would do most of her fighting by telephone." —Captain A. Lincoln Lavine, Air Service. Formerly of the American Telephone and Telegraph Company

Fort Sill, Oklahoma
April 1918

We went in together, all the older students from Armstrong Academy. Tobias Frazier was the oldest at 24. He was only slightly taller than me, with an oval face that came down to a defined jawline. Dark skinned, his hair was nearly black. His education cycle had gotten interrupted, but he was graduating this year. I was glad he'd come to Armstrong. He was one good football player in any position except quarterback.

I held my breath when seventeen-year-old Solomon went through, but he made it fine.

Outside the recruitment office at Fort Sill where we'd

enlisted, Samson took me by the shoulders from behind and shook me until my teeth rattled. He growled in my ear, "*Tvshka homma!*"

Red warrior.

I winced at the jarring. Why did Samson have to speak in Choctaw? I glanced around, thankful no one stood close enough to hear. But then I realized he wasn't the only one speaking our language.

A commotion started in the line on the office steps. Three of the volunteers there to enlist were shoving one fellow out of the line. An Indian.

He was a gritty young man who glared at the big man shoving him. When the Indian tried to rejoin the line, the man and his two buddies blocked him.

While staring down at the younger man, who seemed vaguely familiar to me, the big man spoke loudly for all to hear.

"You gonna have to quit speaking that devil language if you plan to carry a gun around me, Injun."

The younger man pitched his head back. "*Chahta sia hoke!*"

His words struck me in the heart and I gaped in disbelief. I was hearing a voice from my boyhood, taunting me. The pitch was deeper but still belonged to the same lyrical tone I could pick up on the wind a field away—Isaac Hotinlubbi, full-blood Choctaw who had lived in the Ouachita Mountains. I hadn't seen him since he ran away from Armstrong Academy. Back when we were like brothers. Back before that good, bad day changed everything.

Livid, the big man goading Isaac shoved him again.

"You shut that gibberish right now!"

Isaac shoved back. The big man socked him in the jaw. Hard.

Once, a long time ago, I had lied and then watched Isaac whipped for speaking our language. I did nothing.

I did nothing now.

Then Samson jumped in the fight, drawing me in. Before

I knew it, I was leaping on the big man like a dog on the back of a grizzly bear. It wasn't a clean tackle and he shook me off. Samson took him down. I landed flat out and someone planted a boot in my face.

When the haze cleared, I staggered to my feet. An ugly face with possum ears sticking out both sides got in front of me. A finger poked my nose and a voice cleared up the haze.

"I'll tell you when to fight and when not to fight, Chief, do you understand me? Yes, sir!"

"Yes, sir, yes."

I blinked, trying to focus on the sergeant who stood nose-to-nose with me. He had to bend down a considerable bit. His left eye squinted like he was drawing a bead on a buck, ready to squeeze the trigger. He took aim at me.

"One wrong sneeze and you'll be in the guardhouse, do you hear me? Yes, sir!"

"Sir, um, yes."

His squinted eye darted to one side then back at me, drawing another bead. "You speak that gibberish like him?"

He was referring to Isaac, who stood nearby, face bloody. I slowly shook my head. *No.*

That satisfied the sergeant as he went on to his next victim. Samson.

The troublemakers had slid back in line, leaving me standing with Isaac. I avoided looking at him as I fiddled with a rip in the sleeve of the cotton shirt Mama had made me. She'd be disappointed.

Isaac recognized me immediately. "Why are you here, coward?"

He had refused to speak Choctaw to me since that good, bad day, though he understood more English than he could speak. He knew two words well: *coward* and *liar*.

And it had started off as such a good day.

No one but Isaac knew my most painful secret. And there I was, face-to-face with him, joining up to head to the trenches of France together.

In that moment, I acknowledged I hadn't enlisted for all

the noble reasons my friends had. I hadn't joined up to honor my uncle or even to avoid making a decision about my future. I'd joined to deny my cowardice and lies. But there they stood right in front of me like no time had passed.

Isaac had asked why a coward like me was there. I tried to answer honestly.

"I'm here to go fight the Germans." That sounded like a lie.

The sergeant was through with Samson, so my buddy ambled over, grinning from the excitement of the fight. He looked between Isaac and me. I shrugged.

"We were friends."

Isaac took a step toward me. "Liar."

He walked away. Samson got riled, but I told him to forget it.

He wouldn't let it be. "Who was that yokel?"

"Isaac went to Armstrong before you came."

"*He* was in school?"

"Not long. He ran off after the first year." Why was Isaac joining the army? I didn't ask that out loud.

Samson socked my arm. "Come on. We're supposed to meet Jim, Solomon, and the rest of the fellas in town at the soda fountain to see if there are any pretty girls around."

◆ ◆ ◆

We took our basic training at Fort Sill. Being a soldier wasn't so bad, except my sergeant was the same roughneck who had busted us for fighting the day we joined up. He'd been nicknamed "Sergeant Chill" and I had to be ready to meet his wrath each day.

I avoided Isaac, which wasn't difficult since he avoided me, other than his accusing stare whenever we made eye contact.

He got along as a soldier and cooperated with the white officers. Second Lieutenant Carl Edmonds showed him how to pick up his feet when marching. He would take a few steps and Isaac copied him.

Maybe it was just me Isaac despised.

We knew how to drill and that was the main thing they wanted to teach us there, along with bayonet practice and digging trenches. I sprained my wrist trying to drive a pickaxe into the sunbaked prairie soil. Working together, the digging eventually gave us an idea of what fire, support, and reserve trenches might look like.

There were plenty of Indians around and there was talk of forming an all-Indian company. That was something Commissioner of Indian Affairs Cato Sells didn't want. He insisted we blend in with the white soldiers.

That summer, we were placed in the 1st Oklahoma Infantry. I wrote home to my folks about how we were in the proud Oklahoma unit.

Choctaw girls from Wheelock Academy sewed us an American flag and sent it to Captain Locke with the message:

"To Captain Locke and the men of Company L on behalf of the superintendent and young ladies of Wheelock Academy. It comes to you in heart-felt appreciation of the spontaneous patriotism shown by the representative number of men of the Choctaw tribe, and the splendid manhood represented in the entire organization."

I was in Company H with Captain Veach and the boys from the Durant area. Several Choctaws were in Company L under Captain Ben D. Locke, whose brother, Victor M. Locke, Jr., was the presidential-appointed chief of the Choctaw Nation.

My second cousin, Peter, had been in the National Guard under Captain Locke. The division went all the way back to the Spanish-American war. But when I asked Peter if he was going to France with us, he laughed and said he'd get too seasick crossing the ocean.

In truth, he'd gotten injured in a football game while the men were fighting off boredom during the Mexican border crisis. He said the most entertaining thing on the border was a stomp dance Company L staged at San Benito.

He wasn't planning on ever leaving Oklahoma again, and said I'd best come straight back after the war if I wanted to see him. There was that family love and sadness in his eyes. And fear, too. He knew what fighting was like, though not as much as my uncle Matthew who had seen the Mexican border crisis and the trenches in Europe.

Uncle Matthew once wrote Mama to say that anything he'd seen in his life was nothing more than a brawl compared to the carnage over there.

When he had come home to visit last Christmas, he didn't talk about it much, even though my siblings tried to get him to tell stories. Mama asked about Victoria. My uncle said he hadn't seen her when he was in France, and they didn't talk about it anymore. Not in front of us kids.

Funny, I still thought of myself as a kid sometimes, even with getting ready to head off to war.

But I was a warrior. I would be strong and courageous, like Daddy prayed for. I was willing to fight to protect my family, and die if need be. No one really thought they were going to die, but I told myself to be ready just in case.

At Fort Sill, Captain Veach was close by when he wasn't off recruiting or taking leave to be with his new bride. He'd courted Miss Susie Bennett by letter while on the Mexican border, and they planned to marry the next year. Once the United States declared war on Germany, though, they married quick.

Captain Veach helped organize Company H in the 1st Oklahoma Infantry alongside Company L. We would be sent over to France together after training.

But I had no idea there would be so much more to this training than drilling and digging semblances of trenches. And I had no idea we wouldn't stay in Oklahoma. We were shipped out to Texas far too soon.

It was time to overcome my fears of being Indian in a white world.

CHAPTER EIGHT

Paris, France
July 1917

The French people were going mad.

Matthew Teller watched them sing and dance, overjoyed by the arrival of the First American troops to their shattered world. American and French flags flowed side by side from windows throughout Paris.

Standing in the center of the Hôtel national des Invalides complex, the 16th Infantry Band of the 1st Division in the American Expeditionary Forces, in full uniform with field packs strapped on, stood in place as they played the *Star-Spangled Banner* to salutes by the American and French military. The drums vibrated in Matthew's chest and trumpet blasts made his ears ring, but neither gave him the soaring joy he hoped for.

When the band finished, Matthew tried to focus on the speeches given by leading men like Marshal Ferdinand Foch and King Albert of Belgium as they welcomed the American troops to France. But like the green doughboys, Matthew was more interested in the Paris sights than listening to speeches.

Matthew kept his head up in the affair, absorbing the moment, not bothering with notes. This 4th of July would reside in him the remainder of his life, especially with this being his last story of the war.

He felt as battle worn as the Allies and even the Central Powers. Maybe the end was in sight at last. The French certainly hoped so. He recalled one officer summing up his strategic battle plan for the past few months: *we must wait for the Americans.*

Well, the Americans had arrived. And Matthew had decided that morning he was going home for good.

With the arrival of the Americans, Matthew realized how exhausted he felt. They were so fresh and naive and ready to fight. He was ready to quit. He'd been in the heat of combat for three years, from Europe to the Ottoman Empire, all the while fighting censorship and governments to tell the real story of the war. The madness had to end. The Americans were there to do that, and Matthew just wanted to go home. This grand entry of the troops in Paris on July 4th would be his last war story.

He didn't blame his colleague, photographer Tom Alders, for remaining in the Ottoman Empire when Matthew returned to France. Once it was certain the war wouldn't end in swift victory for the Allies, Alders left, not wanting to witness Europe ripped apart piece by bloody piece.

Matthew had wrestled with his decision to leave France after the news he received in a letter from his sister that his nephew, B.B., had joined up and was in training. B.B. would land in France before too long, and face unimaginable hardships and death. It was much for a young man to endure, especially one with Bertram's sensibility. Matthew should stay in France, be there in case his nephew was wounded, or…

After he read the letter, Matthew went to a little shop in Paris and bought a leather-bound journal. He wrote a letter to B.B., wrapped the journal carefully, and dropped them at the post, wondering all the while if he should board the same ship with the package and let it carry him home. B.B. was a strong young man and would make his family proud without his uncle's presence.

Speeches over at last, the green American doughboys set out to march through the principal streets in Paris. Their line was a bit scraggly and rifles were held crooked on their shoulders, but they were there, fresh and polished.

Back home in Oklahoma, a July morning like this would already have sweat running down Matthew's back, especially in a massive crowd of thousands. But in Paris, the sun wasn't unmerciful and the humidity wasn't choking.

He worked his way along with the crowd as the procession headed north across the sparkling Seine River on the extravagant Pont Alexandre III deck arch bridge. The bridge was wider than any road Matthew had traveled.

Four gilt-bronze statues of *Fames* served as stabilizing counterweights for the turn of the century engineering feat. The bridge offered views of the Les Invalides and the Eiffel Tower in the distance.

Matthew had stood on this bridge the night before, watching the sun set behind the ornate wrought iron marvel and thinking of the good he'd tried to do in his life. He hadn't imagined he'd see marvels like this, and would have the opportunity to write about truth in another part of the world. But what good had he really done the past three years?

The procession moved slowly across the bridge and through the Place de la Concorde, one of the major public squares in Paris, known, among more pleasant things, for its guillotine beheadings of such notables as King Louis XVI and Queen Marie Antoinette during the French Revolution. The Luxor Obelisk, a 3,300-year-old piece of Egyptian history, stood watch over the procession pressing through the square.

The obelisk guarded one end of the Avenue des Champs-Élysées while the Arc de Triomphe guarded the other.

Matthew was touching history with every step he took. He would capture all the elegance and tragedy of France to take back home where life still wouldn't make sense or be fair, but there, the vast majority of mountains, hills, and people remained simple and unchanged. He was unchanged. Witnessing the most horrific war in his lifetime had not given him the purpose nor understanding he had hoped it would.

He paused to take in the ornate gold and green tinted fountains as the doughboys scissored around them. People bumped into Matthew from behind, so he worked his way to the outer edge of the crowd and pulled out his writing tablet.

He wanted to sketch the magnificent stone buildings showcasing Louis XV style architecture with the grand arcades on street level. Classical pediments adorned the roofline, the facades balanced by rows of windows and columns and wide-brimmed campaign hats bouncing by.

Though Matthew had time to sketch, he didn't have the spirit. He put away his tablet and made the turn to follow the parade onto Rue de Rivoli, the Napoleon Bonaparte-built street lined on both sides with uniformed, arcade facades that extended for almost a mile with statues and the most fashionable shops. The parade was only beginning. The doughboys had a five-mile march ahead.

Matthew outpaced their speed to get closer to the front again, but it wasn't easy with the enthusiastic crowd. The decorated mounted police on stunning black horses had managed to keep the crowd at bay.

But at the end of Rue de Rivoli, the French people broke through and split the American columns into small groups. Women rushed to walk arm in arm with the soldiers, pressing flowers on them. It looked like a moving flower garden.

Among the friendly chaos as the 1st Division tried to get back to marching, Matthew was drawn to a tight ring of French citizens who had encircled one of the soldiers. There was something different about him.

Moving closer, Matthew picked up excited chatter. Surrounded by centuries of history, war, and foreign cultures, home visited his heart. This tall doughboy was an American Indian.

That could be a story worth writing.

The soldier—with his olive drab uniform, tan campaign hat, wearing a field pack, and at a towering six-foot stature—stood still as people circled him and pointed at his head. The man had a soft smile as he humbly allowed the people to poke at him.

Matthew stepped into the circle. "They want to touch your hair."

The soldier looked down at Matthew, surprised, but he never lost his smile. Removing his wide-brimmed campaign hat, he knelt on the cobblestone street and cocked his head to a little French girl, who squealed in delight.

She lightly fingered the smooth black strands of hair on the first real American Indian she'd met. Her mother reached out to touch his hair, too, opening up the moment for the others to give it a stroke.

The Indian took it calmly, waiting until they were done. Satisfied, the people politely went on their way. When the doughboy rose, he looked at Matthew.

Matthew didn't know what tribe the Indian was, but by his features, he likely was of the Five Civilized Tribes in Oklahoma. He took a chance.

"*Halito, chim achukma?*"

The soldier raised his eyebrows while his smile turned to a grin. "*Vm achukma hoke! Chishnato?*"

"*Vm achukma akinli.*"

The soldier switched to English. "Never imagined I'd hear my language so far from home. It can get you accused of being a spy, you know."

He chuckled and Matthew knew there was a good story he'd have to ask about someday. They shook hands, the doughboy's grip firm and sure.

"I'm Private Otis Leader from Gerty, Oklahoma."

"Matthew Teller, of late from Ireland, Britain, Germany, France, and the Ottoman Empire."

Leader gave a low whistle. "You must be full of all kinds of languages then. You don't happen to speak Chickasaw, do you?"

Whenever in the world he went, people assumed Matthew was half of whatever they were. He'd been addressed in many languages.

"Chikashshanompolili." I speak Chickasaw.

There was something special about this American Indian, the first Matthew had seen in a U.S. Army uniform. Easygoing, Leader didn't command the space he occupied but once people were in his presence, they naturally respected him. There was a softness to his eyes, a maturity.

He looked to be in his mid-thirties, older than most of the fresh, fiery faces of the American soldiers, and he had life experience, but it hadn't beaten him down. Matthew judged he was the kind of man who took life in stride, not in a hurry yet ready to help a friend if called on. He had a family man look about him, too.

"Are you Chickasaw or Choctaw?" Matthew asked.

"Both. Registered on the Dawes as Choctaw on my mother's side. I'm Chickasaw through my father. Never thought I'd meet an Indian already over here, much less one that shared my tribal blood."

He cocked his head, looking as innocently curious as the little girl who'd touched his hair. "You are Choctaw?"

Matthew understood the uncertainty, even from one of his own. Years away from the love and culture of his people, dressed in a French manufactured suit and tie, hair trimmed and styled for the big day, the man reflected in Matthew's mirror that morning had looked astonishingly European. One thing would never change, though—the lyrical sound of speaking in his native language. It anchored him in who he was.

"Chahta sia hoke."

Leader smiled, though this time with a tinge of sadness, the kind Matthew recognized. They both missed home, missed their people, missed a place where speaking their language wasn't foreign.

The moment passed and the men continued to talk about the French people until the parade started moving again.

Leader didn't object when Matthew pulled out his tablet and asked questions, something as second nature to him as breathing.

Leader also had a touch of Scotch and Irish in him, and proved a captivating storyteller in English as well as Choctaw, which he flowed in and out of as they navigated the crowded street.

He told stories of knowing former president Theodore Roosevelt's sons, Major Theodore Roosevelt, Jr. and Lieutenant Archie Roosevelt, both serving in the 1st Division. Leader chronicled crossing the Atlantic while the threat of U-boats still ran high. Matthew didn't interrupt with his own tale of just how dangerous those waters could be.

When the 1st Division had landed, the French town bewildered Leader with its old stone buildings—some with straw roofs—but he was delighted by the warm, welcoming French people. They were fascinated with seeing a real American Indian, one so far removed from the stereotypes in photos, paintings, and films.

In Paris on July 3rd, the 1st Division could hardly get the barrack's gate closed for the crowd wanting to welcome the doughboys.

The soldiers were allowed to go out in rotations to tour the city. Leader's rotation was in the afternoon. He loaded onto a truck with his buddy, Joe, to view sights in Paris but it went entirely too quickly. He and Joe were taken back to the barracks and penned up like cattle for the evening.

That didn't sit well with them, so they tried to bribe every officer they could for permission to go out. No one yielded. There was no way to sneak through the double steel gate with its guards.

Finally, they used an old wagon to crawl over the 18-foot barrack wall. Dropping down the other side, Joe twisted his ankle and Leader stove up his hips to his shoulders. They took off through the city, flat broke, to see the Eiffel Tower and Napoleon's Tomb, and were well fed by the French people. Lots of bread and pastries.

Matthew chuckled at their antics as he made notes.

"You seem to be walking fine now. Good thing, what with…" He didn't finish. He didn't want to think of what lay ahead for Leader. "Have you had *pain au chocolat* yet?"

"Got some in my pack now." Leader motioned to where he wore it on his back. "Help yourself."

Since Matthew had returned to Paris after America officially entered the fray of war, he'd been treated to the country's finest cuisine. He'd grown fond of the breakfast staple *pain au chocolat*, and often wondered if the French would have an appetite for traditional Choctaw foods like *banaha* bread or wild onions in scrambled eggs.

Matthew pulled the smashed pastries from Leader's pack so they could share them as they walked on a carpet of flowers in the parade.

It took several hours, but the procession finally made it to the Picpus Cemetery where the commander of the American Expeditionary Forces General John J. "Blackjack" Pershing had arrived by automobile. The day had been filled with fanfare for Pershing. Matthew had spent some time with the stalwart officer, and knew he would just as soon delegate the sentiments to someone else.

True to form, Pershing saluted Marquis de Lafayette's tomb and took a seat on a small platform. Matthew held his notepad at the ready.

War Minister Paul Painlevé and other dignitaries spoke with the commander, motioning to the front. They were trying to coax Pershing into giving a speech, but he inclined his head toward Lieutenant Colonel Charles E. Stanton.

Facing the hushed crowd, Stanton didn't disappoint. He captured the hearts of the French people by recalling the history between the two countries, waxing eloquent about France's help during the American Revolution.

Near the tomb of the French hero of the American Revolution, Stanton closed with words Matthew knew would land in the pages of history:

"America has joined forces with the Allied Powers, and

what we have of blood and treasure are yours. Therefore, it is with that loving pride we drape the colors in tribute of respect to this citizen of your great republic. And here and now, in the presence of the illustrious dead, we pledge our hearts and our honor in carrying this war to a successful issue. Lafayette, we are here."

Cheers went up along with sobs and laughter. The Franco-American spirit came alive in hearts along with something else—hope.

As the American soldiers were rounded up for departure to the barracks, Matthew and Private Otis Leader shook hands in parting.

"*Chi pisa la chike.*"

"*Ome.*" *Agreed.*

There was no word for goodbye in the Choctaw language, only *I will see you again.*

With those words spoken in their native tongue, clarity for Matthew's near-future came over him with the surety of a mother's embrace.

He stood to the side and watched the American troops march away. He couldn't help but smile, his spirit soaring. This was why he was a writer.

"Good to have an excuse to smile these days, isn't it?"

Jolted, Matthew turned to find the new head of American censorship, Frank Palmer, at his side.

"Yes, it is."

Frank Palmer and Matthew had both invested their lives in pursuit of using words to influence the world. Palmer spent much of his writing career as a war correspondent, covering the gold rush on the Klondike and wars around the globe— Greco-Turkish, the Philippines, Boxer Rebellion, Russo-Japanese, and the Pacific. He was aging well, the face behind his full mustache and eyeglasses unmarred by the strain of constant travel and writing under fire.

Palmer motioned to the departing troops while he spoke to Matthew. "Wish you weren't leaving. The story is just starting for the Americans."

"I'm not leaving."

Palmer turned to him, brow cocked. "But this morning…"

"I've decided I have one more story that has to be told. It'll take awhile, but it'll be worth it."

"And in the meantime?" Palmer asked.

"I'll keep reporting on the war. There are plenty of stories waiting out there with the Americans."

Matthew would write those stories. But Otis Leader had renewed Matthew's purpose and ignited a flame. He was going to tell the American Indian doughboy story.

Palmer nodded as the last of the doughboys filtered out of the cemetery. "Stick with the 1st Division, Teller. I guarantee you won't lack for stories. The 1st will see more action than they can imagine. Those are the stories people back home want to read."

"How much of what I write will they be able to read?" Matthew tried to trim the bitterness from his tone.

He had known Palmer since landing in France in 1914 as they both started reporting on the war. But Palmer was in a different position now.

In a selfless act, he turned down a small fortune to cover the Americans in war for the *New York Herald* and accepted a commission in the U.S. Army with the modest pay of a major. He was now head of the American censorship board. He had privately told Matthew it was worse than war itself.

Palmer held his gaze on the troops. "You know I'd rather be out there. You just tell their story. Let me battle the bureaucrats."

That arrangement suited Matthew. He wouldn't be writing his final story on the war and taking the next ship home after all. People back in America needed to read about Indian soldiers and their service. Matthew had a new story to write during what would hopefully be the final phase of this insane world war.

The French "Blue Devils" had rightly earned their name. Matthew had witnessed their fighting abilities and it made sense they train the first contingent of American soldiers before combat at the front. He didn't know if the American soldiers would agree with the choice.

In the mid-summer heat, they drilled mercilessly near the village of Gondrecourt-le-Château, 25 miles south of the front line at Saint-Mihiel.

But the Americans got on well with the elite 47th Chasseurs Alpins, nicknamed "Blue Devils" by the German soldiers. They drilled the naive Doughboys in weaponry the troops hadn't had ready access to in the States, including machine guns and flamethrowers. They gave them lessons in chemical warfare and drilled eight hours a day, six days a week.

After observing the morning drills and making notes on the performance of the Indian soldiers in the 1st Division—there were only a few—Matthew sought shade and comfort in the American regimental headquarters located in a château. He had wanted to stay out with the Americans, to see them prepare for battle against the backdrop of the lush French farmland and encourage them on, but he had to admit, he wasn't as young as he used to be.

There were no barracks yet, so local establishments served as headquarters, and doughboys billeted in barns heaped with dirt and cobwebs untouched for years.

Matthew justified his action of shirking indoors by examining maps and telling a second lieutenant in the American colonel's office about previous battles at Saint-Mihiel.

While the colonel worked at his desk, Matthew and the lieutenant stood talking near an open window when the roar of an engine came from near the gate. Through the window, they watched a heated exchange between a man in a French official's automobile and the guard. The guard finally waved the automobile through and it wound its way to the office.

Matthew slipped his hand in his pocket to feel for his tablet. Something worth writing about was coming up the road.

A Frenchman bounded from the automobile and straight up the steps. He was dressed in a French uniform with corporal stripes, and wore a blue-grey kepi with its flat circular top and visor and a neatly trimmed mustache. Matthew stepped away from the door as it swished open and admitted the dapper little man.

The colonel jerked to his feet. "What do you think you're doing, barging in here?"

The Frenchman, whipping off his kepi, roared back at the colonel, only his roar was a cat's meow. He spoke in French, which Matthew understood better than he spoke.

I am here on business for the French government!

The colonel, who hadn't understood a word, snapped his fingers at his second lieutenant. "Oust him."

The Frenchman switched to enthusiastic English. "You do not do that, I am here to paint the ideal American *soldat*. I will not leave. I will paint his portrait!"

Matthew started scribbling on his notepad.

The colonel huffed. "These doughboys have no time to pose for pictures if you expect them to help you win a war. Not a one of them is *ideal*, but there are a few thousand more uptown you can pick from."

The Frenchman wasn't derailed.

"The painting, it will be hung at the Musée de l'Armée in Hôtel national des Invalides. I have a commission from the French government and I have come to paint it and I will paint it!"

"What are you talking about, a commission?"

Snapping the kepi under one arm, the dapper man produced a slip of paper from his front pocket.

As the note exchanged hands, Matthew caught sight of the insignia: American General Headquarters. He eased next to the colonel and read the signature at the bottom of the note. It was signed by General Pershing himself.

The colonel huffed. "Well, there are plenty of troops coming in. I don't know why you're here looking for one."

"I found him already! You have him!"

"Who?"

"His name...oh his name! I did not get it. I saw him in Paris in the parade with the American troops. He was with this division in a machine gun company. Tall, handsome. Straight, like an arrow. Keen and calm. Black hair. Naturally bronzed face reflects the spirit you Americans brought across!"

He punched the air with his finger, then lowered it to his lips in thought. "What do you call them? The natives of your land?"

The colonel raised an eyebrow. "An Indian? We have a couple, but they all look the same to me."

Matthew slipped his tablet into his pocket and motioned to the Frenchman. Quietly in passable French, he said, "Come with me. I know who you are speaking of."

It didn't take long to find Private Otis Leader. He was understandably confused by the excited and emotional Frenchman, Raymond Desvarreux, who fell on him with the obligatory kiss to each cheek.

Leader spoke good English but had a hard time understanding the man with his thick accent. Matthew interrupted the artist's chatter and offered to translate—directly from French into Choctaw for Leader.

Though honored, Leader protested the idea of having his portrait done, thinking his Blue Devil commanding officer would be infuriated if he missed training. And though it went unsaid, Matthew knew Leader had come to France to fight, not model his equipment.

In the end, the dapper Frenchman did a sufficient job in convincing Leader to pose for the portrait. Raymond Desvarreux's passion was contagious.

Matthew learned that the artist was the son of American painter James Desvarreux-Larpenteur. Raymond was mobilized in 1914 as a corporal in the 25th Territorial Infantry Regiment, and fought several battles before he was wounded in October, 1914.

After he was declared unfit for service, the Musée de l'Armée sent him out in an automobile to paint portraits of soldiers in the war. He had painted over 100 of them when the Americans arrived, and he set out to find the "ideal" representation of the American doughboy. He believed there was none more appropriate than an American Indian.

It took three days of Leader standing leaned against the château wall of the regimental office for Raymond Desvarreux to make a sketch and paint the portrait. Matthew drifted by several times to observe the process.

Leader wore his full uniform and campaign hat, with cartridge belt and bolo knife strapped on and his French Hotchkiss M1914 machine gun in its canvas case propped against the wall.

What a piece to include in Matthew's article about Indian soldiers, that one of them had been selected to represent the "ideal American doughboy."

In the end, the three stood back to review the painting.

Matthew jotted a note. "It's fine work."

"It is not finished, only a sketch, an outline," Raymond Desvarreux assured them, holding the painting at arm's length with his other fist on his hip. "I will touch it up when I return to Paris."

Leader had the most profound comment. "I don't see how you could improve it with the subject you had to work from, but I suppose ya know what you're talking about."

Matthew laughed. It was good to have someone around who was from his neck of the woods.

As the summer wore on, Matthew began to come alive in his spirit. All the death and anguish and heartache of war had made him numb. But having a fellow American Indian in France made being away from home bearable.

Gradually, with each word Matthew spoke in his native tongue, rocks tumbled from the dam in his heart and he knew a flood was coming. He was starting to feel again and at first, he resisted, thinking of his daughter, Victoria, and his inability to reconcile with her. He'd hold the emotions off as long as he could, maybe until this whole filthy war was over. Then the dam would break and so would he, but he could go home. He'd be ready to return—broken but not shattered. Hurt but healable.

He hoped and prayed that the war would end before his nephew was shipped over. That young B.B. would not begin this horrible journey and have to find his way back home.

God knows.

TEXAS

"Political circumstances allowed the Texans to strip the Regiment of practically all of its Oklahoma officers. Thus, the old First Oklahoma Infantry was swallowed up, devoured, and has faded into the light of a dream of yesterday."

Captain Ben D. Locke

CHAPTER NINE

Journey to Texas
October 1917

We were getting closer to the war every day. But the 1st Oklahoma Infantry was in trouble that summer. Captains Ben D. Locke and Walter Veach worked hard at recruiting for their companies, but we weren't up to war strength when it came time to ship off to Camp Bowie. That was bound to cause problems when we got down to Texas.

The train carrying us Oklahoma boys from Fort Sill huffed across the Red River. Samson stared out the window, and I knew what he was thinking. We were leaving our world far behind. Samson had never been out of Oklahoma. I was comfortable at Fort Sill, surrounded by Indians and those who were used to them. Texas was a different world.

I nudged Samson. "We'll stick together, no matter what."

He nodded.

A cold blast of air greeted us when we got off the train in Fort Worth. It was good football playing weather, and not hard to imagine we had just arrived for a game with a bunch of other players, especially with all the Armstrong Academy boys on the train. But this was no game.

I heard that most of the National Guard units had already arrived at Camp Bowie, along with the regular army for training. There were rumors that the guardsmen and regulars didn't get on well. The National Guard was informal, and the regulars were regimental and well trained. One thing was true with both—they were ready to fight.

This part of Texas wasn't a whole lot different from where I grew up around Durant, 120 miles northeast. But hiking in the mud and freezing wind for three miles was a recipe for disaster. Men started coughing right off. We still wore our summer khaki uniforms. They were all we had.

Once we made it to camp, things got worse. Pyramidal tents had blown down in the recent storm that still lingered above us. We were processed like cattle heading to slaughter—shots, inspection. It was a lot like boarding school. The former Armstrong students had a head start over the other men, many of whom had never been to school.

I was issued a mess kit, plate, cup, knife, fork, spoon, haversack, shelter tent, slicker and two blankets. I knew each item would come in really handy someday.

As the rain—cold as ice-cubes—pelted us, Samson, Jim, Solomon, Mitchell, Tobias, and I worked to get our new quarters out of the mud. The large canvas pyramidal tent that would hold eight soldiers had square sides and a high top like a pyramid with a single pole support in the center. It made me think of a circus tent and we were clumsy clowns fighting it upright. Once up, the roof leaked.

At least we had a river view. That was what Jim called the flooded street that ran in front of our new home.

With the tent anchored, I gathered my new equipment and stomped my numb feet on the wooden floor inside the tent. As my buddies started claiming cots, I tossed my gear on one of the top bunks and started to climb up, but halted when cigarette smoke wafted through the open flap behind me. None of us smoked.

"Hey Injun boy, git your junk off the top bunk."

I turned to see a lanky fellow, who looked a decade older than me, leaned on the pole supporting the opening. A cigarette dangled loose in his lips as he stared at me. I decided it would be in my best interest to give him a wide berth.

I gathered my gear, slid it on the bottom bunk, and glanced back, prepared if he planned to take a swing at me.

He stared back, hard. "I'm Lee Hoade. You stay out of my way, and you'll live to make it to France. Might even make it back."

Samson laid his gear on the bunk at the end of mine. "You been here long?"

"Save your questions. You're gonna know more than you ever wanted by the time this is all over."

Lee Hoade pushed away from the pole, puffed smoke sideways out of his lips, and added, "Wipe your feet good. I don't abide mud on the floor."

He left, slogging through the river road.

Jim backslapped me. "I'll bet there are a lot of nooses up his family tree."

Samson chuckled. We all joined in. It was good to have my buddies there.

◆ ◆ ◆

Cigarette smoke woke me early the next morning. I wasn't used to the smell. No one in my family smoked and it sure wasn't allowed at Armstrong Academy. But from what I'd seen, I'd best get used to it. Seemed just about every man in camp had the habit.

I swung my legs off the cot and squinted in pre-dawn haze. This was always the most subdued, peaceful part of a day and I liked taking it in before any words were spoken into it. But the cigarette smoke didn't belong.

The smoke was drifting from my right, not above from Lee Hoade. I jerked in realization.

"Samson! What do you think you're doing?"

My friend sat cross-legged on his bunk, slowly inhaling another puff. He choked with a terrible cough.

"You…should try one…they aren't so bad…the third time."

A sock-covered foot whacked me in the head. Lee Hoade shoved himself over me and landed on the floor with a thud. He settled and towered over Samson.

"Smokin's for outside, wise guy."

He snatched the cigarette from Samson's lips. Samson was nearly blue. Lee Hoade snuffed the cigarette out on the palm of his hand. "There'll be plenty of ways for you to die in this war without riling me." He sprang back onto his bunk.

Samson slinked out the tent door, barefoot. I hopped my way into my boots before grabbing my coat and following Samson. I reached into my pocket for a rag. I offered it to Samson where he huddled by a depress behind the tent.

"You! Chief!"

I jumped then stretched as tall as I could to block Sergeant Chill's view of Samson as he closed in on us.

It wasn't the first time someone had called me "Chief" and it wasn't just for me. Most of the boys in training camp called the Indians chief no matter which one of us they were speaking to. We had the same thing when we played football. They weren't always mocking us. It just seemed like an apt nickname to them. I accepted it, especially when it came from Sergeant Chill. He was a steam engine in breeches.

"Yes, sir?"

"Don't question me. Here." The sergeant shoved a small gunnysack into my hands. It was tied with a drawstring and contained a few pointy, clanking objects. "You are in charge of this, understand? You take it into the latrine, into No Man's Land, into blazes. When I call for it, you'd better have it."

"Yes, sir."

"Private Coxwell!"

Samson croaked, "Yes, sir?"

"Don't question me, Chief. On your feet!"

I braced as Samson used me as a ladder to climb into a

crouched standing position. The sergeant glared at him.

"Your job is to make sure nothing useful in our outfit gets tossed. Any scrap of anything goes into that sack. It could save our lives someday. Understood?"

"Yes, sir."

"Now beat it before I call a wet nurse."

We scrambled back into our tent, Samson wiping his mouth with the rag. The other boys were stirring. I set the gunnysack on my cot and cautiously peeked into it. Samson, recovered from his bout, grabbed it and dumped the contents onto my cot. The boys, except Lee Hoade, gathered around. Jim hooked his chin over my shoulder.

"What's all this junk?"

That was the right word for the dirty objects scattered over my bed. It was like dumping out a farrier's junk drawer. Rusty horseshoe nails, a heavy bolt with a washer and nut screwed on it, a whetstone, a chipped aqua glass telephone pole insulator, and a leaky can of lubricant.

Samson picked up the bolt and gave the washer a spin. "It's a bag of useful stuff, and the sergeant put me in charge of filling it. Ante up, boys, let's make the sergeant proud!"

Jim contributed a wad of fishing line with hooks and cork bobbers. I protested the hooks since I'd be carrying the sack, but Samson stuffed them in.

Solomon added an old pocketknife. He had taken carpentry at Armstrong, and there were no limits to what he could do with a jackknife and piece of string. Tobias handed over a two-inch oblong magnet.

Lee Hoade came off his bunk and landed hard on the floor. He pulled his last hand-rolled cigarette out of his tobacco bag and tossed the bag on the floor on his way out for a morning smoke.

"Hey!" Samson chided after Lee Hoade, though not loud enough for the man to actually hear. "Get in the spirit, Hoade."

Samson picked up the tobacco bag and tossed it to me. "Put those fish hooks you were complaining about in there."

Mitchell, skinny and hollow-cheeked but more filled out than me, offered to add what was left of a bar of soap to the sack. "This can be useful for washing out the sergeant's mouth!"

We chuckled. Solomon took the corroded piece of soap and turned it over in his hand. "First English word I learned was soap. The matron used it to wash out my mouth when I spoke Choctaw."

We got quiet. I was glad Isaac wasn't in this tent.

"Well," Samson muttered, "The sergeant can hardly speak English himself, so we got nothing to worry about."

◆ ◆ ◆

A few days after we arrived at Camp Bowie, the commanding officers announced a decision that nearly set everyone to fighting one another. The Oklahoma 1st Infantry, whose history went back to the Spanish-American war, was being combined with the 7th Texas Infantry to form a new unit—the 142nd Infantry.

We lost our state pride, damaging morale. The Texans didn't like the merging either, though at least they got to keep Colonel Alfred W. Bloor of Austin, Texas, who was placed in command of the 142nd.

The next big problem was a new all-Indian company that combined Company L—under Captain Locke—and Company H. The army put Captain Veach in charge of forming the new unit of Indians as Company E. The shuffling left Captain Ben D. Locke on the sidelines.

He wouldn't go to France with us, but the men who had fought with Locke in Mexico refused to let things go without a fuss. They put on a fancy gala in Fort Worth for him, and even the captain's brother, Choctaw Chief Victor M. Locke, Jr., came.

The dinner and dance to music of the twenty-seven-piece 1st Oklahoma Infantry Band at the Metropolitan Hotel soothed things, but the men were still bitter. So was Captain

Locke.

After being presented with a loving cup from his men, he gave a speech about the old Oklahoma infantry being swallowed up and devoured by the Texans. But he gave a gracious farewell—of sorts.

"Boys," the captain said, "I never expected anything like this and to express myself frankly, you've got my goat! This thing of parting and farewell I don't like to think of. I'll always cherish fond remembrance in this heart of mine. So, farewell, you men of Company L, I hate like heck to see you go."

Though Captain Locke wasn't going with us, I was at least grateful we still had an Indian—a Choctaw—as our captain in Walter Veach.

There were a few other bright spots in the merging. More officers from the Oklahoma 1st Infantry made it into the new company, including Lieutenants Elijah W. Horner—who was originally from Arkansas—Ben Chastaine, and Carl Edmonds, and 1st Lieutenant Charles H. Barnes, one of our chaplains.

Though most of the soldiers in Company E were Indians from Oklahoma, there were still a few whites. We also had an Irish mechanic and a German cook.

I wouldn't have minded if Sergeant Chill and Lee Hoade had gotten lost in the shuffle, but they didn't. They both landed in Company E. So did Isaac.

CHAPTER TEN

"THE DAILY OKLAHOMAN"

ONLY UNIT OF KIND IN UNITED STATES ARMY

<u>They're Rapidly Learning White Man's Methods of Fighting</u>

CAMP BOWIE FORT WORTH TEXAS NOVEMBER 17—(Special)—Indians from 15 tribes in the state of Oklahoma, among them Cherokees, Chickasaws, Osages, Pawnees, Kiowa, Comanches, Creeks, Potawatomi, Seminole, Cheyenne, and Choctaws, make up the personnel of the most unique infantry company of the United States Army.

As far as can be ascertained there is not another purely Indian company in the army, especially one commanded by an Indian.

As soldiers, the men of this organization already are beginning to attract attention and long before they can be given the title of soldiers they attracted notice wherever they went on account of their ancestry and their swarthy skin.

Learn Modern Warfare Quickly

Officers of the camp are watching the development of the Indian company with the keenest interest to ascertain to what extent the men can master the fine points of discipline, the theory of fighting in trenches and the other points of the modern war game. Up to the present time the Oklahoma tribesmen have shown an aptitude at picking up the necessary knowledge of close order drill that is surprising.

One of the greatest problems facing the officers of the company is the instruction of a few men who cannot speak or understand English. The first task to be carried out in this direction is the establishment of a school at night by which these men may learn to write their names as well as carry on a conversation in English.

Eyes Take Place of English

In many cases where the new soldiers have a scant knowledge of English they are making their eyes do the work of their ears. To a remarkable extent they are picking up the fine points of the foot drill by observation alone. They may not understand the words of the instructor but if he illustrates the movement they do not have to be told twice.

Some Indians Well Educated

Among the members of the company are men of excellent education. Numbers of them have been in school at Carlisle several years while others have been at Haskell and other military schools over the country. Some of them are excellent penmen and a few are able to handle typewriters in the most approved fashion.

Captain Veach, commander of the company, has been in the military service of his state and nation since August 1908. At that time he enlisted in Company H of the old Oklahoma infantry with home rendezvous at Durant, Oklahoma. After about a year of service, he became first lieutenant of this company and by steady efforts gained the rank of captain.

E company's commander obtained the foundation for his military career in the Indian schools and in his new company, he has found several men who attended the same institution where he gained his early education.

◆◆◆

"Listen up, now." Solomon got our attention when we got off track from the discussion he'd started.

We sat on cots and the floor in our tent—everyone except Lee Hoade. He was off playing poker or something. I had been loafing with the others in our tent when Solomon returned with a book for us all to share. It was called *Home Reading Course for Citizen-Soldiers,* and he insisted we study it together and become the best soldiers we could be.

Samson started off the reading, but he kept stopping to poke fun at the book. He had his thumb stuck in the spot where he paused to crack a joke. Solomon motioned to him.

"No more fooling around. This is serious business."

I agreed, taking every word of the book to heart. But I couldn't help laughing when Samson took up the reading again, this time in an exaggerated British accent like we'd heard a few days before when some of their officers arrived to help with training.

Samson lifted his chin and read, "In order to make good in the National Army you must, first of all, fit yourself to carry with credit the simple title of 'American Citizen-Soldier'—one of the proudest titles in the world." He trilled the word, butchering the accent. "This means that you must develop in yourself the qualities of a soldier. The more quickly and thoroughly you cultivate them the greater will be your satisfaction and success."

We couldn't keep our laughter in check. Solomon grabbed the book. "Give it here." He handed it to me. "Let someone with some sense take a turn."

I straightened and flipped through until I found an aptly named section, *Making Use of Spare Time*.

"The use that a man makes of his time off duty is a good test of his character and of his capacity for growth. The good soldier is self-restrained. Don't spend your time repeating indecent stories. They add nothing whatsoever to your standing, either with the men to whom you tell them or with your officers. Avoid boisterousness, vulgarity, and profanity.

"That doesn't mean at all that you should keep yourself in the background or that you should fail to be a good 'mixer.' Let your personality stand out. Broaden your influence by every proper method. But use your personality and your influence to help the men in your own squad and company carry on their work and prepare as possible for the big task ahead of you."

Whether it was the way my monotone voice faded at the end, or if the magnitude of where we were and what we were going to do finally sank in for us schoolboys from Oklahoma, but the inside of the tent grew as somber as a graveside service.

Solomon took the book from my loose fingers. "We should share this with those who can't read."

Trying to get laughter going again, Samson asked, "Who volunteers to read to the sergeant?"

Solomon frowned. "I meant Choctaws. We could translate the important parts for them."

I thought about Isaac, but I had trouble with the qualities on the list at the beginning of the book: loyalty, obedience, and physical fitness. While obedience and physical fitness weren't a problem, when my loyalty was tested, I had failed. Twice. I doubted I had the courage to read to Isaac, doubted he'd sit still for it. Really, I just wanted to avoid Isaac for the rest of my life.

Besides, Isaac was learning to read and write at the special training schools at Camp Bowie. I didn't know how well he was doing, though. He was far more interested in weapons training than English. Always ready to fight like any warrior.

Or so folks thought if they believed all those stories told about Indians.

Everyone had a belief about Indians in the army. The newspapers romanticized our history and culture and boasted about our martial abilities as fierce warriors and scouts more than we ever would. One newspaper said we were blood-thirsty warriors eager to fight. Sensationalized dime novels didn't help either.

One newspaper asked a staff officer why there was such an interest in the Indians and he said it was because there was, "a national craving for a spark of romance in a war whose deep shadows seem unrelieved by color and the higher lights."

If our history was brighter than what we faced over there, no one in America would want to go. Still, pressure from national newspapers, even the Daily Oklahoman—which received stories from former civilian reporter and now officer in Company E, Lieutenant Ben Chastaine—left me with the distinct impression that our home country expected a lot from us Indians.

Being written about, often erroneously, made me have even greater respect for my uncle Matthew. He wrote the truth on both sides, no matter how that made anybody look.

Before leaving Fort Sill, I had received a package from Paris. Uncle Matthew enclosed a letter and blank leather journal like I'd seen him carry all my life. He urged me to write in it, to record this part of history I was in.

I wrote Uncle Matthew back, though I didn't ask all the questions I wanted to ask, like if he let on to those around him that he was Indian. How often did he want to laugh with us over a bowl of *walakshi*, grape dumplings? He had to miss home and speaking our language after three years of surviving the biggest war we'd see in our lifetimes. I wanted to make sure that he was still strong, that Chihowa was with him over there, because that would mean I would be okay, too.

Being the only company of Indians set the whole nation's eyes on us. They showed us a respect I'd never experienced.

Aside from Lee Hoade, fellow soldiers had welcomed us

in with brags of how with a company of Indians in the 36th Division, we'd become the greatest division in the whole U.S. Army. That was a lot to expect from fresh high school graduates whose only battle experience was football.

Several army officers had a genuine appreciation for the aspects that were unique about Indian cultures. Others didn't.

Among those who didn't find special value in 600 Indians filling the 36th, Sergeant Chill complained about our hiking abilities, which the medical officer attributed to us having smaller feet. Choctaws, in particular, were singled out. There were those who thought we wouldn't be able to keep up, not to mention most of us were hardly over five feet six inches.

The sergeant also said we couldn't hold a straight line like white soldiers. Although we had plenty of chances to prove our marching abilities since we did little else at Camp Bowie, half the officers continued to have mixed feelings.

Then there was the young man from Mena, Arkansas.

Second Lieutenant Elijah W. Horner had been under Captain Veach during the Mexican border crisis. He'd joined the National Guard in Oklahoma and now, at age 24, was poised to rise in rank during the war. I admired Lieutenant Horner for his drive and ambition and figured he wouldn't be a bad example to imitate.

And he liked Indians. I was especially glad of that as we lined up for inspection one bright morning in early November.

Lieutenant Horner inspected us, Sergeant Chill at his side. A good six inches taller than most of the Choctaws, Horner had a square jawline, ruddy complexion, and auburn hair. Though he had a disciplined demeanor befitting an officer, his eyes were kind. He wore a large ring on his left hand that often caught a glint in the sun.

They halted in front of me. Horner looked me up and down.

"Private Dunn, what is that bag hanging from your belt?"

My hand dropped self-consciously to the small gunnysack tied to my belt with the drawstrings. Sergeant Chill stiffened. I wondered if he'd get in trouble, too.

I stammered, "This? It's, um, it's our…"

"It's our U.S. bag, sir." Samson, next to me, kept his eyes forward, but I could see the grin creeping across his face.

"U.S.? As in United States?"

"No, sir. As in Useful Stuff."

Lieutenant Horner stared at Samson, then me. He turned away, but not before I caught his side-smile and wink for the first time.

"Carry on."

My camp record stayed clean—up to that day.

We had trouble in the 36th Division that thousands of American soldiers elsewhere didn't deal with. We had Texans and Oklahomans together—cowboys and Indians. Talk about spoiling for a fight.

CHAPTER ELEVEN

Camp Bowie, Texas
November 1917

"Ah! I'm hit!"

Samson slouched against me in the trench, clutching the clumsy steel helmet slouched to one side of his head. Blood trickled down his cheek. I pushed him upright with my shoulder.

"Quit whining."

"Come on, B.B. It hurts."

I crawled up the side of the makeshift trench, finding good footholds in the dirt. The Useful Stuff, or U.S., bag bumped my hip and clanked. Wincing at the noise, I raised my head enough to see where the rock had come from that hit Samson. There he was—a Texas cowboy, in the trench across the pretend No Man's Land.

The Texan grinned at me, bigger than life and daring me to come after him. I had a sudden vision of a Jerry waiting over there. Would he taunt me before shooting real bullets to hit me in the head?

I slid back down to the wood duckboard. Samson had wiped the blood clear and had his helmet on properly.

"He's in the trench to the left. I helped dig that section. There's a jut in a curve we can hide behind and ambush him there."

Most in our unit were confused about what we were supposed to do. Samson and I had left the others to sneak through the trench system the 36th had dug all over the training area.

This practice kind of felt like real war, especially since they pitted Texans and Oklahomans against each other. I don't think the officers knew how real it was. It wasn't just between cowboys and Indians, either. White boys from Oklahoma had taken enough guff from the proud Texans. This was war.

Since I was half Samson's size, I took the lead and made sure the trench was clear before Samson followed.

I figured I'd be a valuable scout but then again, I was just another Oklahoma Choctaw boy, a body to fill a uniform, and I didn't even do that well. My trousers, the smallest the army had, puffed out like bloomers above my canvas leggings.

While digging this trench in a zigzag pattern, just like the ones in France, a boulder sunk deep in the ground had forced us to alter course. The boulder made a perfect dip to hide in, just enough room for Samson and me. I glanced over my shoulder and he nodded.

Together, we gave catcalls to let the Texan know we were challenging him.

Boots shuffled in response, coming fast, then slow. He was looking for us. A few more steps…

I launched and hit him from the side. Samson finished the tackle, taking us both down. But the Texan hadn't come alone.

Two more scooped me up and tossed me at Samson, who was getting ready to charge two others. They all laughed when we collided and went down, tangled up.

Samson shouted for help.

As reinforcements rushed in from the Oklahoma side, the Texans stopped laughing and a real Red River showdown was on. In the flurry, I got slammed, kicked, and trampled. I wondered if we really were bent on killing each other.

My uncle and daddy had taught me to shoot, hunt with a rabbit stick, and play a mean game of stickball, but they neglected to teach me to fistfight like a Texan.

As the ruckus grew, Isaac bumped into me from behind. He was in a bear wrestle with a former cowpuncher. I could see him squeezing hard, and wondered if he'd joined the army just to get some fighting out of his system. Good thing it wasn't me he had a hold of.

Crowded up, the battle boiled over onto ground level, and before long, the whole field was one big fight. Someone snagged the U.S. bag at my waist. Samson shoved him away.

A bugle sounded from somewhere, but I was too dizzy to remember what the call meant. Some of the other men must have recognized it, because man by man, the fighting stopped.

I staggered out of the trench and toward where our commanding officers were gathered, expressions grim. The big guns were all there, including our commander Colonel Alfred W. Bloor.

Except for him, most of these senior officers weren't from this part of the country. They didn't realize they had civilized Indians, open range loving cowboys, and grandsons of Southern confederates under their command. I wondered if we could even become a division disciplined enough to send over to France. They might just send us home.

Bloor strolled up and down the line, inspecting us bloodied, bruised, muddy soldiers. He was a mild-looking man with eyes sunk well back in his slender face, but we knew he meant business. A former attorney, Bloor had military experience at a young age when he graduated Texas A&M in 1895. His service went from Cuba during the Spanish-American war all the way to the rank of colonel when he raised the new 7th Texas Infantry. He claimed moderate fame in Texas football circles as well.

He was not impressed with us.

Colonel Bloor stepped forward to address the hundreds of soldiers before him.

"Men, we are not oblivious to the underlying differences between the social classes among you."

That was a nice way of putting it.

"But we must find a way to unite under a single purpose as a division where we serve as one. I have suggested a solution to General Blakely and he approves. Tomorrow, we will hand out team assignments to mix the units."

Team assignments? It sounded like he was talking about...

"This Saturday, we play football."

CHAPTER TWELVE

Somerville Sector, France
November 1917

"It's ticklish, not knowing the lay of the land."

Otis Leader scratched the back of his neck, likely feeling the bite of his first cootie.

The night was inky and cold. Matthew crouched on the opposite side of the trench from the five-man American machine gun crew and rubbed his hands together, trying to warm them enough to take notes.

The 1st Division was in a so-called "quiet sector," ordered there by Pershing who wanted the first American troops to gain experience at the front before they were used in all-out attacks come spring. The German lines were a few hundred yards across No Man's Land from where the fresh machine gun crew waited. The crew was growing more anxious by the minute while the remainder of the battalion brought up ammunition.

The crew hadn't yet received orders, and huddled in the trench, hunched against a light mist that fell in the darkness.

Other men from the division had gone into dugouts to rest. The division had traversed shell-pocked terrain, digging mules and carts out when they fell in the holes. The crew quickly learned why the French soldiers carried long sticks. They thought it was some kind of odd fad among the French infantrymen, who were called *poilu*. At this point, Matthew doubted this gun crew would ever forego the long sticks they'd rummaged up to feel their way around shell holes.

Matthew had taken Frank Palmer's advice and his authorization letter that got Matthew past the harsh regulations still in place for war correspondents. He planned to stick close to the 1st Division through winter. It had fascinating representatives of many nationalities, from New York Jews and Italians to, well, American Indians.

He wanted to stay particularly close to the 16th Infantry's Machine Gun 2nd Battalion and his new friend, Otis Leader. This was Matthew's first opportunity to observe an American Indian soldier in action. Leader joked that Matthew better keep a close eye out because he planned to do some fighting.

Matthew tried to stay cautious in making friendships with the troops from his home country. He'd seen too much in this war and knew the many grieving widows there would be back home before this was over. Every face he saw under the stars and stripes was one who might not make it home.

Leader wasn't nearly as young as most in the company, but he had no trouble keeping up. He was a gentle man, an Indian Santa Clause of sorts, yet had a toughness that defied the vile conditions of winter and war.

He twirled a long stick between his palms and asked, "What are we supposed to do now?"

His sergeant, Larson, toyed with a loaded ammunition strip. "Might as well do some shooting. That's what we come for."

Matthew wouldn't recommend that, but neither would he say anything. He was there to observe, and technically, not welcome by the higher command. He counted on his long-time relationship with Frank Palmer to give him leeway.

Palmer knew the challenges of being a war correspondent better than anyone. Now head of the American censorship, he had to deal firsthand with the other side of the frustrations. His experience would serve him well. Matthew knew Palmer was determined not to let truth be the first casualty of war.

The five men in the machine gun crew shifted, loaded their Hotchkiss, got into position, and started shooting across No Man's Land. The sharp racket sent a double thump through Matthew's heart. He'd been away from the front for nearly a year. Nothing could steel a man for the jarring sound, even years into war.

After they emptied all four ammunition boxes, Matthew moved up behind Otis Leader. In the quiet, while Sergeant Larson directed the final reloading of the gun, Matthew asked, "What are you shooting at?"

Leader shrugged. "Don't know. Barbed wire, light reflections, anything toward the German line..."

A whiz sounded overhead. This time, Matthew did speak up.

"Artillery barrage, take cover!"

The six men dove to the duckboards at the bottom of the trench as a shell exploded along the south edge. Flashes illuminated the night.

Not knowing what to do, the gun crew stayed hunkered down, listening to the cannons thundering, grenades exploding, rifles rattling, and men down the line howling in fright as they experienced shell explosions shaking the ground beneath their feet.

It was over in less than an hour. The crew checked on their Hotchkiss. Undamaged.

Matthew tipped his steel Brody helmet up his forehead and turned to Otis Leader. The color in the Indian's face had faded in the intensity. It slowly came back and Leader said, "Guess we woke them up."

He started chuckling and Matthew joined in.

Years from now, if they were ever together back home, in the quiet of a conversation, one of them might start chuckling. The other would join in, knowing exactly why when no one around them did. It was a peculiarity some called the "Choctaw chuckle."

Matthew hoped there would be more such moments ahead. But he knew laughter was rare in war.

◆ ◆ ◆

To Matthew Teller—

You are a fool for remaining in Europe. You should have been wise and stayed in the Ottoman Empire. No horrendously cold winter, only sand in your eyes and in every drink you take to forget the bloody carnage and loss.

I hope the Americans you are with do well in the coming spring engagements.

Truly,
Tom Alders

◆ ◆ ◆

No amount of training could prepare the Americans for their first casualties. Matthew was writing a letter to Tom Alders the morning the news arrived, the day after Otis Leader and the gun crew had their first taste of coming under fire.

Before daybreak on November 3, 1917, at Bathelémont, a platoon of Company F in the 2nd Battalion was isolated and caught in a box barrage. German shock troops stormed in.

11 captured. 5 wounded.

3 dead.

Matthew knew the first American casualties would make headlines back home in the States and cause thousands of more men to join up to avenge the doughboy deaths. It was just as well that they didn't fully know what they were getting into. Matthew hoped the war would end before they made it over, especially before B.B. did.

As for Matthew, he wished he was carrying a gun along with a pencil. He still believed the pen was mightier than the sword, but sometimes, one needed to wield both.

A funeral escort formed a square around graves at the foot of a slope at Bathelémont that cold morning on November 4. One soldier stood at the head of Corporal Gresham's casket, holding a rod with a cross at the top.

General Bordeaux, commander of the French 18th Division, conducted the service. Matthew blew on his writing hand to warm it enough to take down the speech. It was in French.

"The deaths of this humble corporal and these two private soldiers appeal to us with extraordinary grandeur. We will, therefore, ask that the mortal remains of these young men remain here: be left to us forever. We will inscribe on their tombs: Here lie the first soldiers of the U.S. to fall on the soil of France for liberty and justice—Corporal Gresham, Private Enright, Private Hay. In the name of France, I thank you. God receive your souls. *Adieu.*"

Shots were fired and taps played. The soldiers disbanded, though Otis Leader remained still next to Matthew. Matthew spoke quietly in Choctaw, asking if he was all right.

Leader tilted his head back to stay the tears in his eyes. The men who'd died were in his battalion. Men who had trained together, swapped stories and photos of family.

"I want to take my brothers home," Leader said. "Cannot leave them here. Not right to leave them here."

Matthew didn't respond except to clasp Leader on the shoulder. The soldiers were a part of each other and to leave their bodies behind was to leave a piece of oneself behind.

The hardest part of that, the part Matthew didn't say aloud, was that these wouldn't be the last soldiers they left buried in this bloody soil.

◆◆◆

Tom,

No sense in saying the censorship is as bad as ever, even with the

Americans.

When this war is over, you and I can join together again for a final review of the Western Front.

I will continue to pray the end comes soon. There has been much loss.

Chi pisa la chike,
Matthew Teller

CHAPTER THIRTEEN

"Nothing will help morale more than immediate action to draw the individual attention of each state represented in one common interest."
—*Colonel Bloor*

Camp Bowie, Texas
November 1917

I played alongside Texans in the football games that brought our division together in a spirit of fair play. Colonel Bloor—from Texas—insisted Chaplain Barnes—from Oklahoma—serve as coach for the 142nd Infantry of the 36th Division.

The whole division got behind the idea of creating teams, and soon a schedule was posted.

Chaplain Barnes had a seasoned expression, heavy eyebrows, a ready smile, and years of coaching experience. He created a team filled with football champions from Texas and Oklahoma to represent the 142nd.

Isaac was on defense when we had team practice. I didn't

know he could play football until he zigged in front of me like a lightning bolt and intercepted a pass.

It was a good thing to be on the Texans' side of this fight. The 2nd Texas Infantry were the football champs during the Mexican border crisis. My cousin Peter had told me how the 2nd Texas Infantry, made up mostly of former college football stars, had walloped every team on the border, from the New York Calvary to the Fort Sam Houston team.

Something I would say about those Texans: most of them were pretty big hearted. I couldn't blame them too much for their big egos. They had a big state and a big history.

But the first football game in the 36th Division wasn't the big news of the season for one of us.

I'd been keeping an eye on Solomon. He'd been acting strange, quiet and serious even for him. He was a thinker, always seeing ahead four or five steps beyond the rest of us. I could tell he was looking ahead to the end of the war. Actually, to the end of his life.

He pulled me aside one day after football practice. "I need a favor, Bertram."

"Yeah?"

"Will you stand with me when I get married tomorrow?"

I jerked to a stop. "You're doing *what* tomorrow?"

"I asked Mary Patterson to be my wife. We're to wed in Fort Worth tomorrow. I already have your pass from Captain Veach."

We'd teased Solomon at his 18th birthday not long ago about how he was finally old enough to enlist in the army. And now?

"But…you…Mary…I mean, we're shipping off to war. You sure you should be getting married just now?"

Solomon faced me square on. His life had been so different from mine. I could never truly understand what had shaped him into the man he was.

"War is the reason. She'll be taken care of if anything happens to me. The army pays death benefits. Did you know that?"

He wasn't really asking me, so I didn't answer. He was thinking on ahead to his wedding day, and his potentially violent death.

Solomon was an orphan with two siblings, though he was the only one to finish school. His sweetheart, Mary, understood him more than anyone. She was mostly alone, too. If they were married, she'd be taken care of whether he made it home or not.

I'd always liked Solomon. Now I understood a little better why.

"I'll stand with you."

On November 30, 1917, Solomon Bond Louis married Mary Patterson. The very next day, he was made a corporal.

Back from the wedding ceremony, I opened the journal my uncle had sent me. I'd better get caught up on all that had happened with trench training, football, and Solomon. But I didn't even know where to begin. Should I write my thoughts, too? What if someone read it?

I was proud of Solomon but had to fight off envy. He was making good in the army, and if he made it home alive, he had his future laid out. It made me feel that maybe I hadn't accomplished all I should have up to that point.

One thing for sure—war would give me plenty of chances to live well or die. It was cut and dry. That should have settled me, but with Isaac around, I couldn't get past the feeling that I was on my way to disappointing everyone.

I closed the journal without writing a word.

♦♦♦

Colonel Bloor was smart when he recommended having the division play football. The 142nd Texans and Oklahomans, once bitter rivals, now visited each other's tents and talked game strategies. We plowed through the 36th Division undefeated, all the way to the grueling division championship game cheered on by thousands of spectators at Panther Park on December 16, 1917.

We lost. But we didn't lose as the 1st Oklahoma Infantry or the 7th Texas Infantry. We were the 142nd Infantry.

It was a good thing the football idea turned out well, because not much else was going right at Camp Bowie.

Cold weather was coming hard-on and we still didn't have our winter uniforms. We drilled with wooden rifle replicas. There was no firing range to practice on for the doughboys who did have rifles or machine guns. Heavy snow halted our training.

And then sickness set in.

Measles and pneumonia didn't scare us nearly as much as meningitis, though that one turned out to be the least worrisome.

Our tent, which had once been crammed with 10 men, was down to 6. It was supposed to house 7 privates with a corporal in charge. Solomon was my corporal now, and Jim had been moved to another tent. He had stripes sewn on his coat sleeve, too. Samson wasn't in my tent anymore, either. He was in the hospital.

He had pneumonia, a respiratory disease, and I couldn't help thinking about Samson filling his lungs with smoke from those cigarettes he took to.

I tried to visit him, but they wouldn't let me in. He sent me a note through one of the nurses, asking me to write Ida Claire Jessop and tell her what a hero he'd been in the championship football game, and that she had better be ready to welcome him home proper after the war.

On a cold December morning, I read my Bible by light coming through a sliver in the tent flap. I knew what had happened from the look on Lieutenant Horner's face when he came into the tent. His expression was tight, though his eyes showed genuine compassion. I sat on the edge of my cot, Bible open across my lap, and stared up at him.

Lee Hoade shifted on the top bunk and swung his feet over the side, knocking me in the head, something I was used to after seven weeks at Camp Bowie. It was oddly comforting.

Solomon, sitting on his cot writing letters, put his pen

aside and stood. Jim, Mitchell, and Tobias stood, too.

I looked down at my Bible. It was Lieutenant Horner's duty to announce it to us.

"Private Samson Coxwell died this morning. We wired his folks."

I kept my head down, wishing I was home.

Lieutenant Horner approached my cot and held out a loosely rolled ball of string to me.

"A nurse said Private Coxwell asked for this to be given to you, and that he hoped it would be useful someday."

I took the medium-sized ball of string and fiddled with it before stuffing it in the U.S. bag.

Lee Hoade's feet rested on each side of my head. Then they swung back up and no one said anything. Grieving would come later.

It had been seven months since I enlisted, and I felt like I had just gotten a taste of what war might mean.

◆ ◆ ◆

Dear Mrs. Coxwell,

I am very sorry for the loss of your son. Samson was my best friend. He may not have died with a gun in his hand, but he was ready to. He was a hero.

Sincerely,
Bertram Robert Dunn

Dear Ida Claire Jessop,

You have most likely heard about Samson. He was a real hero in the football game, a champion player for the 142ⁿᵈ Infantry. Everyone was proud of him.
He missed you a lot.

Respectfully,
Bertram Robert Dunn

◆◆◆

Things got quiet in the 2,200-acre Camp Bowie that winter. Dozens had died from sickness, and we felt the loss of a buddy in every unit.

I spent more time with Choctaws I had met since joining up, but I was reserved with them at first. It was bad enough to be close to my old Armstrong Academy classmates. If I'd lost my best friend before we even shipped out, which of the guys I'd met would be dead before I made it back? If I made it back.

Samson had always been a buffer between me and the world. Now he was gone. I wanted to grieve, but I held off. I needed to have the kind of courage Samson had, the kind that made him able to laugh or fight his way through anything.

The winter froze us stiff. Our commanders gave us protocols to follow to help stop the spread of sickness. Most steps were ignored, like keeping the tent flaps open for ventilation. It was too doggone cold. The little cone-shaped stove was barely enough to keep our tent warm if we didn't go in and out too much.

The weather got so bad near the end of December they had to suspend training. I wished they'd send us home for Christmas, but we were quarantined.

Pokni—grandmother—sent me goodies and traditional Choctaw remedies, and Mama wrote me all the time. She was a prolific writer, but I didn't write back as much as I should have because she just kept asking the same things in different ways.

Folks outside Camp Bowie thought we were all sick and dying. Truth was, there were over 1,800 men in an understaffed hospital that was supposed to hold 1,000. I wrote Mama, trying different ways of explaining how things really were, telling her I was healthy and that not all the men were sick. I also wanted to say I wasn't going to die like Samson had, that I would never touch a cigarette.

I asked Mama to pray for me and of course, she would. I

imagined all the neglected chores because Mama likely wasn't doing anything but praying and asking the Lord Jesus to protect her son.

With training suspended, Jim, Solomon, and I spent days reading the Bible. There was usually a group of us, taking turns reading aloud.

It was times like these I missed Samson most, when we were speaking our beloved language. At Camp Bowie, I only spoke the language when there was no one but Choctaws around.

After reading, Jim would take off preaching in Choctaw and I'd listen and nod and wonder how he could keep so many scriptures in his head. He reminded me a little of Pastor Turner back home.

Rat-a-tat-tat.

Then we'd sing hymns, quiet-like. We hadn't been told not to speak our language at Camp Bowie, but back home, it was something we kept among ourselves. Though truth told, not all Choctaws spoke it even at home.

Buddies of mine from boarding school told stories of how they'd go home and want to speak the language they'd been forbidden to at school only to find their family wouldn't speak it with them, either. They were told it was better to forget the old ways, everything that made them Indian.

My family wasn't that way. They clung to who they were, even in the violent days in the old Choctaw Nation. My uncle Matthew had almost died for publishing truth in his newspaper.

Mama always told that story with a mix of pride and pain in her eyes. She'd say how stubborn her brother was and how bent he was on getting himself killed, that fear never stopped him from doing what was right.

She'd look at me when she said it and I knew she was seeing the future and wondering if my generation would have that kind of courage to fight for our people. Probably hoping we wouldn't have to.

And she'd say, "God knows."

◆◆◆

The Fort Worth Star-Telegram reported there were over 5,000 cases of measles or pneumonia in Fort Worth, yet they insisted there was no pandemic in the town. It reminded me of a newspaper clipping passed down from my great-grandmother who had walked the Choctaw Trail of Tears in the 1830s.

A newspaper in Arkansas had reported that the band of Choctaws camped near town was happy and in good spirits, and that only a few deaths had occurred. Two columns over, the headline read, "Worst winter in history." I never could reconcile those stories.

One quiet day near the end of 1917, I learned just how bad things were at Camp Bowie. Training suspended because of snow and sickness, I laid on my bed in the middle of the day, messing with the ball of string Samson had left us. In the hospital, he'd tied together pieces too short to save. We had used lengths from it to bundle letters from home.

At first, I thought Sergeant Chill was just picking on me by giving me the U.S. bag. But when he used it almost everyday, I realized he did set stock in its value, so I always kept it close. Samson would be proud that I made sure nothing was wasted in our unit.

Hurried footsteps sounded on the wooden walk outside. Jim threw the tent flap open to let in a freezing blast of air and stuck his head inside.

"Hey, look civilized. The governor of Texas is strolling down our street."

Jerking upright, I expected Lee Hoade's feet to whack me, but he didn't share my interest in getting a look at Governor Hobby. I pulled my boots on, tucked my shirt in and looked at least as decent as the other soldiers in our tent.

Corporal Solomon Bond Louis looked us over with a critical eye then let us out. He was meticulous, his uniform clean and pressed, and his boots polished. The only thing he did different from most in the camp was wearing his campaign hat cocked to the side. It looked sharp that way.

I exited and snapped to attention. It wasn't just the Texas governor paying a visit. A fellow with more decorations on his uniform than I'd ever seen walked alongside the governor.

Jim whispered, "Major General W.C. Gorgas, the Surgeon General himself."

Tobias, on my left, asked, *"Pi abeka chiyyohmi ho?" Are we that sick?*

I stiffened, wondering if anyone heard him speaking Choctaw, and glanced at him when the inspectors weren't looking. His dark skin absorbed the winter sunshine. "Shh, Tobe! No Indian talk now."

Governor Hobby and Major General Gorgas made their way down the now gravel road that ran between the rows of tents, nodding at soldiers and peering inside several of the tents. I heard them talking as they came closer.

"Same as other camps across the country," Gorgas told the governor. "Most of the recruits come from rural areas, never exposed to childhood diseases. The transports keep spreading it. It's worse than fighting the Germans."

Governor Hobby stopped in front of our tent. "Are you boys from Oklahoma?"

I nodded, not sure if we were allowed to actually speak to the governor of Texas.

Solomon answered with a stout, "Yes, sir."

"Ever had the measles before?"

We all nodded. We'd been to boarding school. Cramped quarters and shared sicknesses were nothing new to us. Still, pneumonia had killed Samson. That made me blame his smoking. I often found myself being mad at him for smoking and wanting to smack him in the head, then would remember he was gone.

The governor kept staring at us mixed and full-blood Choctaws even when the surgeon general moved on. Then he gave us an awkward salute.

"Make us proud over there, boys."

We saluted and nodded our promise, then he left. I wondered if he had doubts about whether Indians would really fight for a country that had taken theirs.

Indians across America were joining up to prove they were willing. It was our home, too, and we were dedicated to protecting it and our families.

I should have written those things in the journal from Uncle Matthew. But I didn't.

◆ ◆ ◆

Dear Bertram Robert Dunn,

I thank you for the letter. I will truly miss Samson.

Respectfully,
Ida Claire Jessop

CHAPTER FOURTEEN

Gondrecourt and Ansauville, France
Winter 1918

After the 1st Division was relieved at Somerville, Matthew followed them back to Gondrecourt. From green doughboys drilling in their campaigns hats during bayonet training, the division had seasoned up quickly after their experience with German shock troops and burying comrades. But the French Blue Devils had more hardship in store with the winter's grueling training.

Matthew planned to stick close to headquarters that winter. He went among barns that served as billets for the soldiers, collecting stories from them. Otis Leader had plenty to share before spring came. He even wrote down a few to help out with Matthew's article about the Indian doughboy experience.

Handing over a piece of paper, Otis patted Matthew on the back with a grin.

"You're kind of an old Choctaw to be out here doing all this writing by yourself."

They shared a chuckle, knowing many of the doughboys looked at Otis as old at the ripe age of 35. Compared to his comrades barely out of high school, they joked that the oldest soldier among them needed to be seen after.

But as winter went on, Otis wasn't chuckling much. Matthew pieced together the writings Otis had given him. He wouldn't try to send them home, even in a personal letter to Ruth Ann. The little censor scissors would clip out too much of the grim verbiage. He needed to save it for his special article. He needed to save the truth.

Matthew took the pieces of paper and tucked them in an envelope for safekeeping. On the outside, he wrote:

OTIS LEADER'S JOURNAL

Words can't describe the hardships sustained by Officers and men alike during this period, hardships that are inexpressible. It is natural that the 1st Division should suffer from the disadvantage of being the first American division in more than the sense of designation.

These are bitter days of a second "Valley Forge" when men march over frozen grounds through snow, ill-clad, and barefooted. A serious shortage in almost everything essential—equipment, clothing, and lousing of the troops—existed from the first, but no man complained.

Instead of improving with the passage of time, conditions seem to grow worse as the days grow colder and the snow more frequent. The pages of Military history devoted to the record of the American Army will never do justice to these men. Never will a history of the war recorded show a finer spirit than the Division displayed.

In January, the 1st Division marched to Ansauville through 10 inches of snow. Then the weather turned warm, sun shining over the French landscape and turning everything sloshy. The doughboys were soaked to the waist and knee deep in mud and sludge when they relieved the "go-getter" 1st Moroccan Division.

The envelope grew thick with the many cryptic notes Otis shared with Matthew in the following months:

Cooties in the sweaters.
Shell hitting under wall at Chow lines.
Blowing up the graveyard.
Shooting at automobile and killing 1 horse and man.
The Cootie wigwag.
14 Airplane fights, landing in No Man land.
French wind gage with small balloons.
Weigand passing as a German in Hospital or out on detail.
The German Cootie vs. the French Cootie.
Blowing up of our ammunition dump out past from church tower.
Outpost man insane, killing relief and wounding Corporal.
The German Aeroplane on the creek, with dead man in it.
Drowning the Cooties.

We were furnished 35,000 shells for a 45-minute barrage and we shot 30,300 of them, and had to change gun barrel between shelling times as it would not stand the 35,000 rounds. Our guns are the heavy Hotchkiss, air cooled gun by radiators, but we use wet sand bags on them but they get hot in spite of all we can do.

Creepy feeling when the German bombers come over us. One killed my pal.

CHAPTER FIFTEEN

Camp Bowie, Texas
Spring 1917

I didn't like Albert Billy for one reason, and one reason only. He had a blasted bugle he used for reveille, and he took particular delight in blowing it right outside the thin tent wall separating him from me in my cot. I could hear him chuckling afterward, but he always saved me a spot at the front of the chow line.

And that was why I liked Albert. He was a good man. We needed good men for what lay ahead.

Full-blood Choctaw, Albert had been transferred to Company E when it formed, then was transferred to Headquarters Company in November where he got ahold of that bugle. I didn't meet him until springtime because of the quarantine. I learned he was a farmer with a wife and two little children back home. He was tall for a Choctaw, medium-build and kind in disposition. Except when he had that blasted bugle.

I met more Choctaws like him who had joined up or

been drafted. There were quite a few in Company E.

Because of oil royalties some of the Indians received, especially Osage, our unit was referred to as the "Millionaire Company" in newspaper stories. My family didn't fall into that exaggerated bracket, but we did own land through our allotments and that was rich by most standards.

When the 111th Engineers finished the Benbrook trench system in March 1918, training got serious at Camp Bowie. A full-scale system of ten miles, it covered both sides of the Texas and Pacific Railway tracks with barbed wire entanglements, shelters, dugouts, and machine gun emplacements. We were to learn how to place machine guns, follow a rolling barrage, and call in artillery.

The French and British had sent officers to Camp Bowie to train us in warfare techniques that had developed over there. That was the first time I heard foreign accents like theirs, but I didn't notice after a couple of weeks. Neither were as hard to understand as some of the Texans I knew.

They drilled the Americans on the importance of going light with using the telephone at the front because of Jerry listening in. Most of our officers waved it off. America was master of the telephone, and over the past year, the American Telephone and Telegraph Company had set out to prove it with their massive work to lay thousands of miles worth of line all over northeastern France.

The French and British got frustrated with the Americans at times, and they didn't hide it—but they learned quick not to call the Texas and Oklahoma boys "Yanks."

With spring and the Benbrook trench system, we also started receiving adequate training equipment and olive drab uniforms for combat. My new service coat buttoned up to a high collar with the United States seal imprinted on the buttons, but the 36th Division couldn't decide on an insignia, so I didn't have a patch to add to my sleeve.

We no longer had to practice with cannons made of dismantled wagons, sewer pipe, and logs. We didn't need wooden rifle replicas or brooms once they finally issued real rifles—shiny Enfield 1917s. A handy cleaning kit was stored in the butt of the rifle. Some of the 36th would keep the 1903 Springfields they were initially issued to carry over there.

I tried to separate my thoughts of the guns from what they'd be used for. Although most soldiers couldn't wait to start killing the Fritz, I could, which was why I didn't mind still being in training camp nearly a year after I'd enlisted.

When it came time for my company to take part in the "Battle of Benbrook," we went to the front line for our four-day rotation ready to fight. We'd heard stories of how intense the training would be, and it wasn't long before the flares and barrage made us forget it was just practice.

Hanging up the M1917 field telephone where I'd practiced sending a message to another company up the line, I rejoined Company E in an eight-foot-deep trench.

We got quiet as Lieutenant Horner laid out how we were going to take the machine gun nest to the east of us. But my mind was racing too fast to catch much of it.

I kept thinking that I wouldn't have Samson to back me up. I missed him fiercely, and it was all I could do to lock up that feeling in a corner of my heart. That corner held my hurt of what had happened with Isaac, too.

Pokni once told me that losing someone was like falling hard, maybe off a horse, and for a time you're blinded by pain and all you see are black swirls. With a little time, you can open your eyes. The pain is still there, but you can see again. That was what it was like, hitting the ground hard, she said. Then days, maybe years later, the pain was still there, but you could see the world again.

My eyes opened in that trench. I focused on the faces of my fellow soldiers, wondering who would come back alive to see their families. There were the Davenport brothers, George and Joseph. They joined to show they were loyal to their country and wanted to protect their own.

Noel Johnson was in his mid-twenties and squinted. I figured he needed glasses, but he was stout and ready for war.

Then there was Corporal Solomon Bond Louis. What I

was most envious about Solomon being a noncommissioned officer was him getting to carry a sidearm. I trusted him to lead.

He paid close attention as Lieutenant Horner explained why it'd be paramount to capture machine gun nests to keep our troops advancing across No Man's Land. I figured it would save a lot of our boys' lives, but I couldn't imagine the kind of courage it would take to charge a hornet's nest where the stingers were bullets. Solomon was smart, though, and he understood the strategies.

Tobias and Mitchell stood ready. Albert was there from Headquarters Company with his blasted bugle strapped to one side. Corporal James Edwards had a squad with mostly Choctaws. At least Isaac was in his unit instead of with me in Solomon's, though it didn't matter. We were still too close together.

Then there was Lee Hoade settled in the middle of us Choctaws. He chewed tobacco and I was pretty sure he didn't have a girl waiting on him back home. He never talked about it.

Lieutenant Horner finished his instructions and I wondered if the defenders of the machine gun knew our plans or if this really was to see if we could do it.

I read in the Fort Worth Star-Telegram where they said Southwesterners felt "so cheap" having to surrender our identification tags in practice when we got caught, that we'd want to fight to the death to keep them. I didn't know exactly what they meant by "cheap," but I wasn't going to let anyone get mine. I knew how to fight hard on a field. All my buddies from Armstrong did, which was why we ended the last season at Armstrong Academy undefeated.

The small U.S. bag tied to my cartridge belt had continued to fill up and it was getting heavy. We'd added a bent canteen with no lid, a handy pair of tweezers that always came out with the magnet, a thimble, and a lot of metal uniform buttons that I kept organized in little tobacco bags. I was never short on those bags or buttons.

It was, in essence, a bag of junk. But it was our unit's bag of junk and I was proud to bear the burden, especially in honor of Samson.

And maybe it would prove useful when we got over there. I recalled something the sergeant said when he put the full burden of collecting things for the bag on me after Samson died.

"One thing you don't do is question how useful something will be," Sergeant Chill had said. "Just put it in the bag."

Then he'd drawn a bead on me with his squinted eye like I was a piece of scrap and he'd decide later if I had any usefulness.

Shifting the bag so it stayed behind me, I fell in with the middle of the pack that snaked through the trench toward the railroad tracks. A creepy buzz sounded above us. I skittered then realized it was another flyover to get us used to airplanes. They didn't want us distracted by them in battle like I had just been.

Lee Hoade was somewhere behind me, which made me uneasy. I never knew if he was for me or against me. While the other soldiers called all the Indians "Chief," Lee Hoade still called me "Indian boy"—when he talked to me at all. He didn't call anyone else that and I didn't know if it was because he didn't like me or because he did.

We got in position against the wall of the trench, then Solomon and Noel flung flares over to the other side of the enemy machine gun nest. The plan was to distract the gunners so we could charge them before they had a chance to defend themselves.

At the lieutenant's signal, I held my gun like they'd drilled us to and scrambled over the top of the trench. I wanted to whoop and holler, but we weren't supposed to do that. We rushed across the pretend No Man's Land, approaching from the side of the machine gun nest. The gunners wouldn't have time to swing the machine gun toward us before we would reach them. But they did have time for something else.

Ping! Something struck my helmet, a real projectile. As

real as could be sent from a slingshot, which was strictly banned.

"Ah!" A man went to his knees beside me, covering his eye with one hand.

Rocks showered down, and I knew the men in the other trench, our enemies, didn't care to surrender their identity tags either.

But those slingshots made me mad! We had nothing like that to defend ourselves. Instead of retreating, someone down the line let out a war cry. It was so shrill, like a panther, it made my back spasm. It was the cry of Isaac Hotinlubbi.

Stumbling in my run, I went down. I rolled and lay on my back an extra moment, thinking of Isaac and Samson, the black swirls of grief blinding me. But I couldn't grieve, couldn't set things right, not till the war was over.

Pushing to my feet, I ran hard to catch up with my unit as we overwhelmed the machine gun nest. My blood pumped to the tips of my ringing ears, thrills shooting through my body.

I tossed my rifle aside and attacked one of the defenders with both fists. Doughboys down the trench heard the ruckus and came charging to help their buddies, and the whole thing turned into a brawl. One of the defenders shouted that we had to surrender our tags. Lee Hoade laid him out.

Outnumbered four to one, we did the honorable thing and got the blazes out of there. We had to support George Davenport, who had a sprained ankle, and blood splattered our new olive drab uniforms, and we'd lost our shiny Enfield rifles, and we didn't take the nest.

But we still had our identity tags.

◆◆◆

Before long, we were accustomed to the battle exercises and seeing our "enemies" at the next meal, exchanging friendly barbs about how things would be different next time, and who we wanted fighting with us in future battles. We talked about being tougher on each other once we had all of the real equipment.

"We ain't got it so bad. Boys up north are wearing old Union uniforms to drill in!"

"I know someone I'd put in a Yankee uniform, then we'd have something for target practice."

"Watch it. Mama might have raised an idiot, but she didn't raise no fool."

I wished the enemies over in Europe could sit down and eat their meals together and joke and laugh after battle. Better yet, do it before and find out they likely didn't want to fight each other at all. It was the high-powered men that pitted ordinary men against one another.

A lot of people in our country didn't think America should be going over there. I just hoped our part would put an end to the mess and then everyone could sit down for a meal together. And if they didn't, at least they were free to. That was what my uncle believed. We had to keep the world free and to do that, we had to fight, as much as he and so many others didn't want it that way.

After reading his stories about the war for three years, I looked forward to seeing my uncle over there and saying, "We helped put an end to this war, *vmoshi*. We can all go home."

When my first training in the new system ended, I sat down and wrote him a letter along with a pile of others I had neglected to write—one to each of my family members in Durant and one to Peru Farver, who was still superintendent at Armstrong. He wrote his former students regularly.

I kept my letters from home, tied with Samson's string, in the brown leather journal my uncle had given me. Among them was the thin note from Ida Claire Jessop. I'd heard she was going to boarding school in Texas. I remembered the last time I'd seen her, and it made me smile to have a memory of Samson before America declared war and all our lives changed.

I wrote her a letter, though I still hadn't written a word in the journal. I would start on it soon.

◆◆◆

Dear Ida Claire Jessop,

I hope you are getting on well at school. I miss the days at church when you shot at us with your slingshot to protect your cookies. Those were good days. I miss Samson fiercely.

Respectfully,
Bertram Robert Dunn

◆◆◆

Unauthorized slingshots and fistfights that resulted in bruises, black eyes, and cracked heads were nothing compared to the most serious incident before we left Camp Bowie. A Stokes trench mortar shell accidentally exploded in one of the trenches.

That was our first taste of violent death. General Greble and several other officers had been standing ten yards away, but they weren't injured like a dozen others closer to the explosion. A sergeant in the 141st had his left ear torn off and his eye pierced by a fragment. He wouldn't be going over there. One dying soldier asked the men who hurried to his side to wire his mother of his death.

Somehow, I didn't think I'd ever see something so horrible. Maybe the practice trenches really weren't preparing us for war at all.

I thought on that a lot as we got ready to ship out to France.

Before we did though, I received a box of cookies and a note.

Dear Bertram Robert Dunn,

I am getting on well at school. My schoolmates want to know what unit you are in so they will know where you are. They are proud of you

boys. I know Samson is, too, looking down from Heaven.
I hope you enjoy the cookies. Samson would want you to.

Respectfully,
Ida Claire Jessop

CHAPTER SIXTEEN

Cantigny Sector, France
May 1918

With spring came a new addition to Matthew's work, a favor for Frank Palmer. He loaned Matthew a Leica camera along with a tripod and plenty of film. They anticipated a busy spring on the Western Front.

Matthew rode horseback to the Cantigny sector. For a time, he imagined he was traversing the Oklahoma hills through rolling landscape as springtime filled in brown grass and bare limbs. Maybe he was riding through the Kiamichi Mountains to Fort Smith to cover the trial of a crime committed in the lawless Indian Territory, or maybe headed to something better, like his uncle Preston's ranch near the Red River for a wild onion dinner.

His imagination snapped when his mount wisely shied around a gaping shell hole in the road. This was far from Oklahoma. And that life in the old Choctaw Nation was even farther away.

When Matthew arrived where American forces gathered

near Cantigny for their first major engagement in the war, he felt the spirit of movement. General Pershing and the division staff made no plans to spend this spring being bombarded mercilessly in the trenches. Their strategy was to shift the battles to open warfare, a war of movement.

With movement came the need for constant communication through the telephone—the Americans favored form of transmitting messages. But the danger of using the telephone was greater than they realized.

Last winter, Matthew had been there when the 26th "Yankee Division" New England boys relieved the 1st Division in the so-called quiet sector near Bathelémont. The division had gone to great lengths to conceal their transition and identity. But when they arrived and looked across No Man's Land, the Yanks spotted a sign proudly hoisted over the German front line trench:

WELCOME 26TH DIVISION

The American Expeditionary Forces, or AEF, needed secure communications if they wanted to move forward in this war.

It wasn't hard to see the movement from Matthew's vantage point at Cantigny, which lay 70 miles north of Paris. This was the first offensive of the AEF and there would be no holding back. The 1st Division, now known as the Big Red One, was about to face their first major combat experience. Matthew was there to record Otis Leader's story.

The enemy controlled the air around Cantigny, though the French planes were busy, too. The American 28th Infantry had been selected to make the attack, along with a detachment of French flamethrowers. Assault tanks, a mechanical advancement hard to comprehend at Matthew's 47 years of age, rehearsed in conjunction with every detail of the planned attack. And the 1st Division was ready to move in as relief.

Matthew set up his camera on the tripod.

Several photos later, he moved among the soldiers, asking questions, jotting notes. Anxiety built in his chest. So many of these men wouldn't see the end of the week. He hadn't found Otis yet.

Taking a break, he hunkered on the ground with his brown, hard shell suitcase that doubled as his desk and withdrew photographs he'd developed last week. The images were so black and white and flat compared to the vividly real scenes around him.

"Need a hand, *akana*?"

Matthew looked up at Corporal Otis Leader.

"I could use a hand, my friend. You know what an old man I am."

Otis didn't chuckle like Matthew expected. Matthew hadn't seen his friend in nearly a month. Otis' normally soft expression was layered below hard lines from the strain of survival. He'd seen casualties in the "quiet" sector, suffered under fire, and nearly starved, turning over dead men—fellow doughboys—to see if they had any food in the harsh winter.

Matthew had seen the haunted look before. Men reduced to an existence of only one hope—the hope of living. Keen minds grew dull. Essential tasks seemed a useless burden.

Otis squatted next to Matthew and looked at the photographs spread on the suitcase. "Really don't show it, does it?"

Matthew reached into his haversack and pulled out a well-worn envelope. "Your story notes do. I'll see that folks back home know what it was really like, and not just with these images."

Otis looked out over the battle preparations down the road, absently withdrawing an envelope from his coat.

"Will you mail this for me? They're to my babies back in Gerty. I told them I'd see them again if the Almighty was with me."

"I'll send it right off."

"No wife. She died last year."

Matthew felt an immediate kinship in those words, a sense of shared loss and grief. "I am sorry."

"I haven't felt up to writing those sweet American girls

that keep sending me letters. Maybe…maybe it don't matter any at all."

His last sentence made no sense to anyone who hadn't seen what Matthew had over the past four years.

Otis sighed. "My babies, my mama, sisters. They cried. They all cried so hard when I left."

In the distance, an Allied observation balloon floated toward the enemy lines. A German plane rose from behind a hill and a gunner began firing at the balloon from the machine gun mounted on the plane. Matthew held his breath. An Allied plane banked and dove toward the unexpected threat, but it was too far away to save the balloon and its observer.

The enormous balloon ignited in one flaming burst. The prepared observer leaped clear. His parachute carried him behind the enemy lines.

Otis looked at Matthew again, battle readiness in his eyes. "Time to go get 'em, *akana*. This is what I joined up for."

"*Ome.*"

When Otis left, Matthew gathered the photos, thinking of the coming battle to take control of Cantigny. He tucked the photos back in the suitcase and took up what felt most familiar to him, the best way he could tell a story. He started writing.

With the melting pot of nationalities, the rainbow of mankind fighting under one flag, I cannot help but think of our great chief and statesman Pushmataha. Before our people were removed from our homelands in Mississippi, after he himself had led Choctaws in battle alongside the Americans in the War of 1812, Chief Pushmataha predicted something I am witnessing in my lifetime. The great chief once said, "The Choctaw war cry will be heard in foreign lands."

It is being heard now in this foreign, blood-soaked land.

That was to be the beginning of his special article about Indian doughboys, told from the perspective of Otis Leader.

Matthew was ordered to stay away from the battlefield, the first full engagement for the 1st Division. He'd hoped to slip in closer, stay with the American Indian doughboy and his machine gun crew. But Matthew had to satisfy himself with riding horseback between the base hospital—ambulances roaring in and out of it—and the American headquarters. As he went back and forth, he picked up scatterings of casualty numbers, battle successes, and the 72-hour German bombardment.

Those were anxious days and nights. Matthew didn't sleep much, wishing he was on the front line, praying it would soon be over, and waiting for the light of each new day. But the third morning brought one of the most devastating moments of the war for him.

As Matthew scooted out of the way of a stretcher heading to the base hospital, he caught sight of the doughboy slung across it.

Corporal Otis Leader.

CHAPTER SEVENTEEN

Fort Worth, Texas
July 1918

Our time finally came. There was quite a to-do in Fort Worth when we got ready to ship out. The 36th Division had put on a big parade through Fort Worth back in April, a farewell review of sorts. It was a shame we still didn't have an insignia patch for our uniforms to show off.

Because of continued news stories about Indians, the folks cheered—fairly "tore their lungs out" as one reporter put it—when Company E marched by with Captain Veach leading.

I didn't know what to make of all the hoopla, but it seemed best to just enjoy it.

The July troop movements were supposed to be secret, but I guess since we could tell our families we were about to ship out, word spread like wildfire.

Mama and Pokni came to see me right before I left Texas. Daddy was in D.C. again. War kept him there more and more these days.

They got a hotel room in Fort Worth and I received leave to go visit. I should have known they'd busy themselves like women do, fussing about the fit of my uniform and doing everything to not talk about Samson being dead, or the terrifying stories we'd all heard of mustard gas, or how I was about to head into the bloodiest war of our combined lifetimes.

As for mustard gas, I'd never tell them about the intense training we had at Camp Bowie to adjust our gas masks in six seconds, and that they gave us shaving mirrors because it was critical to stay close-shaven so not even a breath could get through the mask.

I knew they wanted to say how proud they were that I was Private First Class Bertram Robert Dunn, but we didn't talk about that either.

Pokni lit into me about the sloppy fit of my olive drab uniform, especially the wide coat sloping off my thin shoulders and the high collar tucking too close to my chin.

Strands of fine silver escaped her tied hair, framing her strong, feminine jawline and prominent cheekbones. She clicked her tongue and snatched at my sleeves. I'd brought along a coat button with its Great Seal of the United States that had popped off the day before, knowing she'd have her sewing kit with her. She always did.

An expert seamstress, she wasn't satisfied with simply restitching the metal button. She had me go straight to the washroom and change into a robe she'd brought for herself. While I waited in the getup, nervous that one of my buddies might make a surprise appearance, I realized I hadn't grown into my man-sized uniform like I should have while training for war. That bothered me.

But I did feel like a man when Pokni finished resizing my uniform before evening. It fit sharply. No one would even notice the parts she left room in. She said, "You'll grow more before you're done."

Pokni could get the right fit without even measuring. She was one good seamstress, and kept our family stitched together, always soft and gentle with the right thing to say.

There was so much to say, yet no one would say it.

I stayed the night with them at the hotel, sleeping on the small sofa. But I knew Mama wouldn't sleep.

Not long after we'd gone to bed, she got up and set a chair near the sofa. I lay there, pretending to sleep, expecting her to start praying and not stop till dawn. I suspected she did, in her heart. But she was quiet as she sat there, staring at me. I could feel her presence and her prayers.

So many mamas had lost their boys over there. My uncle had interviewed a British mother who had lost eight sons in the war. She'd been sitting beside her youngest son—her ninth—in a hospital bed as he lay dying from wounds.

I wished Mama hadn't read that story.

◆ ◆ ◆

I dozed off sometime in the night. Dawn woke me, bright enough to make me turn my face away as it streamed in under the bottom of the curtain by the sofa. The warm light brought a false sense of comfort. I opened my eyes.

Pokni was asleep and Mama was still in that hardback wood chair by me. I figured she'd been thinking on how when I got home, I'd be mature and ready to fulfill my life's calling—do something worthy for our tribe.

I wanted to smile at her, tell her good morning, but she looked like she was finally ready to say whatever it was she'd been thinking on all night.

"When I was a young woman, I went to the Chicago World's Fair. The whole world was there, more than I ever thought I'd see in my lifetime. France, Great Britain, Austria, Belgium. And then there were the Germans. While other countries showed off their wealth and modern inventions, Germany brought its military band and an array of weapons. I will never forget the Krupp monster, the largest canon in the world at the time. The barrel was two train cars long."

I propped myself on one elbow, listening to Mama's soft voice. I'd grown up hearing this story. My younger brothers and sisters and I had gathered around bonfires on summer evenings and listened to her tell stories about the old Choctaw Nation. I especially loved hearing about the Chicago World's Fair in 1893. I held on to the tales, reminding myself that Choctaws could go and do anything in the world. It gave me confidence.

She continued, "I wondered why the Germans were so proud of their weaponry. It seemed like they had enough arms to destroy the world. I hoped then that no country would ever have to face them in war. I wouldn't have admitted it, but deep down, I was grateful they were far, far away, and would never bother us here in America."

Before the sinking of the Lusitania, I'd never given much thought on how American isolationism and war would affect me. Up until then, the war was politics. It was my uncle's stories about horrors far away. And despite training in the Benbrook trench system and live ammunition and losing my best buddy, I hadn't wrapped myself around the fullness of it. Not until now, sitting there with Mama, her acting like she was sending me off to my funeral. I shivered.

Mama looked down at her hands. "I don't want you to go, Bertram."

She always called me B.B.

"But that doesn't mean, I don't want you to go."

I wished Daddy was there to explain what she just said.

Mama looked me in the eyes, long and hard. It was her way. She could sit there all day without hardly blinking. As it was, five minutes felt like eternity brushing by us and I saw her. The wrinkles around her dove-shaped eyes that hadn't been there a few years ago. The strands of white starting to show over her ears. I'd missed a transition in her life somewhere along the way.

At first, I wondered what she saw in me. Did she think I should do more growing before I went over? It was too late. I shipped out tomorrow.

But in that looking, in that quiet, I got to know my mama. I think I understood what she said about not wanting me to go, and then wanting me to go. I nodded to let her know everything was all right, even though we both knew it wasn't. But it was.

She leaned over and took my hand. "God knows."

That was something her daddy used to say, back before he was killed by outlaws when Mama was a girl. He left his family a legacy I was still living. I'd honor him, and all my ancestors, in this war.

That was a promise I made myself, but I couldn't put it into words for my mama. So I fumbled around like I was trying to catch a bad football pass.

"I know I should be scared, and I am, but Mama, Jesus is going with me. It'll be okay. There are stars over there, too."

I reached into my pack lying beside the couch and pulled out the little Bible Pokni had given me when I was born. Mama hugged me. I wasn't afraid of the tears in her eyes or in my heart.

A star full of miracles must have broken up right above us.

♦♦♦

Dear Ida Claire Jessop,

Thank you for the cookies. I enjoyed them.

For your friends who want to know about my unit, I am in Company E, 2nd Battalion, 142nd Infantry, 71st Brigade, in the 36th Division.

We ship out soon.

Sincerely,
Bertram Robert Dunn

CHAPTER EIGHTEEN

Journey to New York
July 1918

Companies in the 142nd Infantry of the 36th Division pulled out of the Fort Worth train station to bugles blasting and bands playing. Albert was in the train car with me, and he returned the calls blast for blast until I was ready to heave him and his bugle out the window.

Other companies tramped around the platform, preparing for departure. One gal ran alongside the train I was on, waving a marriage license. Her intended stuck his head out the window three rows ahead of me, babbling about marrying her as soon as he finished licking the Fritz.

I settled in with the novel a Red Cross worker had handed me when they distributed books for us to read on the voyage.

My mind soon wandered from *Ben-Hur: A Tale of the Christ* to my cousin Victoria, Uncle Matthew's daughter, being a Red Cross volunteer the past three years. She hadn't been on American soil since. I doubted she'd ever come home to

Oklahoma, although maybe she'd settle in New York, some-place exciting and glamorous. Not Choctaw country.

I reread her last letter, which warned me not to come over there—to get a medical excuse, or lie and say I was too young, or run away, like 16 men did as we were preparing to leave Camp Bowie. But I'd made my decision to fight for my country.

In Arlington, girls gave us magazines for the trip, which we were happy to get. Down the line, the Red Cross handed out fruit and cigarettes. I didn't want any part of the latter, but the fruit was good to combat the stifling Texas heat.

The four-day train trip had its own adventures. Though the train chugged straight through without overnight stops, it did halt every six hours for refueling. We bailed at one such stop to take a swim at the YMCA in Atlanta, Georgia. Tobias prodded Isaac into getting off the train. The last time I'd gone swimming with Isaac was on that good, bad day. I stayed clear of him in the pool.

Sometimes I rode on the open flatbed cars to catch a breeze. In one town, I saw a girl looking at all our gear—namely gas masks and rifles. She cooed, "It's so exciting!"

Plenty of young ladies were captivated by the Indian doughboys. That almost led to fights with their menfolk when the women became fascinated with what they called our "swarthy red-tinted skin," but fortunately, the train whistle called us back and pulled out just in time.

Further north, in Jersey City, some of the men went AWOL and had themselves a time. They were welcomed into homes, and a policeman bought them anything they wanted.

It convinced us Southwesterners that Northerners were really more hospitable than we'd always believed. They treated us like heroes just back from the Western Front instead of untested recruits just now heading there. War fever and patriotism had created frenzy from one end of the country to the other, bringing even the north and south together.

We made it to the New York Port of Embarkation after four days of train travel, and I expected to settle in for a stay before shipping out. But once we ferried across the bay to Brooklyn—almost in the shadow of the Statue of Liberty—they hauled us to Camp Mills, where the staff was already experienced in shipping out troops. The processing only took twenty-four hours.

I was nervous when they said the citizenship of each soldier would be "probed." Some of the Indians in the 36th Division weren't citizens of the United States yet. I was afraid they'd get sent home after all the training and sacrifice. But the inspectors were more worried about German spies than American Indians.

We were issued the things we lacked, though I heard Colonel Bloor put in a complaint about motor transportation and draft animals not being sent over with us.

Then they loaded us on trains and transported us back to Brooklyn. From there, we boarded lighters—flat-bottomed barges—and traveled to the Hoboken piers. Jewish Welfare Board workers served hot cocoa and corned beef sandwiches while we waited in the nippy morning air.

Someone shouted it was time to board. We lined up by the narrow ramp leading to the deck of the USS Rijndam, a former passenger liner who had seen her fair share of troubles before the Navy seized her. She'd been rammed once and had struck an underwater mine a few years ago. In her more recent career in the Navy, she'd nearly been torpedoed by a German U-boat.

I wasn't sure whether to be grateful for or worried by her history.

The command "right by file" came. Each man's name rang out clear over the water. I stepped up on the gangplank when mine was shouted. Most of the men had smiling faces at the thought of the exciting times ahead. We would set sail the next day for over there.

The ship blew a long, deep whistle, a tangible signal that my story was about to become intertwined in the annals of history.

♦ ♦ ♦

That evening, we crowded into our bunks. I ended up with Lee Hoade above me again.

The Choctaws I knew were further back. Most of the Indians spoke their native language only in little groups when no one else could hear. There was a common consensus to get quiet when anyone came close. I heard stories about other government-run Indian boarding schools, and what happened to the men around me when they were boys and beaten within an inch of their lives for speaking their language. I knew my own experiences.

"B.B."

Jim waved me over to where he and Solomon sat talking about the Spanish flu and the possibility of it turning into something worse than we experienced at Camp Bowie when Samson died. This new epidemic had spread through the training camps and the civilian population in America and Europe.

Isaac passed by us on his way to claim a bunk further down. Our eyes met, but he gave me a hard look that warned me not to speak to him.

When he was out of earshot, Jim elbowed me. "What's between the two of you, anyway?"

I shrugged.

The conversation shifted to swapping magazines. I glanced up at the bunk where Lee Hoade lay clutching a piece of paper, face red. He looked mighty upset.

I stood and walked over to our bunks in the crowded section. "Hey, Hoade, you got the flu already?"

Lee Hoade sat up quick and swung his feet off the bunk. I ducked.

He gritted his teeth, staring over my head. "I wish I could, but I know I can't."

"Can't what?"

He stared at me. "How old are you?"

"Nineteen."

"I might tell you when you're a man." He shot off the bunk and landed with a thud beside me. Fishing a cigarette from his pocket, he headed to the exit.

Before long, things settled down below deck, everyone waiting for morning when we'd start off to a foreign country. I lay in my bunk, hearing the soft exchanges flow in my native tongue and missing Samson. He'd be fit to bust, all excited about crossing the vast ocean and seeing another continent. I knew, though, he was seeing a lot more beautiful sights in Heaven.

◆◆◆

The next day, I went up on deck with thousands of fellow soldiers to wave a final farewell to the home country. I tried to move closer to the front where I could see, but things were packed tight. So I did what little guys can do that big ones can't. I got down low and quick crawled between legs to get to the front. The men above laughed at my antics. I was so excited and scared, I laughed too.

Bumping into the ship rails, I stuck my head between them and was instantly nauseated. Several stories below was the green-blue water that must have reflected my new facial colors. I pulled my head back and looked straight out. That restored my stomach as I stared in awe at the sight on the wooden platform below.

And the buildings! Every window was crowded with people hanging out and waving handkerchiefs and miniature American flags. We sent back cheer for cheer.

The enormous ship woke, shuddered, and swung away from the dock. As we moved past another section of the city—near Broadway, someone said—a Navy band bid us farewell with the *Star-Spangled Banner*. I was as proud to be an American as ever in my life.

Even as that feeling swelled in my chest, I thought of my father in D.C., arguing with the U.S. government about tribal rights. I thought of my great-grandmother who had walked the Trail of Tears and buried both her parents along the way. I thought of Isaac being whipped for speaking our language.

I sat back on my heels as the cheering and flag-waving continued. I was an American soldier, backed by our shared history, heading out to risk my life for my country and its freedom, wondering if this war might, ironically, bring unity to our country.

In the press of the crowd, I wiggled to a standing position and saluted the majestic Statue of Liberty as we passed her.

FRANCE

"The Choctaw war cry will be heard in foreign lands."

Chief Pushmataha

CHAPTER NINETEEN

Journey to France
July 1918

Company E in the 2nd Battalion of the 142nd Infantry in the 71st Brigade of the 36th Division was on its way over there at last.

A good ninety percent of the soldiers had never seen a ship before and there we were in a convoy of fourteen monster vessels on the tremendous Atlantic Ocean.

It wasn't long before excitement was replaced with that green-blue I feared would come over me. But I started gaining my "sea legs" after the first day.

On the second day, the mess hall was nearly empty. I settled at a table with the few hardy souls who had turned up for chow. But halfway through breakfast, two of the men changed colors and bolted from the table to go hang over the rail. The food was awful.

I nibbled on bread and eyed the man across from me who had just sat down with a plate of fried eggs. The cook must have been okay with a special order, grateful someone was eating at least.

The man, slender face and narrow nose, took the pepper shaker and went to work on the eggs. I stared at him, feeling green. Between lips swelling with an unwanted feeling, I said, "You sure shoot those eggs with pepper."

He shoveled a scoop into his mouth, then asked, "Where are you from?"

"Oklahoma…"

"I'm from the Durant area. Mead. You?"

"Durant…yeah…"

"Family there?"

"Um…"

I shoved away from the table and ran out. I found an empty space among the dozens of tough boys hanging like rag dolls over the rail.

The man next to me shook his head. "They feed us good on this ship. Six meals a day. Three down, three up."

I never wanted to see a fried egg again.

◆ ◆ ◆

By the third day, most of us were on our feet half the time. Things were crowded though. The bunks were small and stacked in tiers four deep. There was standing room only on the deck, with coal carts clogging things up.

I was filthy every day, something Mama would have tanned me for. I was raised that cleanliness was next to godliness, but I was a perfect heathen on the ship.

Despite the filth, and my bland diet of bread and water, there were some bright spots after we got going, like the movies they showed every night—one for the regular guys, one for the officers. I rarely went to the movies while at Armstrong Academy, though Daddy took us to see one when we were in D.C. Most of the Oklahoma boys had never seen the likes of Mary Pickford on the silver screen.

We also had lifeboat drills which, after the sinking of the Lusitania and lack of preparedness that led to over 1,000 deaths, made me feel uneasy and secure at the same time. So far, the United States Navy had done well in protecting the transport ships. The navy wasn't fighting on the front, but they were keeping us safe so we could.

Early on Sunday morning, I went on deck for the service held at the bow. Chaplain Barnes had a congregation gathering and I looked forward to hearing his down-home, Oklahoma Bible preaching.

A shrill call pierced the air. It was the bugle sounding for lifeboat drill. Wild-eyed, everyone took off for the lifeboats. I jumped up, but halted when Chaplain Barnes didn't move. I didn't want him to get left behind.

Chaplain Barnes opened his arms wide as if to draw his flock back. He looked at me—his last parishioner—and said, "Son, that was the church call, not the lifeboats."

I chuckled nervously and listened to his sermon as the congregation drifted back.

One thing I wished for was that our regiment had its own publication. I sheepishly recalled my uncle encouraging me by letter to start one back at Camp Bowie, but I was no writer. Not like him or Mama.

They had accomplished good things with their newspaper back before and after Oklahoma became a state. I was proud of their work, but it didn't light a fire under me. Neither did law, like Daddy's work. But I'd have to do something after the war, and I doubted it would be football.

The ship itself had a publication called the Hatchet, which received bulletins from the radiogram. The publication kept us posted on war zone news and what was going on back home.

One afternoon, I was reading the Hatchet on my bunk when I heard a loud boom. I knew what it was and scrambled with the rest of the boys not too sick to run up the stairs and onto the crowded deck.

I crawled to get close to the rail. Several wooden bobs floated behind one of the ships we traveled with. I craned my neck through the rail to see the gun crew from our ship take aim and cut loose. The wooden targets being pulled behind the other ship exploded, and we cheered.

Those gunners were crack shots. No U-boat stood a chance with them.

The next day, my turn came for the compulsory flu shot. I hated the thought of another needle. I'd never been so poked and prodded in my life.

The young man in front of me looked worse than seasick about the shot. I wondered if he would run off, but there wasn't anywhere to go in the middle of the ocean.

His head trembled like an old dog as he looked straight ahead, stiff as a corpse when the doctor stuck the long needle in his arm. I started to move forward for my turn, but the kid didn't budge. The doctor turned around and reloaded his syringe.

I opened my mouth to say something, but before I could, the doctor turned back and, not realizing it was the same soldier, stuck the kid again!

The kid's head stopped shaking. He went rigid then fell over in a faint. Orderlies gathered him up and the doctor turned to me.

I took my shot and went out on deck for air, feeling woozy. The boys around me would just think it was seasickness. Same result.

CHAPTER TWENTY

St. Nazaire, France
July 1918

We sailed in off the coast of St. Nazaire, France, with a destroyer escort. Up the River Loire, masts stuck out of the water from sunken vessels like old pirate ships. Along the bank, French civilians waved and welcomed us to their country.

After twelve days at sea, not many on the ship were ready to fight, except Lee Hoade. Something ate at him all the way over, something about the letter he carried in his shirt pocket. He pulled it out occasionally when he was by the rail, smoking. One time he wadded it up and started to throw it overboard but stopped. If he'd caught me watching, he would have put his cigarette out in my eye.

Destroyers escorted us in to dock and we went through processing once again. Only this time, we were in France! There I was, a young Choctaw man on the other side of the world, stepping onto foreign soil and into a village filled with houses and shops made of stone.

The French people greeted us as enthusiastically as the Americans had sent us off, but there was a marked difference. The people looked battle worn, hungry, exhausted. They'd been ravaged by war nearly four years and here we'd come to save them. I didn't feel much like a rescuer.

I thought of how my people had been removed from our homelands in Mississippi, and how less than a hundred years later, our tribe was all but gone.

As we marched into St. Nazaire, we could hardly get through the village. People waved French and American flags, cheered, and patted us on the back like we'd already won the war. A group of girls and boys sang out in English, "Hail! Hail! The Gang's All Here!"

We could see that the French were people like us. They had their joys, their sorrows, their pains. And their hopes.

An older woman cried as she clung to Corporal Solomon Bond Louis' arm. The old man behind her, hands on her shoulders and tears in his eyes, spoke.

"Merci beaucoup."

Solomon looked to me for help. I gently tugged the old woman away from him. Her fleshy arm was soft and deep like my grandmother's. I pressed her into the arms of the man, who took her gently as they wept.

Isaac, one of the few who hadn't gotten seasick on the way over, had a death grip on the strap of his rifle. He looked ready to do the fighting we'd come for.

In the last edition of the Hatchet, a woman had written an article saying we needed to blast Germany beyond recognition where they could never do anything like this again for hundreds of years. I'd just set foot on French soil and I was starting to feel that way.

When American boys had first started landing the previous year, the French wanted to whisk them straight to the front lines to replenish their own troops. But General Pershing put a halt to that. He knew the American troops weren't ready for full combat and had set up training camps for us. He wanted proper preparation and a new battle strategy.

That made the French and British mad, but they were already mad at us for being so late to the war—for being "too proud to fight" as President Wilson had unfortunately said—so it didn't much matter.

The Allies and the Central Powers were locked in a bloody stalemate in what I'd heard called a war of "attrition." I looked up the word and learned it meant that rather than trying to take a fortified section, the enemy would make attacks in a way that costs the defenders more lives than a straight-out battle.

The German military had attacked villages and ethnically valuable spots so the French would sacrifice scores of troops to save it. To bleed France white.

Attrition sounded like a mean word.

As we went along, Company E got cut off from the rest of the 142nd. The French people circled us. I disentangled myself from one boy who kept grabbing my coat sleeve and tugging it. I finally understood when Tobias had his foldable overseas cap, with its narrow, tapered crown, prodded off.

He smiled and knelt so the children could touch his hair. The adults eagerly gathered around, and I heard someone say in English, "It is not curly!"

Despite his outgoing personality, Tobias was taken aback by the attention. He looked around, big-eyed in wonder at this country and its people that were so very happy to meet him.

Lieutenant Horner came to our rescue. "They've never seen American Indians in person before. Your people are popular in Europe."

Slowly, Lieutenant Horner and I worked our way ahead of Company E, making a path for the Indian doughboys through the river of emotions sweeping us along the streets of St. Nazaire.

Something was shifting in my being as I encountered the French people, their culture, their current tragedy. Because of the stories and reports I'd heard, nothing surprised me, not even the palpable grief. Yet this experience was changing me.

My being expanded to include this part of the world and

there was something very important about that. Something like what Mama experienced when she went to the Chicago World's Fair. Only instead of the world coming to me, I'd gone to it. I was a part of something bigger than I could have imagined back home.

As I walked side by side with Lieutenant Horner, I saw him differently. He'd joined the State Guard to escape his stepmother. Now there he was, an officer popular with his men, serving his country and the world.

Long after our march through St. Nazaire—after we made it to the barns that would serve as our barracks for the night—those thoughts lingered with me. Lieutenant Horner was making a difference in the world. That was what my folks assumed I'd do, too.

Why couldn't I do it through the U.S. Army, even after there was no massive war threatening the world? As I laid atop hay in the barn loft my first night overseas, that revelation began to shape my thoughts about the future.

I thought about how I should write down everything I was thinking and what I had seen in France that day. But I wasn't ready to commit it to paper.

My journal remained blank.

CHAPTER TWENTY-ONE

Soissons, France
July 1918

"*A*kana! My friend!" Matthew turned his horse to fall in next to the marching American soldiers. "You're out of the hospital already?"

He reached down from the saddle to shake hands with Corporal Otis Leader. Otis looked healthier, having rested from his flesh wound and gassing at the successful taking of Cantigny. But his cheeks still sagged from the strain of war.

At least he smiled.

"Ah, my old, *old* friend. They decided not to attack at Soissons without me. And I was getting fat."

He chuckled at his own joke and patted his flat stomach. At over six-feet-tall, there was plenty of room for extra grub, if there was any.

After walking his horse alongside Otis in the column of marching soldiers, catching up on the past few months, Matthew moved ahead to take a position on a little rise to watch the thousands of doughboys filing by.

All humor soon faded into the night as the troops naturally slowed their pace. Matthew stayed mounted—it was harder and harder to get back up in a saddle—and watched the stream of American soldiers working their way up the muddy road choked with trucks, artillery, and wagon trains.

Bleeding feet, hungry, aching, so utterly exhausted death would have been a joy. That was how Otis had described the march to him. Matthew wrote it down to add to the article.

It would be a long story with some 12,000 American Indians who had volunteered or been drafted for service. Matthew had interviewed many that spring and summer, but the story wasn't finished.

He heard the clatter of a rifle as another doughboy passed out and fell. Two others stopped to help him. The rest pressed on. They didn't know it yet, but Matthew had heard the exhausted troops would be ordered to jump off at Soissons without rest before dawn.

Paris was in danger.

◆◆◆

Matthew was ordered to stay back from the Soissons front. That didn't keep him from hearing that Corporal Otis Leader's gun crew came under a violent barrage and all his men had been killed. The last the reporting soldier saw of him, Otis had scooped up a fallen French soldier's gun and charged across No Man's Land alone.

Matthew got as close as he could to the battle. The earth trembled beneath him, heaving and tossing him to the ground when a series of shells exploded nearby. He was too close but kept moving toward the tricky terrain the Americans fought over. He wasn't concerned about any story; he wanted to know what happened to his friend.

The landscape included a hazardously bare plateau, sloping gradually up from the Forêt de Retz and then abruptly dropping off into Crises Valley, a country cut up by deep ravines, each protected by villages and farm buildings. On its

Eastern edge, where it fell off into the valley, were strong points like Villementaire, the final defenses to the Soissons-Paris highway. If the Allies failed at Soissons, the enemy could march right to Paris.

The houses of the villages and farms were mostly stone, affording excellent cover for German troops. The open spaces were covered with standing grain.

Matthew took refuge with the Marines who marched prisoners back from the front, and that was when he recognized Otis where he stood out in a horde of field gray-clad German prisoners. The tall Indian spotted him as he handed off nearly 20 prisoners.

"What happened?" Matthew asked.

Otis waved a French rifle, eyes bright, skin flushed with wild energy, face split with a grin born of reckless success.

"I took these fellers from their own nest. I poked the gun over the trench and yelled at them. I don't know what I yelled, I just sort of whooped. Their hands went up and I marched them back across No Man's Land, didn't a one of us get shot."

Matthew had to know. "How many bullets did you have left?"

Otis held up a bullet next to the French automatic rifle he carried. "Oh, this was the only one I had, and I didn't know how to load it."

"Is the gun...is it empty?"

"Yep."

"What would you have done if you'd needed to shoot?"

Otis' grin widened as he shrugged. Matthew laughed and Otis joined him, both losing their breath and coughing at the ridiculous notion of the Indian taking prisoners with an empty rifle.

Matthew gripped his friend's shoulder as he regained control of his voice. "That must have been some whoop you let out."

Otis made a good story.

To Matthew Teller—

I hope you are keeping your head down. I heard things are getting hot for the Americans, and Floyd Gibbons, that crazy war correspondent like you, got himself shot up with the Marines in Belleau Woods. A miracle he survived, if you can still believe in miracles after all you've seen in this war. I'm more likely to believe when I'm drunk.

Truly,
Tom Alders

◆ ◆ ◆

Tom,

I spoke with Floyd in the hospital. The arm and shoulder wounds will heal, though he won't get his eye back. In his usual way, focused on the story, he said he had always wondered what it felt like to be shot on the field of battle. Now he knows and can write it more accurately (thankfully he was shot on the left side, not the right) though he made the outlandish claim that it hurt no more than dropping a lit cigarette on the back of his hand. You know Floyd.

I've never been drunk, but yes. I do still believe in miracles.

Chi pisa la chike,
Matthew

CHAPTER TWENTY-TWO

"As an Englishmen remarked: 'They call Americans 'Yanks,' because when they're not yanking themselves into a moving train, they're yanking a telephone toward them.'" —Captain A. Lincoln Lavine, Air Service. Formerly of the American Telephone and Telegraph Company

Bar-sur-Aube, France
August 1918

On the journey to the 13th training zone at Bar-sur-Aube, we were initiated on the French railway system. The boxcars were marked "40-8" meant to carry either 40 men or eight horses. They should have relabeled them to hold a maximum of 20 Texans. None of us would ever forget that ride.

On the way, though, the farmland we traveled through was a sight to behold. Laid out like a patchwork quilt rolling over the hills of central France, the colors ranged from bright yellows to deep green to vineyards of twisting brown vines.

At the training area, Company E billeted at Couvignon.

My quarters were in the loft of a farmer's barn. The family welcomed us and shared small comforts that made the living conditions more bearable.

Piles of manure garnished the farms. I learned the bigger the piles, the wealthier a family was considered, so folks displayed them proudly. The Americans didn't take to that at all. But the people were happy to have us and offered us homemade treats, so we didn't complain.

Special schools throughout the training camp put an emphasis on how to write messages to be transmitted by telephone, runners, dogs, or carrier pigeons. Fast, reliable communication was critical on the front.

I traded the canvas leggings that went over the laced calves of my riding-style breeches for wool puttees. The French told us they were much more suitable for the trenches than the leggings. The puttees were a hassle to put on—similar to wrapping a bandage, which wasn't a comforting thought. But after a few days of practice, I could put them on with my eyes closed.

We were antsier than we'd been in Camp Bowie, but they marched that out of us. Just like there, we dug trenches and drilled for weeks.

No one snickered about how small Choctaws were anymore. We proved to be "exceptional" soldiers, our commanding officers said. We were hardy. Our ancestors had taught us perseverance.

The training was intense—night and daytime maneuvers and target ranges we hadn't had for lack of equipment in Texas. The big, rolling terrain was made up mostly of farmland, though there was still a foreignness about it. I was a long way from home. But despite the language and cultural differences, I felt a kinship with the French people and the land. They were farmers as Choctaws had been for centuries. It was a simple life of hard work. I wondered how long it would take the French to reclaim that life as we had after the long, deadly march from our homelands in Mississippi to Indian Territory.

There was plenty of time for letter writing at the training

camp. I stopped in to deliver a message to Lieutenant Horner one sunshiny day, and he had a stack of his own going. I asked who he was writing, and he said they were to his sisters.

"How many do you have?"

"Three."

I winced, thinking about my mostly sweet, but not always little sisters at home.

Horner smiled. "They raised me after my mother died."

He told me that his father was still around, but not really, because he was always drunk. His siblings were his family. Well, that and a pretty girl in the photograph he showed me. It was a good thing he proposed to her before we shipped out.

Though not Choctaw, his fiancée was born in Talihina in the old Choctaw Nation, Indian Territory. Her family moved to Arkansas where she and Elijah Horner grew up in church together. He sang in the choir and she played the piano. I overheard him singing in camp once. He had a fine voice, and I hoped he'd make it home to marry Maude Katherine Board.

While he talked, I compared his story and Solomon's. They both had lost parents and were the only ones in their family to graduate high school.

The lieutenant asked if I had a girl I was writing to back home. I must have flushed because he laughed good-naturedly, and changed the subject to remind me that every-one needed to submit ideas for the 36th Division insignia or we'd go to the front without one.

I spent those couple of months writing about the French countryside and the farmland and the people in letters to my family, though I didn't mention my thoughts of staying in the army.

Folks from home sent me letters, keeping me up to date on happenings. Mama and Pokni sent me a package with socks and goodies they instructed me to share, while my brothers and sisters sent me drawings, beaded necklaces, and a handmade doll I could gift to French children. Superintendent Peru Farver from Armstrong wrote to say he had resigned his position at the academy to enter the army. I was proud to hear that.

I opened the last letter.

Dear Bertram Robert Dunn,

I have read five books about France and would be pleased if you sent me a letter from there. I would save the postage in my scrapbook.

> *Sincerely,*
> *Ida Claire*

At the next mail call, I received a letter from my uncle Matthew who was near the front. I figured he was pretty tired of all the traveling and the war, but his words came through strong like I remembered him.

> *Somewhere in France*
> *August 14, 1918*

Dear Bertram,

I heard the 36th arrived in France. The navy did an admirable job in getting our boys here, something I especially appreciate after the Lusitania sinking in 1915.

I hope you are writing your experiences in the journal I sent. This is one of the most significant historical events of our time and having accounts from American soldiers will be invaluable for history.

More importantly, we must never forget our own people's sacrifice and tell our stories. We cannot expect anyone to tell them for us.

Writing will help you understand what you have been through in ways your mind alone cannot.

I pray for you every day. God knows.

> *With respect, your uncle,*
> *Matthew Teller*

P.S. Victoria is still serving in the Red Cross on the Western Front, though I do not know where. Perhaps you can look for her if you have the opportunity.

I tucked the letter in the back of the empty journal where I had all my letters from home strapped in. I just didn't know how to start writing in the journal, afraid I'd write the wrong things, thoughts that were too personal, and it would be sent home to my family to read if I was killed, and they wouldn't understand what I was trying to say.

Besides, I was sure someone else would tell our story someday.

♦♦♦

On break from drill, I sat under a tree on a stump with a group of Choctaws where we talked quietly but laughed loud. Isaac had joined us, though he said nothing.

"Looks like you boys are having a good time," came an unfamiliar voice.

A short, scrawny man plopped himself on the ground among us seated on stumps and logs. We quieted. He took off the camera case strapped around his neck and fanned himself with a tablet.

"Whew, it's no cooler here than the Middle East. Not so much sand though. Be grateful you boys weren't sent that way. Hotter than…"

His voice drifted, and he looked around at us. We must have looked like the often thought image of Indians—solemn, stoic. He didn't know it was just our way with strangers.

The man whistled low. "Say, you boys look like you're ready to fight. Mind if I get a picture?"

He scooted back, still seated in the dust, opened the case, and pulled out a camera. Still too close, he leaned back till he was almost laying on the ground, camera mashed against his face, and snapped a picture. We didn't move.

Then he raised up and stuck his hand out to me. "Name's

Kent Powell."

I shook his hand and he, in turn, shook hands with everyone.

"I hope you don't think I look ugly, because you'll be seeing a lot of me. I've been assigned to the 36th."

A war correspondent. I wished they'd put Uncle Matthew with us. But this fellow seemed all right. We even chuckled at his joke.

Ben Carterby, in the 141st Infantry and built stout, was the first to speak to the man still on the ground. "You lay out on the ground like that again, we might accidentally step on you. That'd make you uglier."

Kent Powell cocked his head as the Choctaws elbowed each other with grins. "You'd be surprised how much I can see from down here."

There was a tinge of something in his tone. I saw it in his eyes. Sincerity. Respect. I started to like him as he sat on the ground in the middle of us, having to look up where we sat on stumps.

He laughed easy and wasn't afraid to make fun of or be teased himself. He was early thirties, blue eyes and blonde hair, born and raised in Texas, which we laughed about because we thought all Texans were big and loud and proud. While he wasn't ashamed to put himself right in the middle of things, he wasn't arrogant or puffed up, just quick and scrappy.

He asked questions about our families, our tribal history, and where we were from. I was surprised at some of the answers because we hadn't talked much about it in the year of being together. We would talk about home folks, but didn't tell all the stories.

Albert spoke up. "My grandfather, Simon Billy, was born on the trail from Mississippi. He speaks only Choctaw."

I tensed, afraid the reporter would ask about our language. But the stories continued with Ben Carterby. His round face matched his nose, and his lips settled into a relaxed line when he wasn't smiling. He had been placed in the 141st Infantry rather than Company E with us in the 142nd, but he and Jim were always joking around.

Ben told how his grandparents had been removed from Mississippi and settled the new Carterby home place in the Ouachita Mountains.

Like Solomon, Mitchell Bobb shared that he had been a ward of Hosea L. Fowler prior to his enlistment.

Then there was Benjamin Colbert Jr., the youngest among us. In fact, I suspected he was underage even now, but no one ever mentioned it. Benjamin told about his father being a Rough Rider during the Spanish-American War.

After him, the Davenport brothers talked about growing up around Antlers, Oklahoma. But Jim had the most fun with introducing himself to Kent Powell, who was feverishly writing and trying to spell everyone's name correctly.

"James Edwards?"

"Jim."

"Oh, Jim?"

"Jimpson."

Kent Powell stopped but didn't raise his head. "Jimpson?"

"But you can call me James."

Ben spoke up. "James is short for Jimpson."

Kent Powell knew he was being had. We started chuckling and I felt obliged to explain.

"He was born Jimpson Morrison Edwards, but folks called him Jim. In boarding school, they thought Jim was a nickname for James. For your records, he's Corporal James Edwards."

Kent Powell looked sideways at me, grinning, and I knew he'd look to me in the future to give him the straight story. The fact that the boys teased him, though, was a sign of their acceptance.

Ben elbowed Jim but spoke to Powell. "This Indian wants to be a Methodist preacher when he grows up. Think a congregation will have him?"

"God works in mysterious ways."

We chuckled at Kent Powell's wit before he continued, not wanting to leave anyone out.

Tobias had joined with the rest of us not long after war was declared, along with many current and former Armstrong Academy students. He'd been in the army over a year and had made corporal back in December.

I'd always looked up to Tobe when we were at Armstrong. He was one of the older boys who never got into much trouble, polite and kind, even to the younger boys. He learned patience and tolerance being the oldest of several children.

Kent Powell heard us call Private Benjamin Wilburn Hampton "Bennie." Square-jawed, he had a dark complexion with coal black hair. Bennie had a wife and farm back home.

Noel Johnson, now a corporal, was from Smithville, and had attended Dwight Indian Training School. Then there was Jeff Nelson from Kullituklo.

I had known Corporal Peter P. Maytubby was 26, not married yet, but not how on the Dawes Roll, they had him registered as Chickasaw. He spoke Choctaw fluently.

Robert Taylor from Idabel was full-blood Choctaw.

Corporal Calvin Wilson, shorter than me by an inch, was a farmer from Eagletown, Oklahoma.

A rumble of laughter started when it came around to Solomon Bond Louis, born in Hochatown, Indian Territory. We knew how he'd fibbed about his age to join up, but none of us would give him away except for a chuckle or two. He was serious about his service to his country. Then he let an important detail about his life slip out that few knew but me.

Jim stared at him. "You got married?"

Solomon would never live that down. The guys teased him mercilessly.

Kent Powell grinned, took more pictures, shook hands again and headed off. It was time for us to get back to drill and he had plenty more soldiers to talk to.

Him taking time to interview us like we were the only American soldiers in France instead of a dozen among two million made me like Kent Powell. He'd be a good man to have writing about us.

♦ ♦ ♦

August 1917
Somewhere in France

Dear Ida Claire,

Thank you for writing me. Letters from folks back home mean a great deal to soldiers.
The French countryside is pretty. I hope you enjoy the stamps.

Sincerely,
Bertram

CHAPTER TWENTY-THREE

Western Front, France
September 1918

With nearly two million American troops joining the fight in France, Matthew found himself moving between divisions more. Frank Palmer asked him to help coordinate the American war correspondents on the Western Front. He had finally finished his special article on Indian doughboys after the battle at Soissons, and sent it off to the American newspaper that had purchased the story. There were few articles he'd been so proud to write.

When the battle of Amiens started pushing German forces back, Matthew was occasionally able to snag German propaganda through captured papers passed on to him by acquaintances in the French Army. He was particularly grateful when he obtained nearly an entire copy of *Rhenish Westphalian Gazette*.

Settled at his spot in a barn in Gondrecourt, Matthew read through the bloodstained newspaper, grateful he'd been studying the German and French languages enough to read newspapers and reports.

It wasn't hard to figure out why the officer who gave it to him thought he'd be interested. The articles slandered and downgraded the value of American troops, but what caught his attention—with mild amusement—was the story about a feared ethnic group among the doughboys: American Indians.

Years before, Indians had been popularized in Europe through novels about the American West written by authors like Karl May, who was German. Now the German propaganda machine seemed set on destroying the iconic view of the "noble savage" and his "ghastly" techniques in warfare. Those were tantalizing stories to read at home in front of a cozy fireplace. It was another matter when that reader became the young soldier on a battlefield about to face that vicious, superhuman being.

The writer of the story apparently so feared the demoralizing effect on troops it claimed there were no American Indians in the war at all. The few Indians left, it said, were dying out, "thoroughly degenerated from drink" and could not become soldiers.

Matthew chuckled. How terrified they would be to know thousands of Indian soldiers were camped on the Western Front. He'd have to write a sequel to his article about Indian doughboys.

But when the anticipated American newspaper came in the mail that afternoon, it showed how paltry erroneous reporting on the enemy side was compared to the home front.

Matthew's article was a truthful assessment of Indian soldiers—their strengths and weakness he perceived they would show in battle based on research and questioning new troops as they arrived. He'd reported the personal account of Otis Leader as one of the first doughboys to experience everything except death in the war.

Matthew had labored over the material all summer and sent the article off, satisfied with knowing a good telling would reach the folks back home about their native people's contributions in the war.

But what he wrote and what was printed were two wildly different stories. His sister had sent him a copy with a note of sadness indicating she knew how his article had been butchered. That was putting it politely.

About the only thing left intact was the number of American Indian soldiers Matthew attributed to the various divisions, and those numbers were inflated. But it was the bizarre narrative that made him want to stuff the article down the barrel of a howitzer.

Opposite the bleak picture Germans painted of Indians, Americans romanticized and over-glorified their cunning prowess and abilities, portraying them as having near-supernatural abilities. The story gushed about what fine scouts Indians made, how they could track the Fritz by sniffing the wind, how not even tanks could stop the stoic warriors.

Matthew scrubbed a hand over his face and held it there. When he'd closed his newspaper, the *Choctaw Tribune*, four years ago, that should have been the end of his career as a reporter. He should have just retired his pencil and his determination to write truth. He could have settled on his allotment peacefully and lived to be a really old Choctaw.

Instead, he'd tried to put an ocean between himself and his Indian troubles by becoming a war correspondent. But wherever he went, the truth was loud enough to still call him.

When American troops started pouring into France, he saw an opportunity to tell his people's story while standing on a platform he'd never had nor ever would have again.

All that, and his article had been butchered.

Matthew growled, sat down at his suitcase desk, and did what he always did in a moment like this. He picked up a pencil and started writing.

September 1918
Somewhere in France

Dear Annie,

First, thank you for sending the newspaper clipping.
Second, you'll find a copy of my original article enclosed.
Third, a small printer and printing materials are in the attic at Uncle Preston's. Print and distribute the enclosed story under the banner of the Choctaw Tribune.

With love and respect, your brother,
Matthew Teller

CHAPTER TWENTY-FOUR

Bar-sur-Aube, France
October 1918

When summer surrendered fully to autumn, I was called into Colonel Alfred Bloor's P.C., his Post of Command. The first thought that jumped to mind was that I was in serious trouble. I racked my brain over my training the past few months, wondering if there was any reason for Sergeant Chill to report me for anything. It felt like boarding school, where any wrong twitch could ruin my reputation, and my folks back home would hear.

The P.C. was located in an old farmhouse that must have stood for a hundred years or so. I stepped inside as another man left. He looked happy, so maybe he'd left the colonel in a good mood.

Colonel Alfred Bloor was there along with Captain Veach, Lieutenant Horner, and the dreaded Sergeant Chill. Good thing I had our U.S. bag tied to the back of my belt.

"Have a seat, Private Dunn."

Colonel Bloor motioned to the chair in front of the table

that served as his desk, but he remained standing, flipping through papers as though trying to find something.

He paused once I was seated. "I've reviewed your camp record and your educational background. I've approved Lieutenant Horner's recommendation for your promotion. Congratulations, Corporal Dunn."

It was a mighty good thing I was sitting down, though I partially came out of my seat.

"Sir...are you sure, sir?"

I wished I hadn't spoken. Sergeant Chill glared at me. He sure wouldn't have recommended me for promotion.

Colonel Bloor looked at me over the papers and I felt like a fool. I quickly edited my initial response down to, "Yes, sir."

"Lieutenant Horner will brief you tomorrow. We are no longer looking at months of training, Corporal. We are heading into the thick of combat."

"Yes, sir."

"Any questions?"

"No, sir."

"Dismissed."

I didn't know why the fellow ahead of me had looked happy. I felt like I did the second day on the ship. Blue-green with my lips tingling. At the same time, I couldn't wait to send the news home, and to my uncle there in France.

"Corporal Dunn!"

Halting, I let Lieutenant Horner catch up. He stood in a relaxed manner.

"Corporal, I want to give you a piece of advice before the briefing and our focus is solely on battle."

I waited, trying not to think too far ahead.

"I've watched you the past year. With your exemplary camp record, if you exhibit leadership skills, you have a chance of making sergeant before war's end, and could be looking at an opportunity for military school. There is no faster way to advance than in wartime."

"Yes, sir. Thank you."

Horner nodded and started back toward the P.C. Then he turned back, and I saw the side-smile we knew him for when he wanted to give us a wink.

"Oh, and don't forget to pick up your new sidearm."

I'd finally get to carry an M1911 Colt .45 like Solomon and the others. I grinned. "Yes, sir."

I was now Corporal Bertram Robert Dunn.

The news beat me back to the tents. My friends back-slapped me, and Corporal James Edwards put me in a head-lock and scrubbed my scalp with his knuckles.

"Look at this little Indian! Jerry doesn't stand a chance."

Only two didn't care about my promotion. Isaac was one. I expected that. But I didn't feel too good when Lee Hoade dismissed my news by turning his back on me, spitting, and lighting up a cigarette.

I borrowed Solomon's book, *Home Reading Course for Citizen-Soldiers*, recalling the off-duty times we'd all spent reading it together back in Camp Bowie, back when Samson was alive. I wanted everyone in my new squad to live.

Use your personality and your influence to help the men in your own squad and company carry on their work and prepare as possible for the big task ahead of you.

◆◆◆

The reason for a great many promotions that day was because the whole division was being culled of officers who were reassigned for various reasons, including advanced weapons training. Even a general was removed.

The 36th didn't have much time to adjust to the sudden reassignment of over 100 officers in our ranks, which sadly included Captain Veach, who was sent to advanced training. We were devastated. If not for Captain Veach, I might not have had the courage to join up.

Captain Carter C. Hanner was placed over us in Company E. At least Hanner was an Oklahoma A&M graduate, and we still had Lieutenants Elijah Horner and Carl Edmonds from Oklahoma.

The commander of the 2nd Battalion, encompassing companies E, F, G, and H in the 142nd, was replaced by Major William Morrissey of Philadelphia, Pennsylvania. He was a U.S. Military Academy graduate from West Point.

Just two days after all the switching around, we were on the move toward our first battle. We headed to Saint-Étienne-à-Arnes.

◆◆◆

The 142nd Infantry, under Colonel Alfred Bloor, along with the 141st and our machine gun battalion, made up the 71st Brigade. I was one out of 5,955 men in the brigade, and I wondered what our numbers would be after this battle. I tried not to think about the staggering numbers of killed and wounded my uncle wrote in his stories. In the whole 36th Division, which included the 71st Brigade, we had about 16,000 going into the line. That number should have been about 20,000. We lacked artillery, an ammunition train, and engineers. And we didn't even have a division insignia on our uniforms.

By the time we were ready to leave Bar-sur-Aube, chilly fall weather had set in and most everyone expected the war to shut down for winter. Boys in the 36th complained that we'd spent so much time in training, we wouldn't see action.

The French people who had welcomed us into their homes and villages lined the road to wish us "bonne chance" as we headed for the front. We traveled by train toward Saint-Étienne-à-Arnes. We just wrote "St. Etienne" in reports. I had a lot on my mind, since now, as a corporal, I would be leading a squad. I had almost all Choctaws—Charley Keel, Bennie Hampton, Joseph Davenport, and Benjamin Colbert. Unfortunately, I also had Isaac Hotinlubbi and Lee Hoade, and I didn't know what I was going to do with either of them. I thought about asking Lieutenant Horner if they could put two others with me instead, but I didn't want to be complaining right after my promotion.

Pokni said that Chihowa didn't always change our circumstances. Mostly, He used our circumstances to change us. Personally, I would have rathered He broke open more miracles from the stars. Maybe He was saving them for something more important. Like what we would face in a few days.

We detrained in Epernay, which was south of Reims, in the middle of a drizzly night. We headed to our billets, wet and cold—only to learn there weren't any prepared because the French hadn't been expecting us.

The Germans had.

They started shelling the area after we arrived, although nothing landed too close to me as I marched with part of the division to billet in Châlons-sur-Marne instead. How did the Germans know where the 36th was when the French themselves didn't?

Even in the pitch black, I gaped at the wreckage in the village of Châlons. Six houses in a row had been reduced to rubble. Reports flowed in that women and children and French soldiers were wounded. Flashes of artillery fire continued to light up the sky as we took shelter in the ruins. I tried to find a dry spot to claim. The earth trembled from exploding missiles.

We spent a few days in the damp ruins, getting our first taste of being under fire. On the third night, we loaded into *camions*—trucks—bound for St. Etienne. It was like heading for a football game, all us smelly boys in our uniforms, freezing cold and cracking jokes and giving each other a hand up into the truck. I took the last spot left—right next to Isaac. He stared at me.

I ignored him, adjusting my rifle and making room for Benjamin Colbert. Mitchell and I sat knee to knee. Calvin Wilson, Jim, and Solomon had gotten on this truck, but they kept packing more men on till they were practically hanging over the edges.

I twisted and peered through the open flap of the canvas-covered truck to see Sergeant Chill chewing out an oriental man who'd be driving. In the fading light of evening, I could see the man's red-rimmed eyes and wondered how much sleep he'd gotten with all the troop movements. He nodded anxiously at everything the sergeant barked.

"You keep that truck on the road, hear me, Chinaman?"

He nodded.

"No pulling off for a leak, got it?"

More nodding.

"Make sure the gas tank is full and don't run off the road or get stuck anywhere. *Comprende?*"

Another nod.

Sergeant Chill sneered. "*Hablas español?*"

The oriental man kept nodding vigorously. He hadn't understood one word the big Texan had said, in English or Spanish. I wasn't sure how much confidence we could have in our driver, especially with the no-headlights policy.

As the truck roared to life and jumped into action, I immediately wished we were on foot.

The truck jerked and slid onto the muddy road, and men onboard shouted when we bounced through a crater. Three men got bucked off. They'd have to be picked up by another truck in the caravan because our driver didn't stop. The Oklahoma and Texas boys whooped and waved their helmets like cowboy hats. This must have scared the driver because he sped up.

I felt the bounce when we hit the edge of the road, and the truck tilted dangerously to the side. Then it dipped in the front, like we were going into a ravine. As we shot up the other side, I could have sworn we went airborne. We landed hard, teeth rattling. The truck dove through another mighty dip and I grabbed my stomach.

Anyone behind on their praying got caught up that night, including me.

◆ ◆ ◆

We made it to Somme-Suippe. The driver deposited us

on the road east of town and we marched to camp. After our wet nights in the last village and the chilly ride, those dugouts, shacks, and tents bordering Somme-Suippe looked pretty good.

Once I had settled in, I was talking with Bennie and Calvin when Lieutenant Horner and Major Morrissey passed by our tents. They were heading to an officer meeting, and the major had me come along so I would be handy to run messages to company commanders afterward. They called on Solomon for the same reason.

The meeting was at American commander Lejeune's P.C. located in a former German bunker. American commanding officers General Whitworth, Colonel Bloor, and Colonel Jackson were there at the main conference table.

My uncle had written about how the German commanders made themselves comfortable on the front. That showed in this underground headquarters the French had taken over. The room we entered was small but well-fortified with concrete. Its electric lights brightened the relatively clean, even elegant interior with rugs and a cutout where a religious statue may have been tucked before the Germans abandoned the bunker. The room was small but well-fortified with concrete. A low doorway led into another room with a flickering light where American and French officers conversed in low tones. The light came from a fireplace built into a corner, right in the concrete like it was a log cabin back home.

Solomon and I settled along the outer edge with a few other corporals who were serving as runners for various companies in the 36th Division.

Marine Major General John A. Lejeune was a short, dark French Creole who looked a little too anxious to send us into a fight.

"Gentlemen, the 71st Brigade will relieve the 3rd and 4th Brigades of the American 2nd Division in the line on the night of October 6."

His announcement surprised the others. Colonel Bloor, who stood across the table where I could see his face, spoke up.

"Just a minute, Lejeune. We interpreted Naulin's orders to mean the 71st is to relieve only the 4th Marine Brigade. We don't have adequate supplies. We're short on .30 caliber ammunition, grenades, pyrotechnics—"

Lejeune cut in. "I promise to make up for shortages."

Bloor hadn't stopped. "We lack draft animals and cannot carry our own mortars to the front—"

"The relieved units will leave theirs in place until your weapons can be transported."

Jackson interrupted both of them. "What about the other supplies? We need it all right away."

Lejeune turned to Jackson. "Everything remaining will be brought up in trucks by the 2nd Division. Are there any other questions?"

The arguments went on awhile, but nothing was accomplished. Lejeune had already decided things, and that was that. It was up to the 36th Division to put our training to good use.

It was time to march to the front.

CHAPTER TWENTY-FIVE

Vichy, France
October 1918

The hospital tent at Vichy was overcrowded after the last battle. Matthew stood watching the blind leading the blind. A train of men, bandages covering their eyes, walked single-file from the battlefield, each doughboy holding the shoulder of the man in front of him. They had suffered a severe gas attack that blinded them.

Feeling his heart twist, Matthew shook himself away from the scene and entered the hospital tent. The soldier he was looking for had been wounded—a second time in this war and was gassed three times—on October 1, 1918.

In less than a year of full combat, this soldier was awarded the French Croix de Guerre twice, 2 Silver Stars, and a wound stripe. He had also received Battle Stars for Cantigny, Somerville, Ansauville, Picardy, Second Marne, Saint-Mihiel, Meuse-Argonne, Mouzon-Sedan, and Coblenz Bridgehead. The Oklahoma doughboy had been in practically every major battle the American troops had faced on French soil.

A few questions later, thanks to direction from an orderly, Matthew sat by the sleeping soldier's cot. The soldier had been hit hard this time, but he'd recover after some weeks—more likely months—in the hospital. Maybe the war would be over before Sergeant Otis Leader was sent back into the line of fire.

An American nurse came over to the bed. She was young and pretty, and Matthew wished it was his daughter, Victoria. She must be quite a beautiful young lady in her starched white uniform.

The nurse checked Otis Leader's vitals, waking him in the process, though he hardly moved. He barely had his eyes open by the time she left.

Matthew shifted on the stool to make it easier for Otis to see him. "*Halito.*"

Otis managed that gentle smile of his that told Matthew he'd be one of the ones who'd be all right after the war. "*Chim achukma?*"

"*Vm achukma. Chishnato?*"

"*Vm achukma akinli.*"

"It took some tracking to find you. You decide to sit out the rest of the war?"

"Is it almost over?" Otis was innocent in his question, trust in his eyes. He knew Matthew covered more ground than a soldier and would give him the straight story.

Matthew did. "The fighting will likely go into the spring, according to military strategists. Maybe another year. But who knows? General Pershing isn't slowing up for winter just yet."

"He's a bulldog."

"He has a high opinion of you."

Otis chuckled. Matthew remained serious. "I interviewed him last week. He called you…"

Matthew withdrew a worn writing tablet and read, "'Otis Leader is one of the war's greatest fighting machines.'"

Otis was quiet.

Matthew wondered what had led Otis to enlist when America first declared war. It reminded him of an article he'd read that his sister sent, an editorial in *The American Indian Magazine* called "Reasons Why Indians Should Join the Regular Army." The writer seemed to think their service would help them win respect. That the Indian could prove himself equal to other men. Matthew had heard as much in his many interviews over the past year of Indian doughboys.

He observed Otis.

"Mind if I ask why you joined up?"

Otis pushed himself up to a sitting position. Matthew noted the look of pain that flashed across his face, but Otis was vehement when he answered.

"I wanted to set the record straight. I wanted everyone to know I'm one hundred percent American. I will do whatever I have to do to defend my country."

Matthew fondly recalled their first meeting when the American troops marched in the July 4th grand entry into Paris. "I remember you saying something about a spy accusation?"

Otis harrumphed. "Me? I was tall, dark, and spoke pretty good English, although I looked enough like a foreigner among the cattlemen in Texas. What really got me in trouble were my Swiss bosses."

Matthew settled back for the story.

"It was the start of April 1917. I was in Fort Worth with Arnold Arn and Karl Marty, naturalized U.S. citizens from Switzerland who moved to Oklahoma from Chicago. They owned a ranch in Pittsburg County where I worked. We'd brought a shipment of cattle down to the Fort Worth Stockyards. Their heavy brogue got folks excited, I guess. You weren't in the States right before war was declared, were you? Folks got hysterical, what with the Zimmerman telegram and all.

"My bosses and me didn't know that two federal agents were following us in Fort Worth. They wired ahead to McAlester and when we got off the train, U.S. Marshal Crockett Lee was waiting for a suspected German spy and his 'tall, husky Spanish companion.'"

Otis chuckled again, and Matthew joined in.

"Me and Crockett were old friends and at first we busted out laughing. But it got to me later. I wanted to set the record straight. So, I kissed my babies goodbye, left them with my mama, and enlisted. I trained in Colorado, then ended up on the Mexican border, chasing Pancho Villa with General Pershing before he shipped out to France. You know he's had Indians under him since he was a young officer? He had a company of Lakota from the Pine Ridge Reservation back in 1891."

Matthew had not known that. He made a note to ask Pershing sometime.

"Before we shipped out for France, they paraded us through Fort Worth. Boy, was I hoping those federal agents saw me then!"

Matthew let the laughter die down and sat quietly for awhile. There was more. He waited.

Otis sighed and smiled. "I believe that the Almighty was with me all the way through. It was hard to leave, with my mother, sisters and my babies crying when I left. It was hard on me, to think of giving up my three babies and going away to battle, but I felt it was protection for them. I was determined to go through with it even if it cost my life."

Otis closed his eyes and rested. When he opened them again, his voice was fading.

"My conscience is clear. I set the record straight. I proved I'm one hundred percent American."

Yes, you did, Otis Leader. You most certainly did.

Neither of them knew the "ideal American soldier" had one last critical duty to perform before the war ended.

◆ ◆ ◆

Tom,

You asked once if I could still believe in miracles after all I have seen in this war. I cannot on my own strength. It is by faith alone, which is why I continue to pray for this war's end and for you.

Please write and tell me you are well. I haven't heard from you in quite awhile.

Chi pisa la chike,
Matthew

CHAPTER TWENTY-SIX

"Overhear as much of the enemy's conversation as you can, and be as cautious as possible about your own telephone conversations." —Captain A. Lincoln Lavine

Western Front
October 1918

After the conference in Lejeune's P.C., they passed out marching orders for early the next morning, Sunday. A lot of the men didn't like that because we couldn't have church, but we made do with singing hymns on the march.

The 142nd led the hike as we retraced our route from the Somme-Suippe vicinity to Suippes where we turned and trudged northward.

We didn't march on the main road. It was inundated with traffic flowing to and from the battle zone 10 miles away. A string of combat wagons, water carts, and camions filled with ammunition headed to the front. Leaving the front were ambulances carrying wounded and empty trucks going for supplies. We took the beaten path to the east of the road.

With all the rain, I knew there would be mud, but it was nothing like back home. French mud, a cream-colored, gooey paste, stuck to the sole of my boots like glue. Every step sucked me back to earth and I had to pull extra hard to free myself. It collected so thick on my boots it felt like cement drying on, and I had to stop every so often to peel it off. Camp Bowie hadn't prepared us for the Western Front. This was hard marching.

The Western Front. The words sounded ominous after all the stories I'd read and heard. We needed better preparation than we got back at Camp Bowie, tussling with the Texans. But we truly glimpsed what the last four years had done to this country when we approached a desolate village on the now abandoned Hindenburg Line.

The trenches were blasted to smithereens, mostly collapsed from constant bombardment. I knew countless men had died there, but I didn't see how a single man could have come out uninjured, whether in body or soul.

Our pace slowed. None of the sergeants yelled at us. Even Sergeant Chill knew the importance of the moment. He stared at the devastation, and I heard him murmur something under his breath. It sounded like, *Jesus wept.*

Haunting machine gun emplacements, barbed wire entanglements, lonely graves. Unexploded shells. Equipment smashed to pieces. Discarded guns.

Utterly destroyed, this French countryside likely wouldn't be farmed for years, even if there was anyone left alive to work it. No one was in the village as we approached. Thatched roof homes burned, a giant mill with nothing remaining but pieces of its wooden wheel, the semblance of a quaint market reduced to powder—everything blown to bits by thousands of shells and rounds of ammunition.

That village defined the word attrition.

It must have been a beautiful country once, but I had to use my imagination to fill things in with images from home.

The hill with its top blown off became Nanih Waiya, our

sacred Mother Mound in Mississippi. Jagged trees grew out of mangled soil and into towering pines scattered around my great-uncle's ranch near the Red River. Battle-plowed earth stripped of vegetation for miles turned into lush cornfields at Armstrong Academy.

But none of those images fit. This was no plowed field. It was an upheaval, as though a shovel the size of an airplane had scooped up random spots of the earth and flung them around. The scars ran deep.

It made me think of my people. The decimation of our tribe. Attacks on our cultural identity. The stripping of our language and land.

Attrition was a mean word.

I thought the sting would clear from my eyes once we got through the desolate village, away from the voices I felt echoing from the ground, grieving their losses. But the other side of the village was worse.

There, bodies of men—Americans and Germans—rather than graves met us. They lay where they'd fallen in the recent fighting. I spotted my first "Jerry," a mangled form in a gray uniform that tore me up inside.

I envisioned letters rising from the bodies, telegrams sent to loved ones who had hoped and prayed and begged God to let their daddy, their brother, or their son come home.

I thought of how Samson's mother had gotten that telegram and how they had buried him at the church cemetery in Durant. She could visit his grave. That didn't make her pain any less, but the mothers of these boys might never find their sons' graves—if they got one.

Murmurs started as we walked through those open graves where soldiers and horses lay rotting in the sun. I was ready to burst, and Jim voiced the emotions of the men around us with poetic words that could only come after what we'd witnessed:

"Here, with the sun setting on these uniforms of Uncle Sam's, it's up to us to make good on what we told the folks back home we were going to do."

I thought of the writer who'd said we needed to "blast

Germany beyond recognition."

This village had been blasted beyond recognition. Much of France and Belgium had. It was time to do what we'd come to do.

At some point, we'd seen enough, and we fixed our eyes straight ahead knowing we had a real battle coming. Allied troops and American doughboys had broken the stalemate and were pushing the German soldiers back. But they weren't going without a fight. Our enemies seemed determined to make this year the bloodiest of the war.

We got on a road someone said the Romans built centuries ago. It went straight ahead, up and down the hills, not around them. We were headed straight to our first battle, no curving left or right.

It was time to end this war.

◆ ◆ ◆

The long column halted near the Somme-Py front for rest and supper. I sat in the gooey mud, famished, yet at the same time, wondering how I could eat. To the north, at St. Etienne where we were headed to relieve the Marines, great columns of smoke rose, airplanes skimmed the sky in dog-fights, and observation balloons floated silently against gray clouds. But it was the roar and crash of shell bursts that made it real.

We were in war.

My stomach cramped, and I thought I'd be sick. But remembering the horrors in the village and that we were fighting to keep our own families safe gave me courage, bracing my body and mind for the task.

"Hey, Chief!"

I scrambled to my feet as Sergeant Chill strode up.

"There's an old well 200 yards due north. Take two men and get water."

"Yes, sir."

But the sergeant wasn't done. He looked me right in the

eye, telling me that everything had changed since we arrived at the front.

"There's a heavy concentration of fire because of the well, Chief. You boys keep your heads down."

He went on to get another corporal to form a second water detail. We needed to hurry and draw water before the well was destroyed.

I called on two in my squad, Joseph Davenport and Benjamin Colbert. We took up a water cart and headed for the well. I felt like we were earning the doughboy name. The ground lumped like dough as I punched each step with my boots.

It was tough going over the cratered field with the pale paste holding us in place precious seconds while we tried to maneuver between shell holes. I thought if shells had hit those spots once, they could hit again.

I was right.

An eerie whiz sounded close. I instinctively ducked, but it went over me before it landed. It took out two infantrymen from the other detail.

I stared in amazement as medics rushed to them. Those men had come so far. We crossed an ocean together, and now they were likely dead.

If Sergeant Chill had called on me second instead of first, it would have been me—my long journey, all my training, everything, ended just like that. Just as it had been for Samson who hadn't even made it this far. We could have been together when the shell hit, and both died.

Instead, it was my lot to keep moving, to not get caught in the trap of grief I'd skirted since Samson's death.

We kept on, even as another shell exploded, closer this time. The ground rumbled beneath me, but we didn't stop. We had the only water cart left. We kept going, drew water, and got it back despite the shelling around us.

That was how things would go from now on. No slowing down like back on the old Hindenburg Line. No looking over my shoulder to see which buddy went down. It was ahead, always ahead, to fight and do what we'd come to do like Jim said. That was what mattered and what would help me keep my promise to Mama to come home.

CHAPTER TWENTY-SEVEN

Western Front, France
October 1918

During our halt at Somme-Py, our commanding officers reported to Lejeune at his P.C. for detailed instructions on the relief at St. Etienne. I wasn't in that conference, but it wasn't much more useful than the first time. We didn't have the promised supplies and it looked like we wouldn't get them before we entered the front line.

Lieutenant Horner showed me a map afterward. I looked it over, searching for the front line. I couldn't make out the faded marks, not even enough to read the town names. I started to turn it every which way but didn't want to look foolish.

When I handed the map back to the lieutenant, he folded it with a snap. "Don't worry, Corporal; it doesn't make sense to anyone else, either."

Boy, he wasn't happy. All the maps given out at the meeting were scant. None showed the exact location of the front. Worse, the sector where we were to operate in was encompassed on the corners of four different maps, which made them difficult to read even pasted together.

All we really knew was the 142nd was to relieve the American 4th Marine Brigade on the left. Those Marines had done some fighting! The 2nd Division, victors of Belleau Wood, was a mix of Army and Marine.

The 142nd set off hiking toward the front, four miles away, trying to find our place. That was no easy task with the useless maps and guides from the AEF who couldn't find *us*.

In the chaos that night, battalions got separated from their units, companies from battalions. The guides reported to the wrong units and constant shelling nearby didn't help rattled nerves.

The 142nd finally went back to where we started at Somme-Py, found a guide, and set out again. Colonel Bloor and several from headquarters company were on motorcycles and in automobiles, but they kept getting bogged down in the mud.

By the time we made it to our position on the front, we were exhausted. But we were there, ready to relieve the Marines at St. Etienne. We'd arrived where the growth of pines and underbrush began to thin as they spread out toward the village. The space between the forest and the town was clear and open to draw fire from machine gunners and snipers.

No Man's Land.

If we hadn't marched so hard to get there in time, the ground gained at heavy cost by the American 2nd Division would've been lost.

But this vast front was foreign to us, and even to the 2nd Division. The German soldiers, on the other hand, knew every foot of it.

From the Blanc Mont Ridge, which was won by the Marines shortly before we arrived, you could see for miles. Situated due north of Suippes with Somme-Py at its southern base, the ridge was strategic and we couldn't afford to give it up. That was why the 36th was transferred under French General Gouraud and shoved in to relieve the Marines.

Finally at the front, I didn't rest until my squad was seen after. There was something about the responsibility of being a corporal that made me grow taller. Good thing Pokni left growing room in my uniform.

Artillery, machine gun fire, snipers, and airplanes didn't make it easy for us to sleep that first night. Company E joked on how the little pea shovels we'd complained about having to carry were as good as our weapons now. Some doughboys dug foxholes behind the trenches to crowd into for rest. A shell might get you, but no pesky sniper would.

Solomon and I were kept busy chasing down information. How was sanitation handled? What was our position, and where were the promised supplies? What were we supposed to do next?

The 2nd Division wouldn't give us their maps or data because they were afraid they'd need them. Though technically relieved, they'd been around long enough to know that didn't mean much. They might get called into action anytime.

Exhausted and knowing we'd get no answers, Solomon decided he may as well get some rest. But I was too anxious to sleep by the time we got back to Company E. It'd be dawn soon anyway.

Instead, I found a place at the top of a crater to hunker down in, a ridge-like setting sheltered by a lower rise between me and the trenches. It was a good spot to take in the view.

Across the wide, open expanse of No Man's Land stood the village of St. Etienne. Or what was left of it. I imagined what a pretty place it must have been before the war. Colorful shops, cheery people, love, and a nice life.

Now it stood gray, empty. Instead of lamps and fires illuminating a cozy scene, St. Etienne was lit by German artillery fire coming from the north and northeast. There was little presence of the French, not even airplanes flying. Fog set in and a chilly drizzle began, but that wouldn't stop the Germans from taking to the sky at dawn.

Before the doughboys started stirring—who wanted the

day to start?—movement from a trench caught my attention.

Kent Powell, the sharp and scrappy war correspondent, popped up and trudged through the mess of men huddled in their foxholes. He spotted me, grinned, and headed my way. I didn't know he'd come with the 36th, or maybe he had been there with the Marines beforehand.

The writer didn't look much different than the soldiers, even without a uniform. He wore a gas mask hanging around his neck, steel helmet snug in place, and heavy boots. Instead of a rifle, though, he carried a tablet and pencil. He reminded me of Uncle Matthew who used to say "the pen is mightier than the sword" with such vehemence I never dared ask him what that meant when I was little. I missed him saying it. Maybe I'd write him a letter after we settled into our position and ask him if he still believed that.

Kent Powell worked his way through the churned-up earth to where I was snug in a blasted-out seat in the crater rim. He motioned to me with a steaming tin mug.

"You took my seat."

"Oh. Sorry."

I started to stand, but Kent Powell chuckled and waved me to stay. Settling next to me, he held out the steaming mug.

"Tea?"

I shook my head, wondering how he'd managed a cup of tea on the front. He took a sip and sighed contentedly.

"Nothing like it on a cold morning. I never go without my tea or Pershing himself would hear me hollering."

"You know the general?"

"Son, I've been covering wars the past twenty years. Most of the men leading this mess were no more than knock-kneed soldiers when I started."

"You don't look old."

Kent Powell chuckled into his cup. "Why, thank you. You don't look that old yourself."

I wished I'd finished filling out my uniform. But Kent Powell wasn't paying attention to me. His focus was on St. Etienne and the hill that rose behind her. Coming through the fog, German airplanes emerged. I looked to our side. There weren't many French planes to answer.

One of the airplanes shot across and dropped something further down our front line, a fair distance from where I sat. Another came behind it and did the same. Bombs.

Kent Powell handed me his tea and began writing as he talked.

"Now that you're on the infamous Western Front, let me tell you about life in the trenches. First, you're afraid you're going to die. Then, you're afraid you won't."

He chuckled at my expression. "You learn a devil of a lot in the first five minutes."

We watched more German planes rise, then he went back to writing. "The superiority of the air belongs to the Fritz. No sooner do they spot a target than they're raining down German 150s, or what we call 'G.I. Cans.' You have to watch out for the whizz-bangs. They come at you with no whistle sound, so you don't know when or how to take cover.

"Do you know about the American pilots that came over when the war first started? Poor daredevils. More flyboys died in training than combat in those flimsy things. You heard about the Lafayette Escadrille?"

"Yes, sir. My uncle wrote about them."

"That so?" Powell looked at me as he took his tea back for a sip. "Who's your uncle?"

"Matthew Teller."

"Teller? You're not kidding me, are you?"

I hesitated, uncertain, but then Powell laughed. "Tough fellow. He can write circles around any reporter on the field. Beat me out of an assignment with *Collier's* magazine two years ago."

"Sorry."

"Don't be. He's a fine writer. I didn't realize he's an Indian though…"

Powell sipped his tea and for the first time since I'd met him, he seemed uncomfortable. He seemed to like Indians before, but how did he feel about one who was less of a novelty, someone who had actually shown enough intelligence to beat him out of an assignment? Powell might think twice about his interest in Indians if he knew they were outside their understood place in society.

I shifted to the side as I watched him. "Does that make a difference?"

Powell drained his cup then swirled it in his hand, staring down. He finally looked up at me.

"No, son. It doesn't matter one bit. In fact, I plan on sticking close to you fellows during this war. I'd like to tell your story."

"That'd be fine, sir."

"You boys may get tired of me asking questions. I'm the nosiest fellow you'll ever meet."

"That's fine, sir."

We shook on it, but a shell landing close to the trenches where Company E was reminded me I should be with my squad, getting ready for the day. It was time to get things stirring.

◆◆◆

I found Solomon walking with Sergeant Chill toward Lieutenant Horner where he stood with a Marine lieutenant from the 2nd Division. They were studying a map.

I joined them at the same time as Solomon and the sergeant. Solomon's face was furrowed and beet-red, surprising since he was about the coolest head I knew. But then again, not so surprising given he had to walk with Sergeant Chill.

Lieutenant Horner acknowledged us with a nod, then went back to the map. "So, the American and German lines are only about a hundred yards apart for two and a half miles along here?" He frowned, doubt in his eyes.

The 2nd Division lieutenant—tall, lean and tired— pointed to the west. "See how the scrub and pines just start thinning as they get close to the village? The pines cover the northern slope of Blanc Mont then gradually come down to these scattered woods and brush. The German entrenchments are higher than ours. And you need to know about the machine gun nests. They hide them in heavily wooded areas, and they're arranged in depth. If your boys capture one, they can come under fire from another machine gun.

"There are also belts of barbed wire strung all through the woods and open spaces, right in range of the machine guns. You get hung up in them, Jerry will cut you in pieces."

He drew a line on the map with his finger. "The Arnes rivulet is here. It flows northeast to southeast, touching St. Etienne on its south bank. All through here…" He indicated our area, "observation posts, small hills, and deep dugouts."

Horner shook the other lieutenant's hand. "Thanks. I'll pass the information on to my men." He turned his palm up. "Mind if I borrow that map?"

The 2nd Division lieutenant smiled in a way that said, "try another fool," rolled up the map and tapped Horner's shoulder with it as he walked away.

Horner sighed and turned to address us. More Company E noncoms had joined the informal briefing.

"Okay, you have an idea of the landscape and what we're up against. Relay this information to your men. The better they know the area, the better our chances."

CHAPTER TWENTY-EIGHT

"It seemed that there was not a square foot of air space through which bullets were not flying." —Lieutenant Elijah W. Horner

Saint-Étienne-à-Arnes, France
October 1918

We heard the Germans troops were running low on gasoline for their vehicles, but they sure weren't short on arms and ammunition. We dug in that morning, October 7, not sure how long we'd hole up before seeing action. Turned out, not long.

An unhappy Colonel Bloor briefed us that afternoon. Instead of two or three days to get accustomed to the front, "training under fire," we would be used in an all-out attack—tomorrow, October 8.

We Americans had a reputation for being aggressive in battle. The French had asked General Pershing for our services in the Champagne drive because of that. But parts of the 36th, including the 141st, were still lost between Somme-Py and the front after two days of wandering. They'd better hurry. The French were ready to send us over the top.

The burden of the coming attack wouldn't have been so bad if they planned for our brigade to relieve only the one Marine brigade. Instead, we were relieving two.

They wanted the 36th Division to clean up stubborn enemy resistance. That was a nice way of putting what I imagined morning held for us Oklahoma and Texas boys. We didn't even get breakfast as we waited in the cold, drizzling rain down in the trenches.

◆◆◆

The bombardment lasted all night, lighting up the sky and preventing us from sleep as we huddled in the narrow trench.

In the brilliant flashes of shells exploding, I could see the faces of men around me. In the trenches, ash coating us, we were all the same color—gray.

The scent of death surrounded us, countless men whose blood had spilled right where we were hugged up against the wall of the crumbling trench. The duckboard beneath my feet was sunk well into the mud, doing little good. The rank smell of dead rats was nauseating.

This was it, a real trench on the front. No more training. Across No Man's Land, there wasn't a grinning Texan waiting to sling rocks at me. It was an embittered enemy who had fought four long years, day and night until he was nearly insane. Or so the stories went.

Private Lee Hoade was stretched out on a shelf dug into the trench on the opposite side from where I hugged the wall, waiting to go over the top at the designated jump-off time before dawn. Sergeant Chill had told Lee Hoade to get on his feet, which he did, then went back to the shelf when the sergeant left.

In the sporadic light of artillery fire, he was reading that letter again. I checked both ways—no sergeant in sight—and stepped quietly over to him. Quiet except the mud sucking at my boots. This mud was a richer brown than what we'd marched on to get there.

"Only a few minutes now, Hoade. What are you reading?"

To my surprise, he answered.

"My sister's gettin' married. He's like one of those shells. He'll land and blow her life sky high. Won't be nothing left by the time I git home."

"You met the fellow?"

"He's a filthy German."

I frowned and felt sorry for the Germans who would face Lee Hoade today.

Hoade crumpled the paper in his fist and swung his legs off the shelf, forcing me back. "I know I can't, but I wish I was home to blast him. Ma knows I wish I could."

Stepping away from him before he could take me for a just target, I returned to my spot against the wall.

I tried to breathe easy and not think about what we were about to face. What we were about to do. It was all too real.

Next to me, Jim shifted his Enfield rifle and reached beneath his gas mask case for the pocket of his wool service coat. He pulled out a small Choctaw Bible and read quietly to himself.

Everyone was quiet until a soft voice started singing behind me. It might have been Mitchell. Could have been Tobias or Joseph Davenport or any of the Choctaws. More joined in, barely a hum.

> *Chitokaka ma! chi haksobish a*
> *Et welit, chin tahpahanla li ka*
> *Auet is sa haklo cha, nana ka*
>   *Chim asihilhha li ka et ʊmá;*
> *Klaist a auet is sʊm ihissashke;*
> *Keyukmʊno, sʊlla he banoshke.*

Give me Christ, or else I die.

No one looked scared really. Maybe there would be time to be scared later. I knew Mama was still praying. I hoped that in all the death in No Man's Land, God was there.

We sang softly as a shell soared overhead and burst, spraying deadly shrapnel. A piece clinked against my Brody helmet.

"Ah, I'm hit!" The memory of Samson's words shouted from the locked corner of my heart. I blinked long and refocused on the men who were still alive around me.

To soften up the German line, the American bombardment had started in the night. Time for the attack was almost on us. Once we jumped off, we were supposed to have a rolling barrage, meaning artillery shells would fly ahead of us, further out each time as we moved forward, giving us a screen to cross No Man's Land.

The Marines warned us the German troops were only a hundred yards across from us, yet that was hard to believe. The enemy only a football field away? But sniper fire started in the night, sending bullets around our heads, so we were inclined to believe it.

The countdown began. Sergeant Chill made a pass, checking to see that we were in place. He had a funny smirk when he caught my eye and looked down to make sure I had the bag of Useful Stuff tied to the back of my cartridge belt. Of course I did. He hollered for it every other day.

I checked my watch, which I wore on the inside of my wrist to protect the glass face. The tiny hands showed there were only minutes to go. I felt for my sidearm. Loaded and ready.

Spread through the trench, in dugouts, foxholes and shell holes, Company E waited with Captain Carter Hanner in command. There were Lieutenants Elijah Horner and Carl Edmonds, two 2nd lieutenants, sergeants, a slew of corporals, and plenty of nerves to go around. I was in the first platoon led by Lieutenant Horner.

As the gray dawn fought its way through the tops of the pine trees, runners charged through the trenches, trying to get orders to commanders who in turn tried to get them to their platoon leaders. I wondered if we were the only company ready to go over the top.

I shifted from crouching sideways against the trench wall and faced it straight on. The doughboys around me did the same. All up and down the trench, men were preparing themselves. The Germans might have heard our gear jangling if not for constant shells whistling through the air.

Then it happened.

The sickly drone of an airplane sounded across No Man's Land. I licked my ash coated lips, mouth dry. If the pilot spotted the Americans gathered in the trenches, he would warn his comrades. They'd know we were mounting an attack that morning. We'd be slaughtered.

Another drone sounded, but it came from the opposite direction. A French airplane had soared out to meet the German.

The dogfight was on.

Each airplane was mounted with a machine gun. Engines whining, they made strafing runs at one another. A ball of fire and billow of smoke obscured the French plane momentarily, but it emerged and struck back, sending the German airplane spiraling to earth. It crashed out of sight near St. Etienne.

The French airplane, crippled and smoking, made its way back to us and landed over the hill to our rear.

There was a stir of excitement and I had wanted to cheer when the French plane went over, but we remained quiet. Besides, it seemed wrong to cheer someone's death, even a brutish Jerry.

Distracted by the dogfight, I'd lost track of time. I glanced at my watch. Two minutes left!

I checked my squad, fresh to the front with a year's worth of training. Faces set, determined, ready to fight, waiting for the signal to jump-off.

Sharp machine gun fire exploded around us.

Rat-a-tat-tat.

A shout came from down the way. I tensed and looked.

Word spread quick that two Indian corporals had been hit. Men I knew. Killed.

5:14 a.m.

Five, four, three...

I gripped my Enfield and climbed out of the trench. Thousands of American troops poured over the top, the rolling barrage ahead of us. I heard screams in the explosions behind me.

The German soldiers were ready and waiting.

I tried to keep an eye on my comrades, but it was impossible as we plowed forward into the German machine gun fire that chewed up the ground. We spread out to keep from being a desirable target for a shell, something the Marines advised us to do. I stayed low to the ground.

Getting shot at scared the living daylights out of me, but it also made me mad. I wanted to hunker down and start shooting, but we were to let the rolling barrage be our firepower until we were closer to our objective.

I slipped and slid through the slog of the shell-churned earth—soggy as oatmeal, deadly as quicksand on the Red River if someone didn't come along to pull you out. With its relentless mud, the ground stuck you in one place long enough for German machine gun fire to rip you apart.

Jerking too hard with one step, I lost my balance and tumbled into a shell hole filled with enough water to drown a man. There were soldier's boots along the edge of the slimy water, green scum accumulated on his wool puttees. I scrambled on legs that barely supported me.

Darting out, I came on barbed wire in a gully. I spotted it before it could tangle me in its death trap. Running through the woods at my great-uncle's ranch had taught me to watch for old barbed wire. Those summers saved my life now.

I hunkered down and whipped out my wire cutters, wishing Samson was there to look out for me while I cut through the wire. It was slow going. But I wasn't alone. Benjamin Colbert came up by me, shielding me and watching for German snipers. We stayed low so we wouldn't be spotted.

Snap. Snap. Snap.

The barbed wire coiled away when I snipped each strand, careful not to let it snag our breeches.

I got up to bolt through the cut wire, but someone streaked by me. Isaac Hotinlubbi. He took off, zigzagging and heading for the machine gun nest. Benjamin and I followed.

Behind us, more Company E boys came through the spot we'd cut in the barbed wire. Ahead, Isaac charged the side of the nest, his gun popping away like the machine gun itself.

We came up behind Isaac as gray-uniformed soldiers swarmed in from the backside to defend the nest. Jerry. I was face-to-face with live ones for the first time. They were unkempt, unshaven, and hungry-looking, but they had plenty of fight left in them.

Another machine gunner turned his gun toward us. In the light of flares and coming dawn, I saw his eyes, and will forever wish I hadn't, because that was the first man I killed.

The rapid gunfire around me ceased and the smoke drifted away to reveal the machine gun crew—all dead.

Benjamin, Isaac, Joseph, Lee Hoade, Jim, and Bennie checked the nest and adjoining trench for any more of the enemy. A few rifle pops kept me on guard as I crouched down and looked back over No Man's Land, realizing that we were mostly to the left of it, at the very end of the expanse. How we'd gotten so far down, I wasn't sure.

I turned and squinted up the German trench in the other direction. Soldiers with Stahlhelm helmets marched toward us. Dozens of them!

I gave a shrill whistle and got my comrades' attention. It was just like in the Benbrook trench back in Camp Bowie, and we sure didn't want to give up our identity tags or our lives to the Germans.

The other men saw the threat too and began firing. I snapped a fresh five round stripper clip into my Enfield and fired one bullet after the other, working the bolt action as fast as I could.

Lee Hoade and Bennie jumped behind the German machine gun and turned it sharp. They emptied the ammunition belt.

Rat-a-tat-tat.

Several gray uniforms went down, the rest took cover. We didn't know how to reload the German gun, so Bennie plucked a grenade from his belt, pulled the pin and tossed the live bomb under the machine gun to render it useless. Then we got the blazes out of there.

I glanced over to see Jim charge the other way toward a German dugout. He fired into it several times then dropped off into a shallow trench. That was the last I saw of him.

The rest of us headed for a machine gun-infested copse of pines to join a set of doughboys led by Sergeant Green of Company E. He signaled us forward as those with him lobbed grenades at the closest machine gun. The pine trees ahead blew apart, a flash of imagery on how quick life could splinter.

Five men, along with the sergeant, charged the nest. I scrambled over the heaving earth in time to witness machine gun fire rip into Sergeant Green.

He rolled into a shell hole as his men took the nest. I slid into the hole beside him, not sure if he was breathing. As for me, I wasn't sure if I had taken a breath since we went over the top.

Another corporal grabbed up Green and checked the bullet holes in his chest, gut, and leg. The sergeant pulled his shirt loose from his belt, getting just enough air to cough, "Get those kraut-eating devils."

That was the last thing he ever said.

We took the copse of pines and sent dozens of prisoners back to our lines through the chaos.

Mortars sailed overhead and exploded twenty yards in front of me. Too close. We were too close to our rolling barrage. They didn't know we were there, wherever that was.

Then I remembered the map the 2nd Division lieutenant had shown us.

"This way!" I hollered at a dozen men.

We dodged shattered trees, craters, and severed barbed

wire to slide up to the edge of a trench. Then I signaled the others to lay low while I crawled forward. Reaching into my pouch, I pulled out the shaving mirror and hooked it to the end of my bayonet, then slid it over the lip of the trench. I turned the mirror this way and that until I was reasonably sure the trench was empty. For now.

Motioning the boys forward, I dropped into the trench and checked up and down the parts in sight. The trench systems were in a zigzag pattern, so if you did meet the enemy, he couldn't take out your whole company.

The dozen of us in the trench were mixed up. I didn't have all the men in my squad and they weren't all from Company E. Private Albert Billy and his blasted bugle was with us from Headquarters Company.

But it didn't matter who was with who. We knew who the enemy was and what we were trained to do.

Since there were no officers in the bunch, and I was the only noncom, I hissed, "Colbert, Davenport," not sure why I felt the need to whisper. It seemed a good idea when you were in an enemy trench. My two buddies came up to me.

"Head to the next bend and see what's there. Billy, Hampton, you two see what's the other way."

While they took off to scout, I had the other men stay low—this trench had been blasted so much it was below shoulder high—while I peered over the top. There wasn't much to see of the battle because the edge of a crater rose ahead, blocking my view. We'd need to go further down the trench one way or another to get a look.

A soft whistle came from around the corner. Crouching, I looked toward the sound. Joseph waved me forward. I acknowledged him, and when Albert and Bennie rejoined us—they hadn't seen anyone—I led the men to the curve where Joseph waited.

Benjamin had already gone around the turn, and we soon found out why. In the next section, about two dozen doughboys were crouched with Sergeant Chill. I'd never been more happy to see his sour face. I was relieved to see other familiar faces, too, and tried not to think of the ones I didn't see. Where were Captain Hanner and Lieutenant Horner? Solomon and Jim?

Some of the men with the sergeant were wounded and being cared for with field kits. I wondered how medics would even find us.

Sergeant Chill barked at me, "Report, Chief."

I told him where we'd been, how Sergeant Green had been killed, and how we ended up in that trench. I wanted to ask him where the rest of the 142nd was, or for that matter, the rest of the 71st Brigade. But he didn't look in the mood for questions, just for giving orders.

He assigned men to carry wounded back to the American lines where we had started. The remaining twenty who weren't carrying wounded would hike up the trench and try to get behind the German line and punch a hole somewhere as the full light of morning crept over the battlefield.

CHAPTER TWENTY-NINE

"The job of the Outpost Company, also known as 'The Suicide Club,' is uninterrupted communications between the units, despite all conditions. It is the goal to be striven for, and the subaltern who attains it will have found that he has solved a problem more difficult than that which usually confronts far higher commanders." —Captain A. Lincoln Lavine

Saint-Étienne-à-Arnes, France
October 1918

By mid-day, we hadn't found a spot to punch through, but we also hadn't lost any more men despite taking five machine gun nests and sending dozens of German prisoners behind our lines.

At the edge of the woods overlooking St. Etienne, we met up with more American troops and dug in on the new American line—a terribly thin one. Just ahead, there was a cemetery and remains of a church. The abandoned town had been hard fought for, but it still didn't belong to the Allies. We stayed low in the trench system or dug holes to get situated before the coming night. There were reports of gas shells heading toward us, but the shells fell short and the wind was in our favor.

Sergeant Chill ordered no smoking because German snipers could distinguish the faintest glow or wisp of smoke not from shells. I knew the order would be hard on Lee Hoade and I was right, only it was harder on those around him. He cussed any man that got near the hole he'd burrowed in.

At dusk, Sergeant Chill sent Albert and me to scout the area east of St. Etienne for enemy movement. That included the old cemetery near what was left of the church. The only thing remaining was the high steeple and cross. There had been a machine gun nest in that steeple, but American troops had cleared it out.

We wove through the cemetery, staying low. Albert had told me how before we jumped off that morning, he'd been back behind the line delivering messages when a gas shell exploded near headquarters. He didn't have his mask with him because they thought they were far enough back, and couldn't breathe until he dug a hole with his trench knife and stuck his face in the hole. Said he wouldn't have survived otherwise.

When we came near the cathedral, we must have felt it at the same time. We knelt in respectful silence.

A gunshot disturbed the sacred moment and Albert went down, face first. I did too, scared he was dead, but he raised his head and snapped off a shot with his Enfield. I watched a German sniper fall from the top of the ancient steeple.

We belly crawled behind the largest headstone left intact and looked the place over good. There was no other sign of the enemy.

I hissed to Albert, "That dirty Jerry, using a house of God to kill from. Good thing he was a bad aim."

Albert slowly undid the strap on his steel helmet and took it off. I started to reprimand him, but he held the Brody helmet out for me to see. It had a fresh, deep crease in the side of it.

He spoke in Choctaw. "A happy birthday to me! Guess I will keep wearing this, hoke!"

"This is your birthday?"

"Yep. And it looks like I was reborn here."

He chuckled, and I did, too, knowing it was something we'd chuckle about back home someday—if we made it.

Albert put his helmet back on and looked toward the steeple. "I sure hope he did some praying while he was up there."

I motioned for us to move around to the edge of the cemetery. We discovered a ravine that could conceal the German troop movements to and from the cemetery. They'd done a lot of killing from there.

It was dark when we finished scouting and reported back to Sergeant Chill along with other scouts. That was when we learned we weren't the only ones German snipers had spotted. One soldier on patrol returned carrying the body of his dead partner over his shoulders. A sniper bullet had killed him instantly.

♦♦♦

After all the scouts reported in, I spent a few seconds with Sergeant Chill, trying to figure out exactly where we were compared to the rest of the 142nd. It didn't take but those few seconds to realize he didn't know either and he didn't want me to know that he didn't.

Leaving the sergeant, I found where most of the Choctaws had hunkered down in a crater blown out by an artillery shell, and joined them.

Isaac stared at me, condemning like he always did. *Coward. Liar.*

I was cold, tired, filthy, and feeling I'd proven my mettle today. Feeling it plenty. Isaac had no right to look at me like that after everything we'd been through.

I went up and met him nose to nose. *"Himak ma nukshopa is sv hochefo na."* Never call me a coward again.

I turned but didn't make it all the way around. Isaac's fist sank into my gut, a hard sucker punch that took the wind out of me.

He growled in my ear, "Coward."

I threw my rifle down and slammed into him. We hit the ground and rolled but before I could get in a clean hit, the others were on us. Albert and Joseph grabbed up Isaac and held him back. Lee Hoade—where had he come from?—snagged the back of my collar, yanking me back and choking me.

Bennie stepped between us, looking over his shoulder while motioning for us to calm down. Bennie had a good sense of humor that helped relieve tensions, and besides that, he just had good sense.

"That's no way to act in a uniform! You want to get thrown in the guardhouse for fighting?"

I looked quick to Isaac, who spit years of condemnation from his eyes.

"I am not afraid of punishment," Isaac said.

Those words hit their mark. I stopped straining.

Lee Hoade let me go with a shove. Released too, Isaac took up his gear and moved to the edge of the crater.

I grabbed my gear and went to dig my own foxhole, to bury the memories of actions I didn't know how to set right.

Every day, every time I saw Isaac staring at me, I remembered that first time, that moment when our friendship was destroyed. One bad day, one decision of two nine-year-old Choctaw boys.

And it had started off as such a good day.

CHAPTER THIRTY

No Man's Land, France
October 1918

A distant moan cut through the fogginess of sleep and into the dream I was having that Lee Hoade was crying like a baby for a cigarette.

It took a hand shaking my shoulder to bring me awake enough to realize the moan came from outside the circle of men sleeping in the crater. I shivered. We had no blankets and there was a constant chilly mist coating us.

Private Charley Keel, one of the men in my squad, shook me again and whispered, "Someone's out there, hurt. American. Gotta be."

I sat up sharp, some kind of warning whistling through my mind.

"Could be a trap. Jerry does that, you know."

"He's one of ours, all right. No Jerry could copy that Texas accent."

I crawled with Charley Keel around the sleeping men to the other side of the crater and listened.

After a minute, we heard, "Americans? Hey, Americans?" in a twang only found in one place on earth.

I thought about waking the sergeant, but he'd do one of two things. Order us to stay put until dawn to investigate or send two of us out to bring the wounded man in. The man might die before dawn, and there were already two of us ready to go.

Motioning for Charley to follow me, we left our rifles and anything else that might reflect light. We'd rely on my handgun.

I crawled over the crater rim, an inkling in the back of my mind that we should tell someone where we were going. But it wasn't far, and our comrades would hear if a sniper took a shot at us.

We crawled through the sloppy earth, me thinking about Red River quicksand and how we could get swallowed up in this war.

I came to barbed wire and gingerly followed it with my bare fingers until I came to cut pieces a few feet away. Lifting up on my knees, I rolled the barbed wire back and scooted through, Charley Keel right behind me. The call came again, and we hesitated. It was much closer, right on the other side of a once mighty pine felled by battle. A round Brody helmet poked up above it.

The Texan hadn't stopped dragging himself toward where he must have heard us earlier. When his face appeared over the shattered tree, I recognized this was the same Texan who had taunted Samson and me from the other side of the makeshift trenches when we first started training.

It startled me enough that I couldn't move. Samson wasn't behind me, moaning about the cut in his forehead from not wearing his helmet properly. We were supposed to go through this whole fight together, and maybe one or both of us would die on foreign soil. Suddenly, the unfairness of him dying of some rotten sickness overwhelmed me.

It wasn't right, not right for him to die so young without even getting to fight.

Why? I felt an odd anger toward Chihowa. Bad men had made this war, but the sickness on Samson? Why?

Charley crawled past me and over the pine tree. He lifted the Texan under the armpits and dragged him over the tree. I finally got my senses and helped.

Back through the barbed wire and toward the crater. We let the man rest a minute. He sagged and tried to breathe.

"My buddy…still back there…gotta go…he's a dyin'…"

I could hardly understand his words gasped in bits, but he clearly pointed back where we'd come from.

Movement from the crater caught my eye. Bennie and Albert were coming at a crawl toward us. When they got within whispering range, I told them to take the man in while Charley and I went for the other wounded man. Albert wanted to go with me, but Charley already knew the terrain we'd come over.

We headed back, wondering how far the other soldier was and how long it would take us to find him.

A mist fell, fitting on this chilly night that wrapped the battle up in a tense sleep. The mist would help conceal our movements where shadows were easy to spot in No Man's Land.

We went through the barbed wire and over the tree. Then I lowered and checked the new area.

Boy, it was hard to see in the mist. And it was so quiet. No bombardment on either side, mostly because no one knew where their own troops were. Everything was scattered, disjointed. It felt deadly to me, like no one would make it out alive. I knew I should say a prayer, but that odd anger came on me and I didn't want to think of all I'd been taught about God's sovereignty just then.

The ground was covered with patches of scrub brush like we'd plowed through trying to take the German line. The French soil was still a soggy mess, and getting worse.

I listened for moans or a call for help. Nothing. Motioning Charley to stay close, I raised enough for a quick run over the open space to the next mangled tree. Charley was right behind me. We listened again and he pointed off to our right, toward a crater filled with darkness. He heard or sensed something I didn't. I nodded for him to lead the way.

Charley, bent at the waist, crossed the next open space toward the deep crater.

I followed behind until the crack of a rifle brought us to a standstill. Charley stiffened and collapsed. I flopped to the ground, frantically trying to determine where the sniper's bullet had come from.

We were closer to a mound than I'd realized, likely a machine gun nest not more than thirty yards away. I dragged myself forward with my elbows to Charley's side to see how bad he was hurt. He didn't move. I grabbed his shoulder, shook it, then lifted him enough to see his face. The misty raindrops hit mud that was splattered on his open eyes, and mixed with the blood draining from the hole blasted in his forehead.

I released his shoulder and turned away. My stomach churned and I couldn't hold down my supper rations.

A moan sounded. Was it the Jerry sniper trying to lure me forward? But I'd heard this kind of moan before, from a wounded man.

I wiped my mouth with the back of my coat sleeve and eyed a way to reach the crater without looking at Charley again.

There was no cover for five yards. Without thinking long enough for fear to set in, I shoved to my feet and made a mad dash for the strange end zone. Diving into the crater as a bullet zinged over my head, I hit the inside edge of the deep shell hole and rolled into it.

Touchdown.

When my senses came to me, I looked around to find the wounded American soldier not far from where I landed. I scrambled over to him. His eyes were closed, breathing shallow. I felt guilty being thankful I didn't recognize him.

He was hurt bad. He clenched his hefty gut where his army shirt was soaked with blood. He was an American doughboy with a mama at home, praying for him to come back like he'd promised her.

The soldier opened his eyes enough to squint at me. He tried to speak, but a gurgling sound and blood came out instead. I panicked.

"Listen, soldier, you're going to be all right. We came to get you out of here."

"We" was only "me" now. Others would likely come looking for us soon, especially with the sniper shots, although I hoped they wouldn't.

But it didn't matter what lies I told this soldier. He was dying.

I wanted to speak words of peace like my mama would. I glanced up, looking for the stars and the hope of miracles, but the sky was a cloudy mist spraying my face. When I looked down again, the man was dead.

Using the doughboy's helmet, I covered his face and moved away from him. I fell back against the sloping side of the crater, wondering when a Jerry would emerge over the edge and shoot me.

I remembered the moment I kissed the salty tears on Mama's cheek the day before I shipped out. I'd made a promise only a naive young boy who'd never seen death could when I promised my mama I'd come home. No one came home from this. We were all going to die.

Wiping at the rain on my cheeks, I found only my tears. The mist had stopped and the half moon fought the clouds to cast streams of silver across the battlefield. I couldn't try to leave the filthy, death-ridden hole I was in. It'd be easy to spot someone crawling through the shadows of No Man's Land. No one was coming to rescue me, not until dawn when the bombardment and smoke made it easier to move undetected.

Like Kent Powell had said, you learn a devil of a lot in the first five minutes, which meant I'd learned a century's worth about war in one day.

I listened to the quiet of the battlefield where tens of thousands of men had died. I imagined hearing their moans, their whispers for help, and finally, the silence of release they found in death.

Time floated by like the clouds. I didn't keep track of either until the sky cleared and I was surprised the stars were out. Every night had been so filled with smoke, I hadn't been able to see the sky. After the rain and the halt in fighting, it was so clear I floated in it.

When I was a boy, Victoria told me that if you hummed at just the right pitch, you could make the stars dance.

We were sitting by the lake on Uncle Preston's ranch, back when Victoria had a vivid imagination, back before she turned away from her family, from her people, and from her faith.

Mama had already told me about the stars and miracles, and I thought if I could make the stars dance, I could get miracles to fall whenever I wanted them. But I learned God didn't work that way.

When I couldn't do the right pitch to move the stars, Victoria had convinced me I could make the moon dance. At seven years old and her reaching the double digits, I believed her. I always believed then.

Victoria had taken a pebble and given it a strong toss, landing it in front of the moon's reflection in Uncle Preston's lake. She would have made a fine quarterback. We sat there a good while, watching the moon dance in the ripples.

At some point in life, I knew everyone had to make a decision, had to decide what they really believed. Victoria had decided.

There in the deep night, laying in that shell crater across the way from the enemy's machine gun nest, I needed to make up my mind about life and death.

I was like a child with the memories of an old man. I had to bring that span of time together, had to decide what was worth taking forward in life, and what I should leave behind.

I didn't have the answers for all the tragedies in this corrupted world, but I knew the eternal answer. It was in a hope above the stars. It was in a prayer, the kind of hum Victoria hadn't wanted to believe in.

But I couldn't hum. The sniper might hear and know I was still alive.

And I was alive. I'd never felt more alive than in that moment surrounded by death. I knew why I hadn't been able to make the stars dance. I needed a heavenly pitch, one that reached the very heart of God. Because there He was, up in the stars filled with the hope of miracles. He was all around me, in life and death.

I made the decision to put my trust in Him. I found the right pitch then, and hummed it in my heart. A star shot across the sky as if I had reached the heart of God. Or rather, He reached mine and suddenly all I'd ever known about Him settled peacefully within me. Everything found its place.

Samson and Charley's deaths. My people's trail of tears. Our decimated tribe. Isaac Hotinlubbi's anger. This bloody war. My future, and what it meant to be Choctaw.

God's love didn't mean bad things wouldn't happen. His love was there to comfort me in the face of pain and give me the strength to carry on. And He had a plan for my life and eternity.

God knows.

I truly understood that phrase at last.

Somehow in this mangled mess of humanity, Chihowa was there. The night sky was full of His hope and miracles. They just didn't always look like I thought they would.

In that moment of being, I surrendered my identity tags to God.

CHAPTER THIRTY-ONE

"I was lying down in a little trench with the German artillery fire hitting all around me but I had no fear." —*James Edwards report*

Saint-Étienne-à-Arnes, France
October 1918

At dawn, the Germans began shelling. Gunfire erupted around me as the 142nd started moving again, but I knew how scattered we were. I needed to get back to my comrades. I wasn't scared to die, but I sure didn't want to. Not in that shell hole, alone in No Man's Land.

First, though, I had business to take care of with those machine gunners and sniper. I took up the dead doughboy's Enfield and slung the strap over my shoulder.

I pulled the U.S. bag around to my front only to find two bullet holes in it. I fingered the burnt edges, then opened the bag and pulled out the chipped glass telephone pole cap, Samson's ball of string, and the bent canteen with no lid. I tied the glass cap and canteen together with ample length between them.

Crouched to run, still below the rim of the shell hole, I drew in a deep breath and gobbled like a turkey. The warning was loud enough for the enemy to hear even with the ongoing boom of shell explosions—if they were paying attention. I'd given them the traditional Choctaw warning of what I was about to do.

Just like a fishing line with a heavy lure and the canteen as a bobber, I swung the glass cap in a half circle behind me and then forward, casting it as high and far as I could toward the machine gun nest. As soon as I released the line, I jumped out of the shell hole the other way. Machine gun fire shattered the glass cap and bullets pinged against the canteen.

Samson was still watching out for me.

Rolling into a depress, I flattened myself out of sight of the nest. No gunfire followed me. Still, I waited, thinking of hunting with my rabbit stick in the woods near Armstrong Academy.

I was bold and daring when I was by myself.

When the machine gun fire intensified in the area where the canteen fell, I crawled through thin underbrush until I was a dozen yards from their right flank. Getting a good grip on the Enfield, I leaped up and rushed toward the flaming machine gun still firing in the other direction.

The two soldiers manning the gun kept firing while another soldier reared back and reached for his trench knife. I shot him. Letting out a war cry, I kicked the machine gun over and faced the other two with my fixed bayonet. I did what I had to do, and didn't look back.

With the nest silenced, I ran out and across the open space to the relative safety of the scrub brush. Grieved to leave Charley's body behind and gasping acrid air, I scrambled over the splintered tree, through the cut barbed wire and back to that crest where I'd left the others.

Sliding headfirst to the edge, I came face to face with the barrel of a rifle. The gleaming bayonet almost took out a piece of my nose.

Corporal James Edwards chuckled and lowered his weapon.

"We'll have to call you 'Little Night Horse.'" Then he sobered. "We thought you gave up the ghost out there."

I dropped into the crater and was surrounded by my buddies, backslapping me with chuckles. Jim and his squad had joined our position in the night. Albert tooted his bugle in my ear just loud enough to make it ring.

"The sergeant wouldn't let us go find you fellows until dawn," Joseph said. "Where's Charley?"

I shook my head, accepting the canteen Joseph handed me. I saw the blood splattered on my hands and coat sleeves. Some was Charley's, some the doughboy who'd died in the shell hole, some the enemy's. It couldn't be distinguished.

We spent a moment in silence before more questions came. I told them what happened to Charley, grateful I could talk about it before having to report to Sergeant Chill. I didn't tell them about the machine gun nest, though deep down, I wished Isaac had seen my courage in battle.

Then Sergeant Chill chewed me out, all but blaming me for Charley's death.

The bright memories of the night before and the peace I'd felt threatened to melt away with the morning light. Maybe I wasn't cut out for a military career—any kind of responsibility, for that matter. But there was no time to think about it.

We moved out quick. Sergeant Chill led us to keep exploring for weakness in the German lines but we found none.

Mid-morning, the sergeant settled us for a rest in a trench we hadn't been in before and hollered at me to bring the U.S. bag. He rummaged through it and pulled out the tweezers, then he paused and looked in the bag again. "What happened to that glass cap?"

"I used it, sir."

From the look on his face, I wasn't sure if he was mad it was gone or happy I'd finally found something useful in the U.S. bag. It was hard to tell with the sergeant.

We rested an hour. It was an hour too long. Albert, Benjamin, and Lee Hoade went missing. I asked Bennie if he knew where they were.

He pointed with his square chin up the trench. "They got antsy and decided to go exploring."

I wanted to cuss. I remembered Charley with a hole in his forehead and headed out the way Bennie pointed, telling him not to let anyone follow. We needed to stay together.

Picking my way through the battered trench, I noticed fresh marks that showed this section had been hit by artillery shells yesterday. It'd likely get hit again today.

Staying low, I took each zig and zag carefully, pausing to check for the enemy with my shaving mirror before poking my head around a corner.

There were dead bodies in one section. Five German soldiers lay sprawled on top of each other. Rats had found them in the night and took their fill of flesh.

I felt sick but kept moving. I didn't want the three missing men to meet the same fate.

At the next zig, I peered around the corner. There they were, midway to the next bend. At least two of them, Albert and Benjamin. Hoade was nowhere in sight. I gave a light whistle and they turned, staying low, then grinned and waved. The walls of the trench were so short we had to hump over so we wouldn't be seen.

I caught up with them, holding my gear to keep anything from clanking. "What are you fools doing? Get back with the others, right now!"

Albert nudged me. "Come on, B.B. Let's see where this leads."

Benjamin rounded the next bend. I scrambled after him and slammed into his back. Albert stumbled into me.

We stared, dumb, at a dozen German soldiers grabbing their rifles as they jumped to their feet from where they'd been resting amid the debris.

One of us yelped, I couldn't say who. Scared out of our wits, we turned to run for the next zig. Tangled up, we managed to make the sharp curve and get halfway down the stretch with no bullets chasing us. When I stumbled, Albert turned back to help me.

But then he didn't move, still gripping my arm and facing the direction where the Germans were. I tried to free myself but Albert let out a deep belly laugh. I turned around.

The dozen soldiers had jumped clear out of the trench and were running like madmen across the field. They didn't look back.

We had scared them as bad as they scared us!

Benjamin began chuckling with Albert. I joined in. It was good to laugh.

We made our way back toward our haphazard group, and found Lee Hoade, trench knife in hand, who'd slipped down an offshoot to smoke while the others kept going. He didn't say a word, just pushed to the front and led the way. I had a feeling he had come looking for us, but he'd never say.

We passed the bodies of the five German soldiers again. I was last and stopped cold, trying to remember if they'd been just that way before.

I looked from them to the solid form of Lee Hoade and wondered something fiercely, but I wouldn't dare ask. I kept going, trying not to take a last look at the soldiers, especially the one now missing his scalp.

I couldn't help looking back and wondering.

◆ ◆ ◆

Early afternoon, we found Solomon with more of Company E led by Lieutenant Horner. I was relieved to see them alive and that Horner would be in charge instead of Sergeant Chill. There was a bullet hole in the top shoulder of the lieutenant's coat, but the bullet had missed flesh.

The 142nd had suffered a great number of casualties the first two days of fighting.

Lieutenant Carl Edmonds, who led his Indian soldiers with distinction, had been wounded and sent to the hospital. Worse, our new captain, Carter C. Hanner, had been killed not long after we went over the top. Two sergeants had been killed, along with two Indian corporals. One was full-blood Choctaw Nicholas E. Brown.

Amidst the death and chaos, we'd taken the little strip of woods in between St. Etienne and where we'd jumped off. The village was about a kilometer ahead.

Like us, the men we found had run out of water that day. Thirst was fast becoming the only thing I could think about.

Lieutenant Horner called on me to run a message to Company H where Major Morrissey, our battalion commander, was supposed to be located. The companies were so scattered and shot up, we needed to let them know where we were and how many were left in Company E.

The lieutenant didn't have to warn me not to get caught by the enemy. If they snatched the message I carried, they'd know exactly where Company E was.

I tucked the slip of paper in my inner coat pocket, adjusted my Enfield rifle strap on my shoulder, and headed east.

Darting from pine tree to shell hole to communication trench, I thought things were going pretty good until a whiz sounded close by. I dove to the bottom of the shallow trench and held my breath. The shell landed with a thud. Nothing happened. The words of a joking Marine echoed in my mind: "Another friend of the United States in a German munitions factory."

The next shell wasn't made by a friend. It exploded and shrapnel rained down around me. Then another shell and another. There must have been a group of Americans nearby, and the German artillery was giving them special attention. I lay unmoving for a half an hour until the artillery fire started sending its shells further back.

Taking in a breath of acrid smoke-filled air, I gritted my teeth, jumped from the shallow trench and headed for the pines.

Major Morrissey was in the middle of them, keeping his company together as they advanced toward their objective. I handed the note off to him. He sent me further east to deliver another message, this one to Major Hutchins of the 141st which was on the flank of the 142nd.

The artillery fire was so heavy in the area, I had to crawl a good distance in a communication trench. On my belly, I lifted and looked around to get my bearings. The artillery shells had ripped into a copse of pines, and from my angle, I could see round Brody helmets of men hunkered down. A sharp whistle caught my attention, a loud shrill like the Texans used to get a buddy's attention. It sounded again and I knew it was directed at me.

I jumped up and ran toward them. The raking fire of the machine gun erupted around my feet, causing me to dance to one side then I dove behind scrub for cover. The machine gunners had my number and laid down a strip of fire beside me, plowing a furrow along the length of my body.

American machine gunners answered from the pines, giving me some relief. I crawled forward with my elbows and rolled up to a shell hole beside a set of American doughboys. One grabbed the back of my breeches and hauled me in. It was a Texas cowboy.

He slapped my helmet, making my ears ring. "That just about skins any circus trick I ever peeped at."

Another Texan, a sergeant, crawled up to me. "Hey there, Chief. You lost?"

I took a steadying breath. Machine gun fire continued to rake the rim above us as I answered. "I have a message for Major Hutchins from Major Morrissey."

"Hutchins is dead. Lieutenant Ford is in command. He's all we've got left."

"Where is he?"

"A couple of holes over. Keep low, they've had us pinned down for two days."

He went on to tell me that as soon as Company D of the 141st went over the top the first morning, they'd been shot to pieces. At least two-thirds of their company was dead or wounded, including Major Hutchins and all their officers, except Lieutenant Ford. But they'd plowed on, taking the right and left flank of an enormous cache of enemy machine guns—80 of them—and over 200 prisoners. The doughboys then turned the German machine guns around and were holding the new American line, but Company D was isolated from the rest of the 141st.

They had a bunch of Germans pinned in a dugout, though Company D was pinned down, too, by enemy artillery fire and machine gunners.

I left the sergeant and crawled through the gruesome sight of what was left of Company D of the 141st.

A single rifle pop caught my attention and I raised enough to see one doughboy outside the trench, prone under brush cover and focused on the rim above the dugout. I recognized him as one of the Choctaws I'd met in Camp Bowie, Private Joseph Oklahombi. Black hair, dark eyes, he spoke English only when he had to.

I crawled up beside him, staying behind enough brush to give me cover. Looking around to see if anyone was within earshot, I greeted him in Choctaw. In reply, he asked if I had extra ammunition and I gave him a stripper from my cartridge belt. He loaded it in his Enfield and took aim at the dugout. I followed his bead but didn't see anything. Then he fired and a gray uniformed soldier reared and fell back into the dugout. I whistled low.

"Good shooting."

I left him an extra stripper of bullets.

Ben Carterby, another Choctaw in the 141st who I knew through Jim, was also hunkered down in Company D. He took me to Lieutenant Ford on the front line he'd established with the mere 24 men remaining in his company.

The lieutenant wrote out a message for me to take back to Major Morrissey. He asked them to send relief—water, food, medics. Company D was barely hanging on.

"Private Oklahombi is keeping Fritz pinned in the dugout," Ford said. "That Indian is a sharpshooter. If we can hold out longer than them, we'll be able to take the whole lot prisoner. But we expect a strong counterattack by the Prussian

Guards today."

I tucked the message in its safe place over my heart and headed off again.

I did a lot of running that day, all the while wondering if anyone in the cut-off Company D would make it out alive with facing the elite German fighters.

◆ ◆ ◆

Near nightfall, I returned to Company E, where they had spent a hard day trading shots with Jerry. We settled in for a night in the trenches, still pressed close to St. Etienne. Those who didn't have their pea shovels settled for digging shallow foxholes in the chalky soil with mess pans. They didn't have any better use for the tin plates. What little rations we had left, we divvied up between us, but the hard tack and corned beef only made us thirstier.

A party of men, led by Sergeant Chill, had gone a mile back to the rear and finally made it to us several hours later, staggering under cases of canned tomatoes. There was no water anywhere in the chaos, but Colonel Bloor sent us cases of the tomato cans that supplied enough juice to make us feel like we might survive the night. I couldn't bring myself to scavenge the packs of my dead comrades on the battlefield.

The colonel had also taken personal responsibility in sending up some artillery fire. That helped.

I was so exhausted, I fell out on the first empty spot I found and went right to sleep.

Sometime in the night, I woke to Sergeant Chill kicking my leg. He motioned for me to follow him as he went about waking others in the same fashion.

I had fallen asleep close to Jim. He'd been a runner most of the day, too, which was thoroughly exhausting. He stretched and yawned as he raised up, mumbling, "That sure was a soft piece of ground."

Then he glanced over his shoulder and froze. "B.B."

I crawled to his side. He stared straight ahead, didn't look at me and asked in a soft tone, "Did I just use a dead man for a pillow?"

I looked behind him, grimaced, and gripped him on the shoulder.

We stepped carefully around men—hoping they were just sleeping—to where Sergeant Chill had gathered a little congregation near Lieutenant Horner.

There was Corporal Tobias Frazier, who was like a big brother to me. Corporal Solomon Bond Louis had been summoned, too.

Lieutenant Horner kept his voice low. We leaned in close to hear. "We need three scout patrols to go out. Choose the darkest skinned men you have. They won't reflect light so much."

He assigned the areas we were to scout. Rather than putting me in charge of a patrol, though, the lieutenant put me with Tobias, and I couldn't help wondering if it was because of my getting Charley killed. But I was grateful to be with Tobe who had been a corporal for nearly a year. I was also grateful when Solomon snagged Isaac to join his patrol. My buddies didn't know what had happened between the two of us or when, but they made an effort to keep us separated that day after the fight in the shell hole. I wanted to say something to Isaac, wanted to make things right with him. But I didn't have the words.

Two Choctaws in Tobe's squad, Jeff Nelson and Robert Taylor, were a part of our scouting party. I wasn't the darkest skinned, but with mud coating my face, only my mama could see me in the night.

Indians were used as scouts a lot in this war. Some officers thought we possessed innate cunningness unique to our race. Maybe, but it was also because we were boys raised in the woods since we could crawl. That was naturally a part of who we were as soldiers.

Lieutenant Horner took time to get to know us. He understood our strengths and weaknesses better than most. Those who had been with him and Captain Veach in Mexico knew Elijah Horner treated Indians as equals.

That was a good thing, because Indians were often assigned the most dangerous scout and runner jobs because of the hyperbole surrounding us.

Our assigned area took us closer to St. Etienne than I'd been since the night in the cemetery. We stayed low with Tobias leading the way through the trench until it sloped up to an end. Then we slipped out and stayed in the shadows of blown apart trees, weaving our way to what was left of the village.

Behind us, the nighttime bombardment began. That gave us light to see by but also exposed us to sniper fire.

We scrambled over a shorn off wall and landed in a once magnificent structure. Only one fully standing wall rose several stories in the air. The many windows in the wall made me think this had likely been a hotel.

Jeff must have thought so, too. He leaned close to me and whispered, "Think they'd give us a free room for the night?"

I smiled without showing my teeth, turning in a cautious circle. Near the blown apart trees, I caught movement just before a flash burst from the shadows. The report of the sniper rifle was swallowed by the roar of the bombardment.

"Ah!"

I jerked around. "Tobe!"

Tobias went down, clutching his leg. Robert jumped in front of him, firing at the tree where the sniper hid. Jeff and I grabbed Tobe's arms and dragged him behind a crumbling interior wall.

As we settled him against it, Tobe gritted his teeth and muttered, "We weren't even complaining about the upkeep of the place."

I leaned my rifle next to him and drew my Colt .45. Leaving Jeff to bandage the leg wound, I crept over to where Robert, the tallest in our patrol, was hunkered against a pile of bricks. He peered around it and shook his head. No more gunfire from the trees.

Explosions sounded beyond the village, and I could tell from my vantage point they were coming from behind the German lines. Were they blowing up their own ammunition? Their artillery fire seemed to be coming from further back. Maybe they were retreating.

There was movement in the upper branches of the sniper's tree. I raised my pistol, took aim, and fired. In the light of the bombardment, a figure fell, turning a flip mid-air. I might have thought it was a Jerry trick except for the sickening thud when he landed on the hard ground.

Shuffling sounds came from behind me. Jeff supported Tobias as they made their way to us.

I signaled them to stay low. "I think we got him, but we better make sure."

Tobias pointed with his chin for us to go ahead.

Through rubble and broken glass outside the hotel, I led the way through the shadows until we halted where the sniper had fallen. He was dead all right. But after closer inspection we found it wasn't a "he" after all.

Tobe, dragging his left leg with Jeff under his arm, took a peek and grimaced.

"Well, I'll be."

He was kind of embarrassed and shamed. We all were. I would never tell my family back home what I'd done with my Colt .45.

The sniper was a young woman.

♦ ♦ ♦

We barely made it back to our company before dawn. In fact, Corporal Louis' group met us coming in. Lieutenant Horner had sent them to find us. Robert and Jeff supported Tobe while I scouted in the lead.

Lieutenant Horner assessed the casualties and dead. Jim, serving as a runner, brought word back that the regiment was being recalled to the American line where we had jumped off two days before. I wondered if Joseph Oklahombi, Ben

Carterby, and Company D had made it out from where they were cut off, holding back the elite Prussian Guard.

While we waited for scouts to make sure the way was clear before bringing the wounded through one of the trenches, I knelt by Corporal Tobias Frazier. He was on a stretcher since we'd met up with orderlies from the medical corps. They sent out search parties in regular intervals to find the wounded.

Tobe's leg was wrapped in a clean bandage and he didn't look too bad. I wondered what it was like to get shot. Everyone I'd seen shot was dead, so I asked him, "Does it hurt bad, Tobe?"

He chuckled. "I got hurt worse playing football back at Armstrong. And you know how that feels."

A strange sense of relief came over me. I'd gotten busted by boys twice my size on the football field. And Samson always seemed to land on my head.

I missed him fiercely, but I'd see him again someday. Maybe sooner than natural because of this war.

God knows.

◆ ◆ ◆

Around noon, we stumbled on more of the 142nd and the 141st. Colonel Bloor was in charge of the chaotic situation and ordered us to stay put once we settled in the trench where we started on October 8. The 142nd had taken over 500 prisoners and 50 machine guns. The 141st took a great many as well. I asked some 141st boys if they knew anything about Company D, but heard they were still cut off.

Colonel Bloor had done his best to keep things in order during the battle. We knew he was proud of our grit and determination. There were no shirkers in our line. Bloor was fast gaining a reputation in the 36th as someone who looked after his men and took initiative when it mattered. He was cool and calm on the front line, showing sound judgment.

The greatest problem of the whole operation, he reported, was with communications. Most of the Headquarters Company had gotten lost with their guides and not arrived on the line until the night before we jumped off. They hadn't had the chance to locate P.C.s, and the telephone section had no opportunity to locate or lay wires. The lack of secure communication cost a lot of lives in the 142nd especially.

Later that day, we learned we were supposed to lead an attack to take a mile and a half of trench by St. Etienne, but General Whitworth failed to carry out that order because things were too chaotic with the 36th Division scattered all over and exhausted. He'd sent word to Lejeune, who ordered the abandonment of the contemplated attack.

Colonel Bloor told us to rest. Apparently the Germans were retreating from St. Etienne, and the Americans were working on moving the fresh 72nd Brigade through the 71st to take up pursuing the Germans. We in the 71st were in no condition to do it.

I settled in a narrow trench with a few dozen men where at least there was room to lounge and trade battle stories and eat. I couldn't eat though, not since I'd sat on something when we first got back. I thought it was a dead rat, but checking, found a decaying human hand.

I got sick and searched for another place to sit, but ended up just leaning against the worn gabions—wicker cylinders—of the wall, nauseated and ready for a real night's sleep.

Sergeant Chill came by and tossed a scrap of barbed wire at me. I caught it and winced. One of the spikes had nicked me. "Barbed wire in the U.S. bag, sir?"

"Don't question me."

Kent Powell found his way to us, but he didn't ask much. He seemed serious and I wondered what he'd seen in the battle, keeping up with the troops and writing stories. He was a top reporter. Not as good as my uncle, of course, but I was glad he was there. If I died, he'd shed an honest tear over my grave, provided there was anything left of me to bury.

Kent Powell asked us Choctaws a few questions then moved on, distracted. I wanted to tell him about Private Albert Billy being shot in the head but his helmet saved him, and how Tobias was shot by a woman sniper. Another time.

While the remainder of the 142nd was rounded up and wounded brought in, we stayed on guard for a counterattack, though we were hardly ready for one. Good thing was, the Germans weren't either. We just needed to "sit pretty" like Sergeant Chill told us.

The troops were so mixed up, we had Fourth Army French soldiers keeping guard alongside us. They couldn't speak English. Though between us Indians we could speak a couple dozen tribal dialects, we couldn't speak a lick of French.

The silence was awkward as I sat next to Albert, a *poilu* on his other side who wore an Adrian helmet—with its insignia of a pair of crossed cannons behind the flaming bomb—and drab blue uniform.

The Frenchman nodded at Albert. "*Bonjour, monsieur.*"

Albert whispered to me, "What did he say?"

"Bonjour, monsieur."

Albert elbowed me and reached into his coat pocket. He pulled out a photograph of his wife and two children, a sweet-looking Choctaw family. When he showed it to the French soldier, the man grinned, reached into his coat pocket and withdrew a photograph of his own family. We looked at it and smiled. The silence wasn't awkward anymore.

I showed my family's photograph, then we took turns showing letters that the other couldn't read because we could feel love in the words written by those waiting and praying for us to come home, both French and American. I imagined the German soldiers did the same.

When I pulled out my journal where I kept my letters tucked safely, I realized it was still blank. I should write about what happened to me, alone out in No Man's Land, but didn't want anyone reading that if they found the journal on my body. I couldn't write it well, and wanted to make sure no one misunderstood what it had done inside me. I didn't understand it all, but I'd never be the same. When I was ready, I'd write it out. I was too tired now.

No wonder the 2nd Division had looked worn out when we relieved them. We'd only been at the front a few days, and I already felt we deserved a long break.

The French military leaders had other plans for us.

CHAPTER THIRTY-TWO

Chitokaka ma! chi haksobish a
Et welit, chin tahpahanla li ka
Auet is sa haklo cha, nana ka
   Chim asihilhha li ka et ʊmá;
Klaist a auet is sʊm ihissashke;
Keyukmʊno, sʊlla he banoshke.

Saint-Étienne-à-Arnes, France
October 1918

The night was birthing something beautiful, something that drew Matthew away from the hubbub of the 141st Infantry of the 36th Division. They were settled on the outer edge of St. Etienne where he'd just arrived. Soft strains of singing soothed Matthew's heart. He halted in the shadows near the singer and let his ears pick out the words as he listened in wonder.

Tʋli hollisso, micha nanasi
Yakni 'ʋppa asha, yohmi kʋno
Is sʋmakbano, chi ahni la wa;
Klaist ak bano, ho sa bahannʋshke
Klaist a auet is sʋm ihissashke;
Keyukmʋno, sʋlla he banoshke.

Give me Christ, or else I die.

The American soldier seated under a splintered pine, singing the Choctaw hymn, paused and looked Matthew's way.

Matthew stepped out of the shadows. "Halito."

The young man grinned and returned the greeting. He had a full head of black hair beneath his helmet, and a wide nose, oval face, dark skin. A taste of home for Matthew.

The doughboy introduced himself as Joseph Oklahombi and continued speaking in Choctaw. "Where are you from?"

"Durant area," Matthew said. "You?"

"Kiamichi Mountains, near Wright City."

"Family?"

"A wife and son. I send them everything I make in the army."

Oklahombi looked tired after combat but peaceful. Matthew lowered himself to the ground beside the soldier, wincing as pain shot through his body. Three days in the saddle had done him no good. He rubbed his left arm.

"Has it been tough going?"

The young Choctaw turned somber then, that shadowed expression Matthew had seen on every soldier after they had killed for the first time in war.

"I thought many times I could not go on. I long for hunting and fishing back home. The farm. My family. It is Chihowa who gives me strength." Joseph Oklahombi looked skyward, seconds then minutes passing. There was no hurry.

Still looking at the stars, he continued. "When I'm hungry, I start to pray and He strengthens me and I go a little further. I do what I have to do for our country."

Matthew wanted to pull out his tablet and write down those words, but he restrained his reporter instinct. Besides, he would remember those words.

Joseph Oklahombi and Matthew talked awhile longer, mostly about home. The old Choctaw Nation visited them and they sat up in the quiet Kiamichi Mountains with a panther's distant scream in the night and the sweep of stars blanketing their lives in peace. They sang a hymn together.

Matthew never once heard Private First Class Joseph Oklahombi speak a word of English.

◆ ◆ ◆

Tom,

As the Allies and Americans push back the German forces, I cannot help but hope the end will come within the next year. When you return to Europe, we can put your photos and my stories together for something truly remarkable. I have much to tell you that will not make it through the censors.

I hope you are well. I pray for you often.

Chi pisa la chike,
Matthew

◆ ◆ ◆

Matthew settled in the tent loaned to him by a French officer he was acquainted with who was on the move that night. Matthew had finally caught up with the 36th Division at St. Etienne, but he was exhausted. A few weeks ago, when he heard the 36th was being sent to the front, he notified Palmer to forward his mail to that division for awhile. He spent a week with another division before he was finally able to ride two days straight to catch up with the famous all-Indian Company E. He had a new story to write about Indian doughboys.

That wasn't his only reason for seeking out Company E in the 142nd Infantry. Somewhere among the thousands of soldiers was the nephew he'd come to find. He hadn't written B.B. in awhile, knowing he'd see him soon. But his search would have to wait for morning. The 142nd was beyond where he was with the 141st, and most of the soldiers would bed down soon, exhausted by four days of chaos and hard fighting.

It had been a baptism of fire for the new troops. Matthew hoped, prayed, dared believe that B.B. was alive and not among the scores of casualties and dead.

Matthew put his brown hard shell suitcase on a table under the light of a lantern inside the French officer's tent. He opened it, withdrew a thin stack of papers, and thumbed through his notes from the past few weeks.

One story he'd put off writing for awhile was about a German soldier in the village of Romagne who had made new soles for the children's shoes during the occupation. Since the Americans liberated the village that month, most of the stories coming out of it were horrible. But the shoes were one story that showed not all the enemy was barbaric. They had humanity, like ones Matthew had met in the German trenches four years ago. He wondered if young Ernst Gustav Hubschmann had made it out of the trenches alive after his feet had nearly been shot off by French machine gun fire. Matthew could still visualize the blood coming from the soles of his boots.

Truthfully, Matthew wanted to write about the Romagne shoes for his own healing.

Earlier that week, he had stood atop Montsec, one of the highest hills in the Saint-Mihiel region. The village had been occupied by German troops since 1914, and they fortified the Montsec hill as an outlook. Since the 1st Division, with Sergeant Otis Leader, and the 26th Division had helped cut off the supply lines, the fortification fell to the Allies.

Atop the hill, Matthew finally understood why it was so valuable. To the west lay Saint-Mihiel, to the northwest Verdun, northeast Metz, the southeast Nancy. So many points where brutal fighting took place, costing millions of lives, soldier and civilian, from all around the world. The ruin from the four year war spread out before him. How long would the horror burn fresh for the French people?

On his way to St. Etienne, Matthew stopped at a Cistercian abbey in Lachalade. The structure showed the ill-effects of war with bullet marks pecked into the 800 year old walls. The French countryside was dotted with ancient churches and abbeys in every village, some hundreds of years old. Many were the last building standing of leveled villages, if anything stood at all.

France held centuries of world history. But how would history remember this war? That was one reason Matthew was there, to write truth to the best of his ability. The pen would tell generations to come what the sword could do and perhaps they would choose wiser paths.

Matthew stretched and leaned back in the hard chair by the table where his suitcase rested. He rubbed his eyes, then his left arm, but the pain persisted. The war better end soon. He didn't have many months of war corresponding remaining in him.

"Knock, knock."

Matthew raised his eyes as reporter Kent Powell popped through the tent door.

"I heard there was a great writer among us, and I asked for the privilege of delivering his mail."

"Have a seat, Powell."

Matthew motioned to the vacant stool across the table where his suitcase lay open. He hadn't seen the ambitious reporter since early summer. He was relieved Powell had a steaming cup of tea in hand so he didn't have to dredge up hospitality.

Powell took the seat, handing a string-tied bundle of envelopes to Matthew. Matthew took it and laid it beside the suitcase. He didn't have the energy to talk and read at the same time. Powell saluted Matthew with his tin cup.

"You're late. Rumor has it the 36th is going to leapfrog past St. Etienne soon."

Matthew liked Powell. Sharp reporter. Accurate. Just right now, Matthew would rather be rolling into the French officer's empty cot than trading stories with a fellow writer. But he forced himself through the question he most wanted an answer to.

"Have you been with the 142nd?"

"You want to know about the all-Indian Company E, right?"

"Pardon?"

"I met your nephew, Bertram Dunn, at the training camp in Bar-sur-Aube. Fine boy. They all are. And yes, he fought hard and came through the battle without a scratch. You can be proud of him."

Matthew was grateful Powell answered the question he didn't have the courage to ask.

"Thank you."

"Now, about this censorship hogwash. I understand you're good friends with Frank Palmer and I don't see why he can't let things slide…"

Matthew cocked his head, Kent Powell sighed, and that was the end of it. They knew there was no fighting the Allied governments from their low positions.

Matthew thumbed his bundle of mail, fanning the paper without looking at the stack. "How are communications here?"

"Not good." Powell took a sip of tea. "The Fritz left plenty of hardware handy, by which means they are tapping messages. They capture one in four runners. Carrier pigeons and dogs are easy to catch. The telephone is the most effective means for communicating." He gave a humorless laugh. "As the Fritz are well aware of."

Matthew knew these problems with communications were up and down the front, especially with the AEF setting a fast pace, a war of movement, always pushing forward. If the Allies couldn't find a safe way to communicate, this war could last another year. Or longer.

Powell shifted on his stool. "If you want a story, I saw you talking to one of the best potentials."

"Private Oklahombi?"

"He and his buddies took two hundred prisoners. He's a real marksman. They say he kept the Fritz pinned for days in a dugout, picking off any that showed his head. He killed 79 and took a hundred prisoners there. He also crossed No Man's Land several times, carrying wounded and taking prisoners back. They say a Marine officer watched him bringing two prisoners in, but by the time he got all the way up, Oklahombi only had one. The officer asked him where the other one was, and he said, 'I killed him. Want me to go back and kill him more?'" Powell shook his head. "Better get the story before someone else does."

"You're not going to write it?"

Powell grinned. "I have another big one coming down the line. A special story."

"Share?"

"Not a chance. This is book material."

Matthew would talk to Joseph Oklahombi first thing in the morning. Something he did know that Powell didn't. The name Oklahombi loosely meant "man killer" in Choctaw. No prisoner had better try to escape under his watch.

The story called to mind one Matthew caught wind of on his way to St. Etienne about a man from Tennessee who killed and captured a slew of German soldiers and officers on his own. Matthew flipped through his notes then scribbled Private Joseph Oklahombi's name next to Corporal Alvin York.

Matthew had book material of his own working in the back of his mind. He'd already talked with Otis Leader about the potential and encouraged Otis to finish his journal covering all of his war experiences.

Powell eyed the field notes Matthew held. "I heard you were able to interview General Pershing a few days ago."

"I did."

"Share?"

"Not a chance."

Powell grinned, drained his tea, and tapped the tied packet of mail. "Don't go to sleep without reading those. There's a piece you'll find particularly interesting."

"You read my mail?"

"Good reading material is scarce."

Powell winked and left. Matthew chuckled softly, then winced, rubbing his chest with his free hand. Sharp pains had pestered him there all day.

He started to rise, then eased back down and reached for the packet. His curiosity would never let him sleep.

On top were letters from his sister Ruth Ann, his mother, and from newspapers who wanted stories. Beneath that was a copy of a captured document forwarded by a contact he had in the 1st Division.

At the bottom of the mail lay something that made Matthew drop everything else. It seemed foreign, yet so, so familiar, and he stared at it a long time. Lifting his hand, his fingers hovered over the banner emblazoned across the top of sturdy newspaper. The page was slightly crooked—Annie never could quite get the paper straight in the printing press—but it was there, dated, with bold headlines across the front page.

CHOCTAW TRIBUNE

Durant, Oklahoma

September 27, 1918

AMERICAN INDIANS SERVE THEIR COUNTRY

By Matthew Teller

There was his article—every word—beneath the banner of the newspaper he'd started in his early twenties to report the truth of what went on in his world—the old Choctaw Nation, Indian Territory. And there was that banner again, serving the same purpose.

God bless his sister.

But she didn't stop with his story. She added her own, including the enthusiastic efforts for the war cause by American Indians at home. Indian women on reservations planted Victory Gardens and ran liberty bond drives. An estimated ten thousand of them joined the Red Cross. Families and churches throughout Indian country sent countless Christmas boxes and knitted sweaters for the doughboys.

In the editorial section, Ruth Ann had added a quote from *American Notes* by Charles Dickens. On his tour of the States in the 1840s, Dickens had met Choctaw Chief Peter Pitchlynn and wrote about the encounter. She had added commentary at the end.

"He would very much like, he said, to see England before he died; and spoke with much interest about the great things to be seen there. When I told him of that chamber in the British Museum wherein are preserved household memorials of a race that ceased to be, thousands of years ago, he was very attentive, and it was not hard to see that he had a reference in his mind to the gradual fading away of his own people."
—*Charles Dickens.*

We are still here, Chief Pitchlynn. And now, we are on foreign soil. Choctaws have fought alongside American soldiers for our country in every war since Independence.

We have not faded away, Chief Pitchlynn. And we will not fade away.

She included an image of the Great Seal of the Choctaw Nation. Its smoking pipe hatchet with an unstrung bow represented peace yet a preparedness to go to war at a moment's notice.

Matthew's other articles had made it to her in time for publication, too. He could have sold them to any newspaper in America or France or Britain for a tidy sum. But money never meant anything to him when there was truth to be told.

Bless you, Annie.

He had written about the battle waged over American citizenship for Indians and how the war might effect it. A third of the Indians Matthew had interviewed weren't even U.S. citizens. Not all of them wanted to be. With citizenship came land taxes and swindlers who would steal the rest of Indian land as they'd often done after the Dawes allotments. Many politicians and Indian agents argued for competency testing of Indians before citizenship. They said they wanted to make certain Indians were educated enough to protect themselves from being swindled by unscrupulous citizens.

Matthew had witnessed his share of irony in life.

Annie also printed his story of Sergeant John Northrup, a Chippewa. He'd lost a leg in battle. Matthew interviewed him in the hospital where the man told the gruesome story of how, as he laid on a stretcher waiting for an ambulance, another Indian crawled by with a severely wounded soldier on his back. The crawling Indian's feet had been shot off.

There was also a quote from Major Tom Reilly of the 165th. Nearly half his men were cut down in a single battle:

"The Indians in the front ranks were thoroughly swept away," he reported grimly. "When an Indian went down, another Indian stepped immediately to the front."

The major commended the men in the fight. "If a battle was on, and you wanted to find the Indians, you would always find them at the front."

Matthew closed his eyes, rubbed his left arm, and sighed.

This moment summed up his life, his service to God, and his fellow man. The fight for truth.

He bowed his head and time slipped away in the prayer he sent up to the Creator. He thought of Joseph Oklahombi's words.

I start to pray and He strengthens me and I go a little further. I do what I have to do for our country.

A quarter of an hour passed. Matthew laid aside the *Choctaw Tribune* and opened the letter from his sister. He smiled at her gushing tone, one she hadn't taken during the whole war.

Instead of seeing her graying hair and full waistline, he envisioned the sparky eighteen-year-old who had been at his side when he first launched the newspaper. Back then, they were two crazy Indian kids on a grand though dangerous adventure.

She laughed easy then, cried easy. She had enough heart for both of them, and took delight in echoing their mother's words to him.

Stubborn, stubborn Choctaw.

Matthew laid the memories aside in his heart for a time when he would need to draw upon the beauty and strength of life shaped by time, love, and family.

He took up the captured German dispatch and read it next. Then, fingers pressed against his temple, he read it again. He'd thought Powell was referring to the *Choctaw Tribune* as the interesting piece of mail, but this qualified as well.

It was an order issued from a German colonel in the 97th Landwehrs during the Saint-Mihiel offensive. The paranoia among German soldiers about American Indian troops only heightened with the arrival of fresh troops and rumors of an all-Indian company—Company E of the 142nd Infantry. The company Matthew's nephew served in.

The order was issued to 97th commanders that additional snipers be assigned with the primary task of killing Indian soldiers, especially when they served as night workers, scouts, and runners. They were a special target.

Matthew put the dispatch aside with one last look at the *Choctaw Tribune*. He started to blow out the lamp, but paused. The dispatch glared at him.

No one was promised tomorrow.

Matthew headed for the tent door. He'd find B.B. tonight, tell him he was proud of him, tell him...

Sharp pain opened up Matthew's chest, like a bullet ripping through. But this wasn't an attack from outside. This was one within his own body.

He tripped on the stool and fell, his breath raspy, pain

blinding his vision. Disoriented, he reached back for a pencil on his suitcase desk. His last thought was to write a letter to his little sister and tell her how much the newspaper had meant in the final moments of his life.

CHAPTER THIRTY-THREE

KILLED IN ACTION
Dedicated to the Heroic Dead of the 142nd Infantry
by Chaplain C. H. Barnes

Killed in action—oh, sacred thing!
Treasure it dearly and to this cling;
He gave his life for you and me,
He paid a great price for humanity.
He's sleeping the last sleep, somewhere today,
So treasure the price he had to pay.

Saint-Étienne-à-Arnes, France
October 1918

We learned from prisoners that the German troops were pulling out all along the Champagne front. They had already pulled back from the French lines to the east. Fires and explosions during the night told us they were getting ready to move from the American zone, destroying everything they couldn't carry. Like I'd suspected, their artillery fire was coming from further back as they retreated. The American commanders instructed us to keep "close contact" with the enemy.

"Close contact" meant Colonel Bloor sending out patrols from the 142nd and 141st. Boys in the 141st were met with gas and light machine gun fire, but they didn't have much trouble advancing up the road. It was a different story for our patrols in the 142nd.

Under Lieutenant Horner, Company E advanced with other companies in the 142nd toward St. Etienne.

Machine gun fire coming from north of the village was so fierce, we couldn't do much except hunker down in the trench or in foxholes we'd dug for shelter. I ended up digging in near Lee Hoade, who was in a better mood since he could smoke in his foxhole, blocked from enemy sight.

I raised my head enough to talk to him. "That smoking will kill you before any Jerry."

"Fine by me." Lee Hoade puffed the smoke in a ring, and raised his cigarette. "I'd rather die by my friend here than a dirty kraut-eater."

Machine gun fire sprayed the dirt above our heads.

From behind me, Jim muttered, "I thought they said Jerry was retreating!"

A creepy buzz in the sky caught my attention. I scooted down in the foxhole to take a look without raising up. The hum materialized as an airplane above us. It made a sweep and disappeared.

"Let's get out of here!"

We'd just made it to the crowded trench when artillery shells started dropping right where those foxholes were. The scout plane had revealed our position and Jerry was a good shot.

Close contact.

The 72nd Brigade finished slipping through our ranks to take up the pursuit, relieving us at last. Four days of combat had aged me ten years. I'd be an old man by the end of the month.

We retreated to the line where we'd originally jumped off. The Germans were in retreat and we could relax while the 72nd chased them down.

But the rest wouldn't last long. Lieutenant Horner informed us that as soon as the 71st Brigade had reorganized, we'd be on the move again.

The lieutenant was the highest ranking officer left in Company E. The others had been killed or wounded. Lieutenant Elijah W. Horner from Mena, Arkansas was now our commanding officer.

CHAPTER THIRTY-FOUR

"THE STARS AND STRIPES"

Official Newspaper of the
American Expeditionary Forces

Prussian Guard is Tamed Again

It was the Prussian Guard against the American Indian on the morning of October 8 in the hills of Champagne.

When it was all over, after the wire protected slopes had been trampled as though they were no more than bramble patches of thorny and leafless berry bushes, and there were no more German gunners left in the earth-baked machine gun nests, the Prussian Guards were farther on their way back toward the Aisne River, and going fast, and warriors of thirteen Indian tribes looked down on the town of St. Etienne.

The Indians—one company of them—were fighting with the 36th Division, made up of Texas and Oklahoma rangers and oil men, for the most part, and with the French this division was pushing away forever the German menace to Reims.

The Marines told us that the German lines were only a hundred yards in front; but we were inclined to be skeptical until the bullets from sniper's guns began singing by our heads. Then we knew it must be so.

No sooner had our barrage started than the Germans started firing on our positions. It was an accurate and deadly fire both from artillery and machine guns. I lost two of the best Indians I had—two corporals— right in the holes where they had kept watch before we jumped off.

My men advanced by short rushes until the first machine guns were reached. It seemed that there was not a square foot of air space through which bullets were not flying.

—Lieutenant Elijah W. Horner's report

Arrived on front line on the morning of Oct. 7th, 1918 and received an order to make an attack on October 8th, 1918. Went over the top at 5:43 a.m. I went over and saw Germans in a dugout and I shot them and killed 4 Germans.

I was lying down in a little trench with the German artillery fire hitting all around me but I had no fear so I kept on going with the Platoon and saw many comrades falling down wounded and killed from machine gun fire. I advanced on through the open country from the woods and dug in where we established our front line northeast of the town.

About 6 o'clock the Germans laid down the barrage and we retreated to the end of the woods and established our new line and held it for two days and nights. I was acting runner for awhile and I went through the artillery fire where they were falling all around and one hit about 25 yards from me and I got some of the high explosion of gas and didn't go any further for about 30 minutes.

Every time I hear the shell I always fall and go again when it's over.

—Corporal James Edwards' report

CHAPTER THIRTY-FIVE

"When the 2nd and 36th Divisions were sent over above Somme-Py to break the tenacious clutch of the enemy, the following radio message was received at a divisional P.C. from a brigadier general commanding the attacking brigade: "I am absolutely out of communication." The loss of telephone communication was equivalent to the loss of all communication." —*Captain A. Lincoln Lavine*

Western Front, France
October 1918

We reorganized and moved out on October 12 to follow the 72nd Brigade. The Germans had pulled out, and the 72nd had a hard time in the chase. Through the liaison system, we learned the brigade had been sprayed by machine gun fire from upper stories and roofs of houses still standing in St. Etienne and from nests in the outskirts. But accidental shelling of its own troops finally silenced the German guns and they quietly withdrew from St. Etienne.

The 142nd got on the battered Machault-Dricourt road, a

miserable experience. Congested with guns, ambulances, marching men, motorcycles, and potholes, the road also over-flowed with hundreds of French civilians—old men, women, and children. Families were torn apart, their belongings packed in carts and on their backs.

This must have been how it was for my great-grandmother with her folks during the Indian Removal, forced to pack what they could carry and leave the rest behind to cross 400 miles to reach their new homeland in Indian Territory. As one Choctaw chief put it, "this has been a trail of tears and death."

I guessed the French people were feeling that way now.

On the night of October 13th, the 71st Brigade was inserted to the right of the 72nd. We were near Attigny and the Aisne River. Colonel Bloor established his P.C. in an old brick warehouse at Vaux-Champagne.

We'd outrun our supply base, meaning no hot meals, tents, or changes of clothes until it caught up to us. Solomon, Jim, and I worked together to dig holes for each other and cover them with pine boughs for shelter from the rain. I might have to sleep in the mud but at least the rain wouldn't pelt my face.

We couldn't attack at the Aisne River until our supply base caught up. And we needed to get good and ready before we launched an attack at this river. I didn't know how we could do it without getting slaughtered.

On the north bank, the Germans were well prepared. Trees on our side had been chopped down and hauled to their side to build machine gun emplacements and give them a clear line of fire across the river. The Ardennes Canal stood between us and the Aisne River, and the bridges had been destroyed.

I was no military strategist, but this didn't look good.

Snipers and intermittent artillery fire from across the river sent a lot of American boys to the field hospital or the grave. But we needed to know more about the enemy's position and movements, so several patrols were sent to take prisoners. Too often they were discovered and sent scampering back across the river.

But the 36th prevailed and took live prisoners on October 16th. It involved some Company C boys and a determined lieutenant who hadn't changed his clothes in seventeen days. A lot of us hadn't. The division hadn't stopped long enough for common comforts.

When the prisoners were interrogated, they revealed how terrified they had been. Their commanding officer had warned them not to be taken alive by Indian troops, that we would torture then scalp them. The American officers laughed.

I recalled the rumors I'd heard that some Indian soldiers had taken German scalps in battle. It also called to mind that moment in the trench with the German bodies and Lee Hoade.

Some rumors had roots in truth.

◆ ◆ ◆

Major Morrissey sent me to gather reports from three of the artillery guns. The major's telephone was out, much to his chagrin, and they had to rely on runners all day. I hiked to the first gun, jittery because of shells flying overhead. But I'd learned to listen to the whistle and get a good idea if I needed to take cover or not. I didn't duck for the one flying overhead, but I did pick up my pace.

I found the lieutenant in a dugout with a telephone, and held up the message from Major Morrissey. It requested information on the number of German guns they faced. The lieutenant waved me to wait while he finished his call.

"Yes, sir, the Fritz have consistently sent the bombs 200 yards over us all day. We shouldn't need to move until morning."

When he was finished, he handed me off a written report with a grin on his dirt-streaked lips. "Here you go, Chief. Too bad about the major's telephone. Can't expect to win this war without one."

I took his report and headed off for the next gun, and the next. It was on my way back that a warning whistle sent me to the ground.

The shell exploded, shaking the earth beneath me. Three more were right behind it. I covered the back of my neck as dirt clods rained down. There was stillness for a split second, then urgent shouts. I jumped up and ran for the first gun I'd gone to. Only it was no longer there. Neither was the dugout. Neither was the lieutenant.

I thought about the telephone call he'd made when I was there, telling his C.O. exactly how much the Fritz missed his position by. Had he told Germans listening-in exactly where he was? They hadn't missed again.

We might not be able to win the war without the telephone, but I didn't see how we could win with it, either.

◆ ◆ ◆

Mail finally caught up with us. At mail call, I found letters from family, and a package from Mama with homemade persimmon leather and *nipi shila*—salt pork. I wasn't happy with her instruction to share the treats with my buddies.

There was also a letter postmarked in Texas.

Dear Bertram,

Thank you for the letter from France. I saved the stamps in my scrapbook along with a clipping from your uncle's newspaper story.
I wish he had written about you.

Sincerely,
Ida Claire

But the letter that surprised me most was from Victoria.

My dearest cousin Bertram,

I hope this letter finds you alive and well. I haven't much time, but there is something I must tell you about.

I wrote a friend in New York about your talent in academics and she informed me of a wealthy businessman who is interested in sponsoring Indian youth for higher education.

Please consider this opportunity. It begins at the Ivy League preparatory school, Mercersburg Academy in Pennsylvania. From there, you may expect sponsorship for an Ivy League education.

This is the opportunity for you to be successful. Please consider it carefully as I did when I made the decision to improve my status. You do not have to remain in Indian country all of your life.

Lovingly, your cousin,
Victoria Teller

I knew what she meant, that there were places in the world who thought Indians were novelties. Some places even had a detached appreciation for our unique heritage. But that respect was often only earned with distancing oneself from one's culture, heritage, and even family—to be a showpiece, not someone still fighting for their people's rights in the twentieth century as a lawyer like my daddy.

Still, what would it be like to escape the realities of being Indian, of the expectation of doing good for my tribe? I could even play football with the top schools in the country.

I wrote replies to the letters, except Victoria's. I didn't have an answer and she'd expect one. She never deliberated long on making a decision, and nothing stopped her once she did. She was like her father in that.

I was careful with what I wrote to Mama. She'd notice if I didn't put in a lot of details, especially after stories she'd soon read in the Oklahoma newspapers about the 36th Division's first engagement. All the killing, the shells and machine gun bullets flying around me, human beings blown to atoms. Mamas didn't need to hear things like that, knowing their sons had been only steps away from the explosion.

As I wrote to her, I thought about how it had been over

a month since I'd last heard from Uncle Matthew. He normally wrote me often, but I figured he was pretty busy lately, keeping up with the whole American Expeditionary Forces as the Meuse-Argonne offensive pushed on. When the pace slowed with coming winter and the troops rested to start fighting again come spring, I'd hopefully get a chance to see him.

Somewhere in France
October 20, 1918

Dear Ida Claire,

You are welcome for the stamps. I have not seen my uncle. He is a busy writer and there is a lot happening, but I am not allowed to write about it. They won't let us send those things in case the enemy captures the mail.

War is hard. We crawl, work, and sleep in mud, and that's not the worst of it. But when you have something you have to do, you just have to do it. I just wish Samson was here with me.

I hope this letter reaches you so you have more stamps.

Sincerely,
Bertram

◆ ◆ ◆

I thought I'd get a good rest while we waited for the coming attack at the Aisne River. But a couple of officers in the 142nd wanted to prove that Indians were better crawlers than whites. They picked five of us from Company E—Jim and myself included—and five white soldiers from Company H to compete by crawling to one of the supply trucks.

I sized up the competition and was feeling pretty confident. Until they blindfolded us.

Bets were on as our fellow soldiers whooped and hollered at the start. I began crawling in the direction of the truck they designated as the finish line. Before they put the blindfold on me, I'd gotten a good look at the area and knew I was close when my fingers encountered a scraggly bush. I heard moans of disappointment and second guessed myself. But no, this was the right way.

More moans and then catcalls. Someone was close to me, elbow to elbow. I crawled faster, pulling myself forward as quick as I could. Then I slowed and put out my hand, crawled closer, and felt the rubber tire of the truck.

I rolled over and sat up, pulling off my blindfold to see Jim beside me, grinning as we watched the others crawl in every direction but the right one.

The fun was short lived. Sergeant Chill called Jim and me up to support a company in the 2nd Artillery as they made their daily change to move their guns, because German shells always seemed able to find them. Too often, it seemed Jerry knew more what we were going to do than we did.

We were assigned to take three men each and help move the monster guns. I gathered Joseph Davenport, Benjamin Colbert, and Lee Hoade. We didn't make it.

The haunting whistle of a shell tickled my ear. We all hit the dirt and waited to see if we'd die.

The shell burst close, shaking the ground beneath my belly and sending muddy debris over me.

Not hearing another whistle, I raised up to check on the men around me, but didn't get a chance to see if they were alive. My eyes started burning and I screamed. Voices around me shouted. There was something important I had to do but I couldn't think as thick gas surrounded me.

Gas. My gas mask!

I always kept my gas mask case around my neck in terror of the Yellow Cross. I shouted something about putting on the monkey face and I think the other men did. I got my mask out of its case and put it on as I staggered up. I bumped into Lee Hoade, who was helping Joseph to his feet. Benjamin was ready to run.

We all hightailed it away from where the mustard gas shell had landed. Terror pumped through my brain as I remembered the training and fear they'd stoked us with in Camp Bowie, warning us about the horrors of gas.

The air inside the mask choked me. Part of the gas was trapped inside and my lungs burned unmercifully.

We ran to the gas station along with dozens of other men who had survived several shells exploding. Many had already been turned away as false alarms and I could tell the medics were ready to do the same with us. But when I yanked my mask down to get a breath away from the stale, fumigated air trapped in my lungs, they set to work on me. I stripped down to nothing and stood under one of the showers.

The water was freezing cold, making it harder to breathe. I shook uncontrollably but stayed on my feet. Jim was in the showers too. His lips had turned blue.

"Just like a football game, huh?" His teeth clenched against the chatter created a funny grin. I made a face at him.

"Come on, B.B., you'll walk it off."

I trusted Jim Edwards, but I sure didn't believe him then.

The medics cleaned us up. Once medicated, they put us on cots for the night. I didn't get the gas bad and gradually, the terror faded.

Fortunately we had been in open country, not like men in the trenches who'd experienced gas for the first time in the history of war. This gas hadn't been concentrated but the way my eyes and lungs felt, I couldn't imagine wanting to survive if it'd been worse.

That night, Chaplain Barnes stopped to see me in the hospital tent. His eyes were sunk deeper in his face, squinted by the bags under them. Still, he had a smile for me and asked if I needed anything. I asked him to read from the book of Joshua, about being strong and courageous.

He did and prayed for me. Before he left, I gathered the courage to tell him something that had gnawed at me since the fight with Isaac in the shell crater at St. Etienne. It wasn't until I was lying on my back in the hospital tent that I'd been still long enough to think it through.

"Chaplain Barnes?"

"Yes, Corporal?"

I hesitated. I'd never confessed to anyone, but since I'd been given the gift of air back, I wanted to clear it. "When I was a kid, I lied."

He tried not to smile.

"No, sir, not about sneaking dessert before dinner or anything like that. This lie hurt my best friend. We did a kind of bad thing, at least the white man at school thought it was bad, but I lied and said I didn't. My friend told the truth.

"He was whipped for what we did. Whipped bad and locked in a closet. He hated me for lying, and now, well, we joined up at the same time and he's here and he still hates me."

Chaplain Barnes said nothing for a time. He closed his Bible and stared at it.

"Was he punished for speaking his native language?"

The chaplain might as well have gassed me again. I took a quick breath.

"Yes, sir."

"I am sorry that happened."

I didn't know what to say. Chaplain Barnes looked right at me.

"For the offender, the first step toward reconciliation begins with a sincere apology. For the victim, it is forgiveness."

He asked if I wanted to talk more about it, but I shook my head and he headed off soon after.

I was left alone to contemplate the fact that I'd never once told Isaac how very sorry I was for lying.

CHAPTER THIRTY-SIX

Western Front, France
October 1918

"What's this?" The orderly outside the hospital tent muttered to himself.

It was the middle of the night and I couldn't sleep for all the constant coming and going in the hospital tent. A large truck, visible through the open tent flap where my cot was, had rolled up to the back of the tent with supplies. Someone laid flat out in the bed of the truck.

The orderly grabbed the two ankles and pulled them until the man's legs dangled over the tail-gate. Then he fetched a cup of water and tossed it on the doughboy's face. A fountain of spittle caught moonlight before the soldier tried to raise up. Latching onto one arm, the orderly pulled him into a sitting position.

"All right, soldier, off to bed before your commanding officer catches you drunk."

The soldier slipped off the truck and into the orderly's supporting arms. He shook himself and stumbled off, his face turned down but I recognized him anyway.

Isaac Hotinlubbi.

Surely the good Lord didn't want me making things up to Isaac right then? I dove under the covers, willing my mind to forget what I had seen. Isaac had never drank the whole time we were in the army.

Hours passed and when dawn crept out of hiding, so did I. But it was Lieutenant Horner who drew me out of bed.

"Corporal Dunn?"

I squinted through swollen eyelids.

"Do you speak Choctaw fluently?"

My head trembled, tongue frozen. What kind of trouble would I be in if I said yes?

"I need you to come with me."

Crawling out of bed and into my boots, I staggered forward with a lingering fear. Lieutenant Horner led the way outside and around to another tent. In front of it stood Isaac and Sergeant Chill. They glared at me. For someone who always wanted to do what was right, I had a knack for making enemies.

Lieutenant Horner took my arm, bringing me fully alert, wondering what would happen. Then I realized I was swaying and had nearly fallen. My head pounded.

"Corporal Dunn, I need you to ask Private Hotinlubbi where he was last night."

I looked at Isaac, feeling dumb. "Where were you last night?"

Sergeant Chill barked, "Use your gibberish, Chief."

"Sergeant." Horner's hold on my arm loosened.

In the sergeant's expression, I glimpsed the stern look of Mr. Watson, the teacher who had whipped Isaac for speaking Choctaw and would have whipped me if I hadn't lied. What would happen if I said I didn't speak Choctaw? What would happen if I did?

I glanced at Lieutenant Horner, who nodded. He wanted me to do it. I didn't want to. Even though no one had been punished for speaking their language in the army, the terrible memory of Isaac being whipped while I watched froze my tongue.

"Corporal Dunn," Lieutenant Horner urged.

I finally repeated the question in Choctaw.

"Ninakash, katimma ish aya tuk?" Where were you last night?

Isaac's expression didn't change. The sergeant shook his head, squinting one eye like he did when he was annoyed, which was most of the time. "Still drunk," he muttered.

Lieutenant Horner turned me toward himself and spoke confidentially. "A Frenchman was stabbed to death at a farmhouse last night. Hotinlubbi was seen in the vicinity beforehand. I need to know exactly where he was and what he was doing."

"He was passed out drunk when I found him this morning," Sergeant Chill insisted.

"Corporal Dunn?" Lieutenant Horner waited for me to continue.

I turned and spoke to Isaac again in Choctaw. "I know you do not want to speak to me, but a man has been killed. They need to know who did it."

No change.

"Isaac, you were in the truck bed last night. An orderly pulled you out. What happened?"

A moment of contemplation passed. Isaac was puzzling it out. Now he fully comprehended the gravity of the situation. But being a full-blood Choctaw, it was unlikely he'd defend himself, even with the truth. It was an old tradition among our people to simply accept a verdict and whatever punishment that was decreed.

Still, I had to try. I couldn't believe he had done it.

"A nakfi, hattak a ish vbi tuk o?" My brother, did you kill the man?

"Keyu." No.

His response came automatically, then he spit, disgusted.

I blinked my swollen eyes as they watered up. Gas was nasty. That was the cause of the tears, not hearing my old friend speak to me in Choctaw for the first time since we were

253

nine.

"Corporal?" Horner watched me.

"He did not do it."

My neck ached, stiff from the fetal position I'd spent the night in, so I turned my body to face Lieutenant Horner, who still steadied me.

"Speak with the orderly who unloaded the supply truck. About 3 a.m. Isaac was in the back."

"3 a.m.?" The lieutenant looked to Sergeant Chill.

The sergeant nodded. "That's about the time the farmhand said a soldier was there wanting another drink, and he found his boss inside, stabbed. The money jar was gone."

"He drunk."

We turned to Isaac. He looked at me and spoke in Choctaw. "I carried a message for the field hospital in the night. A soldier passed me on the path. He was drunk and wanted money. When I walked away, he hit me. I do not remember anything until the water splashed my face."

I recalled what I'd seen last night, and everything made sense. Isaac had been knocked unconscious by the drunk soldier who went on to rob and kill the farmer. Someone must have found Isaac and put him on the hospital truck, where the orderly merely thought he had hitched a ride, and passed out from drinking.

I translated Isaac's story and his description of the other soldier.

Lieutenant Horner looked over my head to Sergeant Chill. "Did Private Hotinlubbi have money on him when you found him?"

The sergeant shook his head. "Not a cent."

"I'd say it's fair to assume that another soldier is the killer. We'll find him."

"*He's* likely passed out drunk somewhere," Sergeant Chill said.

Lieutenant Horner squeezed his free hand into a fist. He'd told me once how his father was an alcoholic, and why he never drank because of it. There were good reasons why liquor sale to AEF troops was prohibited by French law and U.S. Army regulations.

The lieutenant released my arm. "You are both dismissed."

I swayed. Lieutenant Horner steadied me with a hand on my shoulder and gave me a side-smile and wink. "Can you two sober Indians make it to the hospital tent together?"

"Yes, sir."

It was a partial lie. We wouldn't go back together. Isaac was already several paces away, though still unsteady from the blow to his head.

Behind me, Sergeant Chill said, "So, Dunn can speak that gibberish fluently too."

I quickened my steps.

◆ ◆ ◆

A few days later, I was back by the Aisne River, helping cover for the engineers while they established a bridgehead at Attigny. We didn't make the crossing there though.

Orders came for our division to shift east and take over the sector where the French 73rd Division had been.

We marched all night through mud to our new position, worn out by the time we reached it. But by dawn, we were ready for whatever we had to do next. Except no one knew what that was.

We did learn what we were up against. From Attigny, the river made a decided horseshoe bend to avoid the hilly terrain surrounding a farm called Forest Ferme. The bend was a perfect U-shape and the Germans had fortified the mouth of the U with a double band of coiled barbed wire that stretched two miles from west to east. The barbed wire was low enough to step over—cautiously—if you had time before the machine gunners behind it or riflemen in the trenches got you.

The Germans commanded the higher ground as usual and their strong points gave them a view of the entire plain to the south.

Facing this line was deadly enough, but that wasn't the worst. Across the canal and the river, all behind the horseshoe bend, rose several high hills. Jerry artillery stood sentry duty on those hills, looking down on the river loop and protecting their troops. If we tried to cross at Attigny, our flank would be exposed to gunners inside the river loop. If we tried to attack the river loop, the gunners and artillery north and east on the high hills above the Aisne River would get us.

No wonder the French had failed twice to take the salient, which was a bulge in the German line of defense.

The first French attack was supposed to be a surprise. It wasn't. The enemy had been ready and met them with heavy machine gun fire. The second time, the French used an artillery barrage. They took heavy casualties in their retreat.

And still, the American 36th Division was expected to clear out the river loop by October 27th.

The 142nd Infantry sat across from the far east end of the river loop line. To our right, high on a hill, stood the occupied town of Voncq. I imagined you could see the whole battlefield from there. Jerry could watch us trying to get into position.

Artillery fire increased when we moved positions. The medical corps set up a field hospital north of Machault. Casualties went there every day.

That evening after we had moved east, I sat on the ground with Solomon and Mitchell alongside our row of pup tents, talking in Choctaw. I was facing the road and saw a tall, lean figure heading by at a good clip. Major William Morrissey. He looked our way and slowed. Solomon had just asked me a question, but I fell silent. Had Morrissey heard us speaking our language?

The major veered off the road and came over to us. We quickly stood and saluted.

He asked, "What language were you speaking? It didn't sound French or Spanish?"

The officers from Texas and Oklahoma were used to us, but being from Pennsylvania, our new major of the 2nd Battalion had never been around Indians.

Solomon told the major we were speaking Choctaw, the common language of our people. Major Morrissey looked stunned. "This language still exists? How many of the soldiers here speak it?"

He glanced past Solomon and our eyes met. I looked down, trying to make up my mind about what had happened with Isaac and if that had changed me at all.

Lieutenant Horner came up the road then, and I shifted a little behind Mitchell. Horner had a written statement concerning the stabbing for Isaac Hotinlubbi to sign. Solomon offered to find Isaac and translate the statement.

The three of them headed off with Major Morrissey asking Horner exactly how many Indians they had in the 142nd.

I crawled into the pup tent I shared with Noel and laid on my side. I'd used fishing hooks and line from the U.S. bag to hang a photograph of my family by my bedroll, and it dangled before me now. I was getting really homesick in France and tired of trying to be white with whites and Choctaw with Choctaws—not knowing which to be when I was around both.

But there was no time for moping. We had another battle coming up quick.

Our division commander hollered for more replacements. Few came. We were low on men in the infantry, and we needed more for the coming attack on the river loop, but there was no help on the horizon. And that was just one problem—the whole area was netted with German wires and cables. That set off rumors about a threat that put the entire Meuse-Argonne campaign at risk, even as the 36th Division prepared for major battle to take the river loop and Forest Ferme.

Someone in our division decided to test the suspicion every officer had, and gave out false coordinates to our supply dump. Within an hour, enemy shells rained down on that location. Just like the lieutenant with the artillery gun, the Germans knew our every move, and met us with deadly G.I. cans and whizzbangs.

As Sergeant Chill put it, the telephone was way too leaky of a bucket to put water in.

If the Allies couldn't find a secure code for our messages, and quick, the whole operation could come to a grinding halt. And cost still more lives.

We needed a code the Germans could never break.

CHAPTER THIRTY-SEVEN

"Battles are now being fought by telephone; and, to be able to manage the telephone, to get messages back and forth, to have a good understanding at the different ends of the line, and to be a good telephone operator, is now becoming a part of the duty of the commanding general." —Captain A. Lincoln Lavine

Aisne River near Roche, France
October 1918

"We need to make food plans before we take the river in case we get surrounded by Jerry," Ben Carterby said in Choctaw.

I was seated with my brothers around a fire, eating out of my foldable tin mess kit. Jim had goaded his buddy, Ben Carterby from Company D of the 141st, into telling a story.

Ben had survived four days in the battle with artillery barrages, machine gun fire, snipers, and a fierce counterattack on his company. Those four days cost three-fourths of the company's men and officers. But it didn't take much to get him going on telling traditional stories from home.

"We should make *tanchi labona*," Ben continued, but then quieted and looked up as Kent Powell joined our circle with his cup of tea and writing tablet.

"Evening, boys. Mind if I sit down for a bit?"

We nodded and he took a seat on the log next to me. I explained that Ben was about to tell a story, knowing Ben would do it in English so Kent Powell could understand.

"Once during the long ago war between the Choctaws and the Creeks, five Choctaws made their camp on Nanih Waiya Creek. One day, four of them went a hunting, leaving the remaining comrade in camp as a cook. An hour or so afterwards, when the cook was busy with a pot of *tanchi labona*, he suddenly found himself surrounded by five Creek warriors, who ordered him to serve dinner for them. The Choctaw consented. The pot was placed at a convenient spot on the ground. The self-invited Muscogee Creek guests seated themselves around it in the usual Indian circle, while the Choctaw stood in the center, ready to play the role of an officious host. He was quick-witted and knew the Creeks intended to kill him as soon as they were through with their dinner.

"Standing by the pot with a big gourd as a ladle, the Choctaw began to dip up the *tanchi labona* and pour it back into the pot so as to cool it sufficiently for the stomachs of his guests. While the Creeks were regaling themselves with some venison, which he had served them, all at once the Choctaw swung the gourd full of scalding hot *tanchi labona*, and threw it full in the faces of his guests. The blinded Creeks, smarting with pain, clapped their hands to their eyes to remove the hot, sticking plaster.

"The Choctaw bounded away like a deer and made good his escape. He soon found his companions, and they all returned to the camp. They saw that the Creeks had decamped in a hurry, for the remaining *tanchi labona* was untouched. The cook henceforth was reckoned as a 'Nakni fehna,' a real brave."

We chuckled again and Kent Powell grinned as he took a

sip of tea.

"You better make a big pot for the Fritz." He set his tea aside. "Do you mind if I write that story down?"

Ben exchanged looks with the rest of us, and we came to a consensus. He nodded at Kent Powell, who picked up his cup and saluted us with it before heading off to the next group of soldiers.

Two Choctaws from the 141st and 143rd found us and joined the circle: Corporal Victor Brown and Private First Class Joseph Oklahombi. Corporal Victor Brown was 27, and had graduated Armstrong Academy not long after I started attending. He went on to graduate from Haskell University, and took classes at Tyler Commercial College and Southeastern State College, too. His school record brought to mind my cousin's urging about my future. I hadn't replied to her letter yet.

As they sat and talked with us, Victor shared his pride of being in France. He was one-fourth French and three-quarters Choctaw. The Choctaws and French had a long history going back to the fur trading days, and they even fought together against the British before the American Revolution. Now we were fighting alongside the French again, only this time, we were in their homeland. And the British were on our side.

Joseph Oklahombi had made it out of St. Etienne alive. He told us he lived in the Kiamichi Mountains in Oklahoma with his wife and young son.

Isaac joined the circle, though he didn't look my way. That was better than him staring at me with contempt. I had to talk with him before the next battle, had to try to make things right. But I couldn't do it in front of everyone. Could I?

As stories went on, I sensed competition rising when the topic turned to family histories and we tried to best each other.

"My pa was a Lighthorseman. He rode with Marshal Bass Reeves once. Bass said he was the best shooter he'd ever seen."

"My grandpa was wounded at the Battle of Poison

Springs in the War of Northern Aggression. Saved a whole company of his men."

"Well, *my* granddaddy helped lead a lost band of 100 starving Choctaws out of a swamp on the old trail from Mississippi."

"My great-grandparents met and fell in love on the trail."

"My grandpa was born on the trail in a blizzard."

Things quieted, each of us casting back in our memories for a tall tale. I was named after my great-grandfather who crossed on the trail, but I couldn't think of anything tall about him.

Mitchell came up with the ringer of the night.

"A deer followed my grandpa all the way from Mississippi to Indian Territory."

No one could respond to that. Jim started chuckling. We all joined in, and that was the end of our entertainment.

Coming into our circle was Major Morrissey, with Lieutenant Horner accompanying him. We quieted and stood.

If it were just Horner, I wouldn't have had jitters in my spine. But we didn't know the major well. He showed courage on the battlefield at St. Etienne, was being decorated for it, but what did he think about Indians?

I recalled Morrissey asking about our language. Was he there to put a stop to our "heathen" tongue?

But the major looked more curious than upset. "Was that your Indian language you were speaking?"

Lieutenant Horner interjected, "The Choctaw language."

Morrissey nodded and looked straight at me. I'd delivered many messages to and from him. "Yes. Choctaw. Is that what you were speaking?"

It was an echo of the same question I'd heard so long ago, the one I'd answered with an unforgivable lie. I looked across the way and met Isaac's bold, steady gaze. The anger in his eyes was gone, but he was still challenging me. It was time to make things right.

I nodded at Major Morrissey. "Yes, sir. *Chahta anumpa.* We were speaking in the language of our ancestors."

Isaac stood and spoke to the major. "We..." He motioned around the circle. "...Chahta."

And there we were, Isaac and I standing together, being Choctaw. Things were finally right between us. Almost.

Major Morrissey exchanged looks with the lieutenant. "I believe this is the answer."

Lieutenant Horner addressed us. "Corporal Louis, gather eight who speak your language fluently."

Solomon didn't hesitate. He picked out Mitchell Bobb, Ben Carterby, James Edwards, Calvin Wilson, Joseph Davenport, and Noel Johnson. Then he motioned to me. My tongue felt frozen again. What would happen now? As the officers turned, I glanced up at the night sky coming on, but there were no stars out.

As we followed our commanding officers, I whispered to Solomon, "What do you think they want with us?"

He looked at me, his expression puzzled for the first time since I could remember. "You don't know?"

I shook my head.

"You'll understand soon enough."

I went cold all over.

We loaded in a truck and traveled to Colonel Alfred Bloor's headquarters at Vaux-Champagne. His P.C. was like most of the Americans'—former German headquarters. Instead of an underground concrete bunker, though, his P.C. was located in an old warehouse. Still, it had been outfitted with all the comforts of home, even more so than most of the folks I grew up with—electric lights, baths, and pianos. It even had a billiard table.

Lieutenant Horner had us gather around the billiard table where he spread a huge map over the taut green cloth. Sergeant Chill was there, looking pretty sour even for him. I felt like I'd been called by Mr. Watson into Principal Fair's office to await punishment for breaking a rule—namely, speaking Choctaw.

The officers conversed in a tight circle near the stone fireplace, the flames in it casting warmth into the room. Morrissey was doing most of the talking. Then they came to the table and Colonel Bloor spoke calmly, though the steadiness and cool head he'd proved at St. Etienne didn't relieve the tension.

"A rumor is out that the division gave false coordinates for our supply dump, and in thirty minutes, the enemy's shells fell on that point."

He motioned to the map. "The Germans deliberately laid telephone lines close to where they knew we'd be, hoping for us to use them so they could easily intercept our messages. We are indeed going to use those lines to coordinate a delicate withdrawal of two companies in the 2nd Battalion from Chufilly to Chardonnay."

Bloor nodded for Major Morrissey to take over.

"The enemy shelled Chufilly with mustard gas and we have to evacuate our men," Morrissey said. "We need to co-ordinate getting them out without the Germans detecting their movements."

He met our gazes. "I recently learned there are some 26 dialects or languages spoken by the Indians in Company E, few of which have ever been written. There is hardly one chance in a million that the Fritz will be able to understand these dialects. We want to use the Choctaw language to send coded messages over the telephones."

The present time froze as an image overcame me— young Isaac Hotinlubbi, bent over, getting the Choctaw language whipped out of him.

Solomon was quick to answer, like he'd been expecting this. "Yes, sir. We can do it."

Major Morrissey nodded at Solomon. "We are attempting this tonight. Only Company E can get our boys out of Chufilly."

Stars must have exploded.

◆ ◆ ◆

Lieutenant Horner arranged sets of Choctaws to transmit

messages over the phones. Some of us would go to the front line, some to the hospital message center, and one to the gassed area where our 2nd Battalion companies were trapped.

"Corporal Dunn, I'm sending you to Chufilly," Lieutenant Horner said. "Keep your head down and your gas mask close."

I gulped, thinking about the last time I'd been gassed, but steadied myself as I moved out with Lieutenant Temple Black, 142nd liaison officer, and two line operators. They quietly relayed to me their challenges of the past few days and what I was headed into.

Colonel Bloor, Major Morrissey, and Lieutenant Horner had been calm, so calm I hadn't realized how badly they needed this to work. We had to get our comrades in the 2nd Battalion out. If the Germans learned of our movements, we could all be killed. It would also mean we couldn't take the salient at Forest Ferme. We couldn't move forward. The Meuse-Argonne offensive—the war itself—would cost far more lives.

Under cover of darkness, I traversed the woods with Lieutenant Black and the line operators who knew every tree and trap from their time of risking their necks to keep the telephone lines operational. All of which did no good if we didn't have a code Jerry couldn't break.

We crept along quietly, single file, until we reached Chufilly an hour later. We wore our gas masks until we climbed into a blown-apart building. The medical officer had cleared it as a safe area, so we removed our masks but tension in the air felt as heavy as gas.

The former post held an American field telephone connected to the German wires I would use. Jerry had graciously left the lines intact for us, all the while snatching our messages and killing our troops with them. But like the old Choctaw cook in our traditional story, I was about to outsmart the enemy. At least that was what I hoped.

I knelt next to the field phone box which sat on a wood crate near a captain who was helping coordinate the with-

SARAH ELISABETH SAWYER

drawal from Chufilly.

The captain, a stout man with a furrowed brow, addressed me. "I understand you speak English and an Indian dialect?"

"Yes, sir."

"I will relay a message to you, Corporal. You must interpret and relay it accurately over the telephone. Let's see if this works."

Those were the words he used. His tone said, "Let's see if you can do it."

I inhaled deeply. *Chihowa, help me do what You brought me to this place for. Hear my prayer as You did of my ancestors, my family, and all people who call on Your name.*

I lifted the heavy receiver from its hook on the portable field phone box. Something monumental was happening, as critical to our people's history in the twentieth century as anything that had or might be. Our existence as native people was stamped into our language and young Choctaws had to carry that forward wherever in the world they went. I had to carry it forward.

I recalled memories of sitting in church, of being within those four walls, and feeling safe to sing our Choctaw hymns.

But those songs didn't depend on four walls. They were within me. Christ was within me. Anywhere in the world was safe for me to speak my language as long as I never lost sight of that truth.

The captain handed me a message marked for the medical corps. I read it, rolling the words over in my mind, trying to translate them into Choctaw.

Pressing the cold receiver to my ear, I connected to the message center of the medical corps. The line cracked and popped and I thought about the enemy hearing the same sounds. They would also hear what came next.

Noel Johnson answered on the other end. "Halito?"

I began transmitting the captain's message to Noel in Choctaw, but halted when I came on the word "gas." We didn't have that in our language.

The captain stared at me, at my hesitation, at my literal loss for words. Lieutenant Black stopped making notes.

The line popped then Noel said, "*Peh makachi.*" *Just say it.*

How could I explain the word in Choctaw?

Gas filled the air outside the blown-out building, threatening hundreds of lives. It was deadly air.

Air. Bad wind, bad air. *Mahli okpulo.*

I spoke the Choctaw term to Noel and continued the message, hoping he would understand.

The captain kept staring at me. I finished and set the message aside. The stillness in the blown-out building was palpable. No one but me knew what I had just said.

In that moment, I realized the American officers trusted us. They put their lives, the whole war effort for this sector, in the hands—or rather the tongues—of Indians.

What a monumental responsibility rested on our language.

In a dugout, I knew Mitchell relayed messages to Ben who would translate it for Major Morrissey. From the front line, Jim relayed messages to Solomon who was stationed in another field company headquarters.

The telephone clicked. It was Noel with a message from Captain Byron Bruce of the medical corps.

Hattak abeka aiasha ya abeka shali apitta cha Marqueny isht ia tuk. Alikchi micha tanchi tikba hikia im anoli, okla kochichit tivbli.

I wrote it down, then thought a few moments, analyzing the words Noel had chosen in place of their potential English counterparts. I carefully wrote out the message in English and handed it to the captain.

Hospital Corps men removed to Marqueny taking ambulance. Notify Surgeon, Advance Battalion, to evacuate by litter to that point.

Lieutenant Black looked over the captain's shoulder and nodded, the tense lines on his face relaxing at last. The captain gave me another message. Back and forth. Over and over.

A shift took place in my soul. Speaking the rhythm of my language soothed my spirit. Speaking it in front of white men healed my heart.

My Choctaw and white cultures were converging, and the world needed me to be both, to be exactly who I was created to be.

I knew then what I was to do with the rest of my life, however long that would be.

CHAPTER THIRTY-EIGHT

"These code and language specialists from the land of Kultur boasted that no code or language known to man could pass through their scrutiny and remain unintelligible." —Captain A. Lincoln Lavine

Aisne River, France
October 1918

It worked. It worked!

As far as we could tell, the Germans hadn't deciphered our code. We didn't lose a man withdrawing the two companies in the 2nd Battalion.

Keep those Choctaws on the telephones. Colonel Bloor's message went out to each of us. All through the night, they kept us busy with communications and as runners to get the 71st Brigade in position for the coming attack.

Solomon organized us to go over ideas for transmitting messages on the telephone. Even though he was among the youngest of the Choctaw soldiers, he was smart, always that five steps ahead of us. He rounded up other Choctaws he knew in the 36th Division: Albert Billy, Benjamin Hampton, George Davenport, Robert Taylor, Benjamin Colbert, Jeff Nelson, Victor Brown, Pete Maytubby, and Joseph Oklahombi. Only a few who couldn't speak English well were chosen, but Isaac wasn't one. Though he'd learned more English since being in the army, he wasn't fluent enough for the work.

They even pulled Choctaws out of the hospitals to do code talking. Tobias was up for it, manning a phone near where he was laid up, and I heard there was a Choctaw-Chickasaw in the 1st Division also pulled out of a hospital. His name was Otis Leader.

Speaking in Choctaw over the telephone seemed simple in concept, but when we did those first messages, we quickly realized we needed words to communicate things we didn't have in our language. *Machine gun* became *tanampushi tushpat tokahli*—little gun shoot fast—and *uski naki*—arrow—was used for ammunition.

Someone suggested we throw in English words like pork and beans to add to the confusion. Even the folks back home wouldn't know what we were talking about if they listened in alongside the Germans!

As we were coordinating in the darkness near our row of pup tents, Kent Powell sidled up next to me. When there was a lull in our discussion, he spoke up.

"The Fritz will be feverish. This could be the first time they've been stumped. I hope you boys realize the significance of this."

We shrugged and smiled. We were mighty proud of using our language to fool the Germans, but this wasn't the time to say so.

We didn't have much time to work on our "code" either. They sent us out faster than we could talk.

Lieutenant Horner had given assignments of where they wanted us. Company E would serve as support for two of our other companies in the Forest Ferme attack. Some Choctaws would stay with the company, some would go to various headquarters and continue transmitting messages during the battle. I was to go with the attacking force to deliver messages as a runner.

We dispersed to attend to last minute preparations and take position at the front before dawn. Kent Powell walked with me to where I'd left my rifle and cartridge belt by my tent.

"Corporal Dunn, you remember how I said it didn't matter that your uncle was an Indian?"

"Yes, sir."

"I lied."

Silently waiting for the war correspondent to continue, I picked up my heavy cartridge belt and cinched it on, realizing my uniform fit just about right now.

Kent Powell settled his arms at his sides, still holding his tablet but looking directly at me.

"It did matter and it does because it shows the world that it's not so important what race a man is—it matters who the man is. I don't believe in Richard Pratt's 'kill the Indian, save the man' policy. An Indian can be as good a man as any and your uncle is proving that. So are you."

I looked away. "There's a lot of history, you know. A lot."

"And I want to learn it. I'm considering Indian soldiers—particularly Choctaws—as a subject for my book about the war. Would you be willing to help?"

"I'm no writer, sir."

"Leave that part to me. I just need input. I've heard different stories of how this coded messaging with your language got started. Some say Major Morrissey overheard Solomon Bond Louis and Mitchell Bobb speaking in Choctaw, latched onto the idea of using it to transmit messages, and asked Louis how many of you spoke the same dialect. Then I heard others had suggested it to him, like Albert Billy in the Headquarter Company or Corporal James Edwards, maybe? I want to make sure we get the story right. This could be a hit in the States."

My first instinct was to doubt that. But then I recalled the words of a scholarly Choctaw, Second Lieutenant Charles McGilberry, who was back in America in officer training. He published articles my uncle liked to send to me. The last snippet said:

Words spoken are fodder for the wind. Words written are eternal to remain in the heart.

I couldn't help but think of what a difference a book like Kent Powell's would make back home. The next round of football players at Armstrong Academy might not get mud clods slung at them after a game.

But those things didn't make me angry. I'd learned I had to forgive each time a mud clod came my way to keep them from sticking.

Kent Powell was still making notes. The way he kept glancing at me said he was describing me, what an Indian soldier looked like. Then he paused and seemed to think. Finally, he started writing again.

"I've seen some of you praying like Christians. I suppose that's what you were taught in boarding school?"

He was nice about it, but he only knew the side that history books often told about Indians, the idea that since we'd been treated like children for more than a century, we couldn't discern spiritual matters for ourselves. In our childlike state, we took in every shiny thing around us, like Christianity, and simply believed whatever we were told.

"Choctaws who go to boarding school are taught to pray. Not all accept it, though."

I thought of Isaac and hurried on. "But we knew what we believed long before Europeans came to our land. We believed in the Creator and thanked Him for the land and knew that we were to take care of everything in it."

"Your people were sun worshippers, weren't they?"

I laughed. "No, sir. When the missionaries first came to us, they tried to ask if we believed in a superior being. Since they couldn't speak our language, we pointed to the sun. The missionaries thought that meant we looked at the sun as our god. But the story my great-grandmother told to me, that was told to her by hers, is that we believed the Creator lived behind the sun. But the story that we were sun worshipers was recorded as our belief. Once my people could understand the missionaries—especially when the ministers learned our language—my ancestors accepted the gospel of Jesus Christ as the Creator's Son."

Kent Powell had gone back to scribbling and there was a feeling, a deep push from my heart.

"Do you, sir?"

"Hmm?"

"Do you believe in the Son of God?"

Kent Powell kept writing as he asked, "You really do, don't you?"

I felt the filth and death and hopelessness around me, but my feelings went back much further, back to Armstrong Academy and beyond to the tragic Removal of our people from our homelands. Then I recalled laying in the shell hole in No Man's Land, the understanding that came to me, and how I now looked ahead to eternity, to the hope beyond the stars.

"Yes, sir. I do."

Kent Powell stared in a different direction. "I'm thinking of titling it 'Trench Talkers.' What do you think?"

"Sir?"

"The title of book I'm going to write about you boys using your language here. You may not realize it now, but you Indians are doing something special. The world needs to know."

"I'm just doing what God gives me to do."

"I won't leave that part out."

Quietly, I thanked him. "*Yakoke.*"

He wrote down the Choctaw word then tucked his pencil away in his coat pocket.

"This isn't the best time, but I need to tell you something. I was going to wait until after your relief, but that just doesn't seem right. You need to know. It's about your uncle."

The Spanish Flu was wreaking havoc all around the

world, especially in the AEF. My uncle had a bad habit of putting himself in harm's way, and the look on Kent Powell's face had me holding my breath.

He didn't meet my gaze. "Heart attack."

I thought I was prepared for bad news, but this wasn't what I'd braced for.

Kent Powell added, "He's in a hospital in Paris. They said…well, you need to get there as soon as you can."

I still didn't breathe. I imagined Mama at home, getting the news. She'd thought it was her son who might not come home. But Uncle Matthew…no. He was one tough, tough Choctaw. This war wasn't going to kill him, not by U-boat, bullet, or his own heart. I was determined to believe that, even as my own heart warned me I couldn't keep grief at bay forever.

Powell reached inside his bag and pulled out a thin stack of letters.

"I almost forgot. I picked up your mail earlier. You were a little busy."

After Kent Powell left, I stood alone awhile, then crawled into my tent and reached inside my haversack. I pulled out the journal Uncle Matthew had given me and wrote my first entry.

Then I read the last letter in the stack.

Dear B.B.,

I heard there have been a lot of casualties in the 36th Division. I pray for you every day. I wish Samson was there with you.
I don't know what else to say.

Your friend,
Ida

CHAPTER THIRTY-NINE

"Although this book was read by a white man, I believe there is some-thing better in it than the way the white man acts. This book sets the heart right. I know. It makes a new man if he be red, white, or black."
—*Kanchi, full-blood Choctaw on the Trail of Tears*

Forest Ferme, France
October 1918

Though Isaac wasn't used on the field telephones, I think he valued the importance of the work. He was ready to fight when the time came.

That fight for us was the river loop to the east of Forest Ferme.

Our commanding officers were planning a surprise attack on the afternoon of October 27th. The attack was up to the doughboys. The surprise was up to the Choctaw doughboys.

We delivered all the communications—transmitting over the telephone lines and with messages written in Choctaw that we carried as field runners.

Everyone knew exactly where they were to be. We knew where the engineers would open holes in the enemy barbed wires, and the mop up crews knew what the infantry routes were so they could follow and transport prisoners back.

In the darkness of the early morning on October 27th, I crept into position with Company E right under the forward of the German position, below the first belt of barbed wire. We lay shoulder to shoulder in a single line, camouflaged in the brush and foxholes as the sun rose then traveled across the blue sky. Quietly, quietly, all day long, the pulse of thousands of soldiers seemed as one. None of my Choctaw brothers were close by, but all the men around me were my brothers.

The man next to me was whisper-talking to the doughboy on his other side as we lay on our backs awhile, squinting against the sunlight. What was left of his hair was shockingly white, something he said ran in his family. The premature color earned him the nickname "Granny." We were on the same side once during trench practice in Camp Bowie and he saved me from being captured. He flashed me a great big homely grin.

"Hey Chief, who you got waiting on you back home?" His voice was hoarse and scratchy, made worse by whispering.

I didn't think we should be talking much. Those Germans were good listeners, but I answered Granny anyway.

"My folks. Brothers and sisters, too."

"My little girl, she'll be nine come spring. Think this could be our last fight?"

He chuckled to himself. We all knew it wouldn't be.

I rolled to my side and munched on the bit of persimmon leather I'd saved. Before we went to the line, I worked on writing a letter to Mama with the news about Uncle Matthew. I had tucked the unfinished letter in my coat pocket under my gas mask case and over my heart. I felt for it now, wishing I didn't have all day of laying still to think about how he might already be gone. I had to get to him as soon as I could get leave.

We didn't know exactly what time we would attack. No one did until it was almost time. We'd learned the importance of secrecy from St. Etienne. I began to wonder if we were going to attack at all. The sun would start sliding down soon. It was already hovering in the west.

Albert crawled past my feet and hissed, "4:30!" before crawling on.

At 4:10 p.m., a lone gun opened fire, breaking the silence. I gripped my Enfield rifle then flexed my fingers to relax them. Our artillery began to lay down a terrific barrage that would last twenty minutes, softening the enemy lines and hopefully holding them in their dugouts until the infantry could take them. The 142nd was to take the right side of the two-mile river loop opening while the 141st took the left.

In conjunction with a rolling barrage, our artillery fire would concentrate on the machine gun emplacements on the heights of the north and east banks of the Aisne River where they guarded the salient in the river loop. I realized why the attack was set for late afternoon. The sun was to our advantage in the west.

Minutes ticked down. The rolling barrage began. Smoke shells exploded in front of the hills above the river, and the smoke drifted up and over enemy positions on the heights, providing a perfect screen between the river loop and its protectors.

Then it was time.

We jumped off from our hiding places behind the rolling barrage and smoke screen. I wanted to whoop just to reinforce the German's terror of Indian soldiers, to let them know we were coming over there. But I refrained. We needed to keep quiet in the charge.

Wire cutters from the 2nd Engineers went in the first wave, rapidly cutting enemy wire and clearing a path for the 142nd. Compared to our first combat experience at St. Etienne, we were organized veterans. We went through the first cut barbed wire entanglement, then the second. Instead of men screaming and dropping dead all around me, we rolled forward as a unit, hardly a man getting hit.

From there, we pressed up the hill toward the trenches, following our barrage so close we almost leaned into it. There was random artillery fire from the enemy but that didn't faze the 142nd nearly as much as what happened next.

A shell from behind us landed just to my left, sending two men airborne. Several men yelled and halted, some going to a knee, looking around, confused. More American shells landed around us!

But we didn't stop the advance. We regrouped and moved forward to the first dugouts.

A group of us surrounded a dugout as the occupants rushed out. We didn't have to shoot these soldiers. As soon as they saw us, they threw their hands up, shouting, "Comrade, comrade!"

They hadn't known we were so close. Germans on the heights above the river didn't know it was happening, either.

When the prisoners were secure, Major Morrissey flagged me and gave me a message to transmit on a field telephone located back where we'd jumped off. He wanted the American artillery to know exactly where we were, and he wanted me to obtain information on how the 141st was progressing.

I ran fast back to the line and slid down into the trench where Albert was talking rapidly in Choctaw over the telephone. He finished and handed the receiver to me, his face flush with excitement.

"There are a bunch of Fritz by a train near the canal. If we can get Company D of the 141st up there, we can take the whole lot!"

I transmitted my message then joined Albert as he headed out to carry messages sent from HQ to the 141st inside the river loop. When we reached Company D, Lieutenant Ford sent us with Joseph Oklahombi and Ben Carterby to scout the train rumored to have Germans waiting as replacements. Ford had sent us with Joseph and Ben so we could carry back the information.

Turned out, the train, which was sitting on a track near

the canal, was just a few box cars on a siding. The area looked abandoned.

Albert and me stuck close together to flank one end of the cars while Ben and Joseph got in position at the other end.

We charged at the same time, only to halt in surprise. Albert started chuckling. German soldiers were leaned against the cars' wheels, asleep despite the barrage of artillery in the distance.

Albert kicked one of the soldier's legs while I kept them covered with my rifle. Ben and Joseph worked their way up the line from the other end, rousing each of the thirty soldiers we'd captured.

One by one, they startled awake, hands going in the air, most drawing back in terror. They recognized us as the dreaded American Indian soldiers they'd been warned about.

Ben called to Albert, "You want to scalp them or should I?"

"Ah, I scalped the last bunch. You go ahead."

Ben drew his long trench knife and one of the prisoners screeched. Ben laughed and put his knife away.

I shook my head. "I'll let Lieutenant Ford know we got them. You boys be civilized."

Everything seemed to be going as planned in the river loop. After reporting to Lieutenant Ford, I ran messages to the 142nd relaying that the 141st were achieving their objectives. Then I delivered messages from the 141st to Major Morrissey, who sent me back to Company E.

Approaching the area where my company would be coming up from the woods, I spotted one of our sergeants. Davis, a stout Indian, stood outside a German dugout, two enemy soldiers laying on the ground, bleeding. A third one came out, waving his hands.

"Comrade, comrade!"

Sergeant Davis bayoneted him.

I lurched forward. "Hey!"

Another Jerry popped out of the dugout, hands in the air. The sergeant drew his rifle back, preparing to plunge it into the soldier.

Lieutenant Horner, emerging from the woods, saw it and shouted at the sergeant to stop. Davis didn't. The soldier crumpled to the ground.

Reaching them before I could, Horner put himself between the sergeant and whatever Germans remained huddled in the dugout.

"Sergeant." Lieutenant Horner sounded dangerously calm.

Granny, who I had waited with all day, came up behind Horner and ordered the rest of the Germans out. Two other Company E men took charge of the prisoners, glancing cautiously at the sergeant and lieutenant.

Davis, slinging blood from his bayonet as he motioned with it, shouted at Lieutenant Horner, "I enlisted to kill Germans and now that I can, you will not let me do it!"

"You cannot kill them when they are surrendering."

Davis wasn't convinced, but he took his place at the back of the company like Horner ordered. He was still mad.

I joined up with Granny, who gave me a thumbs up to go with his homely grin as we split off to charge through the woods toward another dugout. We kept pace alongside one another until the explosive force of an enemy shell tossed us apart.

I stumbled into a hole, rolled, and crawled back to Granny. I grabbed the front of his wool coat and shook him. His eyes were closed, sunk into his pudgy face.

"No!" I roared.

The mop up crew was close behind. They edged me aside and I got moving, but in my heart, I knew Granny wouldn't be alive to see his little girl's birthday.

Something inside me snapped. For the first time in my life, I wanted to kill.

I snuck up behind a machine gun nest and the lone gunner turned and threw his hands in the air.

"Comrade, comrade!"

He was German—with a bushy but trim black mustache

contrasting his gray uniform—surrendering to me.

I visualized Sergeant Davis bayoneting the other soldier. This soldier's life was mine. Mine for all the buddies who had died because of this war, starting with Samson.

I could just kill him, like I could have beat that Newkirk football player after I tackled him by the creek bed. Samson and I let him get away, but maybe we shouldn't have.

No. We did the right thing and it caused a change in that boy. I lowered my rifle. My identity tags belonged to God.

Turning my prisoner over to the mop up crew, I kept moving, and found the same thing at the next nest. The Germans were surrendering all over the place. Many of them were still in their shelters, not realizing the American infantry had taken over their position. The American machine gun battalion had kept them pinned in their dugouts until we got there.

Rat-a-tat-tat.

Our boys just waited outside the dugouts for them to surrender. We could hardly keep up with taking prisoners.

That was better than killing.

◆◆◆

In just a few hours, the battle was over. Green star shells were fired in the air to signal we had accomplished our mission, which we answered with a loud holler. The operation went "by the book," as one captain said. Everything went nearly exactly as the field orders we'd transmitted in Choctaw. The Oklahoma and Texas boys had cleared out the river loop.

Patrols were sent through the rest of the loop. One Jerry messenger was taken down by shotgun-wielding Sergeant Chill before he could get away with the news. The messenger admitted it was the first time he'd been wounded in all the war.

The German artillery on the high hills to the north and east behind the river had no idea we'd taken the area. Still, with the coming night, we dug in and prepared for a counter-attack.

The day's battle at Forest Ferme had resulted in complete destruction of a Prussian Guard battalion, reputed to be one of the best in the German Army. These soldiers looked well-groomed and fed compared to the ones we captured at St. Etienne. Judging by the stockpile of stores, they had thought they would be there a good long while.

Sergeant Chill wasn't impressed with them. One lagged, taking his time as the clean-up crew prepared to march the prisoners back. Chill gave the soldier a swift kick in the pants that would have earned him a spot on the Armstrong football team.

Late that night, fires on the hills around Voncq and Semuy told us the Germans knew we were close. They were likely preparing for a fighting retreat.

The next day, October 28th, we hunkered down, waiting for a counter-attack, shelling, something.

Something did happen.

Later afternoon, German airplanes hummed overhead, dropping pieces of white paper. One piece landed beside me.

Propaganda leaflets. Printed in French and English, they said there was a new German government being set up, and they had accepted President Wilson's fourteen points for peace, and why should the useless fighting continue?

Most of the doughboys had a good laugh out of it. I wished it was true. I knew it wasn't when the Fritz batteries sprayed our position with machine gun fire and shells that exploded all night. There were few casualties, but enough. Ben Carterby was wounded, and the valiant, well-loved Lieutenant Ford of Company D was killed.

CHAPTER FORTY

Forest Ferme, France
October 1918

Once we were relieved by the French and pulled out of the river loop, I hunted for Kent Powell in the darkness as the 36th Division prepared for transportation. We were being relieved and sent for rest.

But the reporter wasn't among the troops, gathering stories of the swift victory. I asked around for him, eventually ending near the dressing station.

Someone there I hadn't expected was Lee Hoade. He had taken a piece of shrapnel in the thigh, though it didn't seem to have any more effect on him than a blister on a wooden leg. He was sitting on a long box outside the medical tent, smoking while a nurse scolded him for not being in bed. Lee Hoade was smoking and I knew nothing would move him—he wouldn't put it out nor would he smoke inside. But it was the cadence of the nurse's voice that caught my attention.

"Victoria?"

She turned, her Red Cross cap perfectly pinned, every

hair in place, not like she'd been through a war. Except her eyes. Her eyes held an earnest but detached look. When they landed on me though, and she recognized me in my uniform and dirty face four years older, she lit up with astonishment.

She rushed into me with her exuberant hug, knocking my unstrapped steel helmet off. She'd done what no Jerry had been able to do.

After she squeezed the air from my lungs and nearly fractured my ribs, she stepped back and gripped my shoulders, shaking me till my teeth rattled. She was a strong Choctaw woman, even though she denied her blood.

"I so wish you weren't here, you foolish boy!"

"Then why are you acting happy to see me?"

"Silly boy."

She hugged me tight and cried against my muddy coat. We were still the same height, something that had bothered me when I was younger. It didn't mean anything now.

Hooking my chin on her shoulder, I met eyes with Lee Hoade, who looked disgusted.

I shook away from Victoria and asked her, "Have you gotten the news?"

"Bertram, I have been moved around so much with the advancement of the troops..."

She halted. Nothing mattered but our silent communication. We understood things like siblings.

"My father?"

"It's his heart. He's in Paris at the hospital. You need to get to him."

"How bad?"

"I don't know. Just need to pray. And hurry."

Victoria's expression cooled, and I knew it was what I'd said about praying. But she grasped my shoulder and gave it a warm squeeze.

"Bertram, as soon as you receive a leave, come to Paris. You'll find me there."

She turned to look back at Lee Hoade. "That is, *after* I treat the difficult patients here. Really, soldier, you must get

284

inside out of the damp."

Lee Hoade didn't budge. Victoria gave me a quick peck on my dirty cheek and left. In and out of my life so fast, but that was the way of living through a war. She'd expect an answer to the question in her letter when I saw her next.

After she left, I picked up my helmet and settled by Lee Hoade on the long box, waving away the cigarette smoke that drifted toward me.

I'd already visited Ben Carterby, who was recovering from a shoulder wound he received when Lieutenant Ford was killed in the river loop, and also heard Corporal Victor Brown had a broken nose and head injuries. Everyone else I knew came through all right.

I had no one else to see, and this was the first time I was okay with just sitting and being quiet with Lee Hoade. When you go through a couple of battles with someone, you get a different feeling being around them. I wondered if that could happen for me and Isaac.

I was thinking back to when Lee Hoade threatened to kill Samson and me when Lee finally spoke. But it wasn't in English.

"*Wakarée.*"

I stared at him. He kept smoking and looking out at the coming and going of the medics with wounded.

"Pardon?"

"*Wakarée.* You're like a turtle. Slow, but you get where you're going. You turned into a real warrior."

"I...what...?" I couldn't form my thoughts or words to respond to the Comanche word I'd picked up from being in Company E.

"What? You the same as others, ain't you? Judging a fellow by the skin he's wrapped in? You wouldn't imagine a white-looking man like me was half-Comanche."

I dropped my gaze in disbelief and shame. I thought back to when I met Lee Hoade, and wondered if I'd treated him different, thinking he was a white man in an Indian company. But Lee Hoade hadn't wanted to shame me. I felt that. He just had something important to say.

He lit another cigarette. "You need to know this, *wakarée*. It don't matter if no one a hundred years from now knows what you did using your Indian language to help win a war. You'll know and it'll change you. That's what you need to know."

I raised my head, holding my breath. Lee Hoade still wouldn't look at me. He motioned to his injured leg. "I wasn't a dozen yards away. Heard the whistle, knew where the shell would land. Tried to get to him in time." He stared at his bandage. "They said we did real good, kept our wits. 'Friendly fire' they've coined it. Nothing friendly about your own shell falling short and a man you know being blown to bits by it."

"Who?"

"The reporter feller. Kent Powell."

I stood and walked away.

◆ ◆ ◆

"Halito, B.B.!"

Albert snagged my arm when I walked by him on my way to pack up my tent. It was the middle of the night, but no one slept. There was too much to do with organizing the German prisoners and getting ready to transport the field hospitals to the rear as we vacated the area.

I looked numbly at Albert who didn't seem to notice my grief. We'd all been through it the past three weeks, but nothing felt quite like this. Uncle Matthew's condition was settling heavy on me, and Kent Powell was gone. Writers weren't supposed to die in war.

"Most everyone came through all right," Albert continued as we walked. "Only a few casualties in the whole 142nd. Could have been a lot worse. It worked, B.B. The Fritz weren't able to decode our language. *Tvshka anumpa*. We are language warriors."

My mind went to the memory of Kent Powell and his enthusiasm to write our story. But the loss of having someone write our story wasn't what I was grieving. I'd liked Kent Powell. He had been a good white man.

No. He was as good a man as any.

Albert elbowed me as we walked. "Hey, did you know Lee Hoade is Comanche? They had him and another one on the telephone a few hours ago, transmitting messages in their language. Isn't that something?"

It certainly was.

"They're putting Indians out everywhere—Cherokee, Comanche, Cheyenne, Osage, Sioux—helping win battles up and down the line. There's a 'use them if you have them' policy spreading through the AEF."

"Hey, Chief!" Sergeant Chill barked at me. We halted. "Bring me the U.S. bag."

He was supervising the guards herding German prisoners into a pen surrounded by barbed wire. Albert and I veered over to him, and I offered him the bag, but he was distracted by one of the linemen.

The lineman, who could speak German, was being put to use communicating with the prisoners. He said to the sergeant, "Sir, this officer has a question."

Sergeant Chill drew a bead on the German officer with his squinted eye. "Does he, now?"

"He wants to know what nationality we had on the telephones. He couldn't break the code."

Sergeant Chill glanced at me and Albert and said, "You tell him, 'Americans, boy. Just Americans.'"

It took a moment, but I actually returned Sergeant Chill's grin.

◆◆◆

At our pup tents, we prepared to load onto trucks that would take us as far as Somme-Py so we wouldn't have to march that far. We'd go by foot after that to our relief area.

Near the line of heavy transport trucks, I spotted Major Morrissey and Lieutenant Horner talking with Colonel Bloor and moved closer where I overheard that Horner had just received his battlefield commission to captain of Company E. I was proud of him. As for Major William Morrissey, he was now a lieutenant colonel.

He'd come to admire the Indians under his command and I had a feeling he'd have good things to say about us when he got back home to Pennsylvania.

They talked about the fact that we'd taken the Germans in the river loop completely by surprise. Thanks to the Choctaw language, the enemy hadn't had any idea we were about to attack, which resulted in far fewer casualties on both sides. That was good with me.

Colonel Bloor noticed me standing behind Captain Elijah Horner's shoulder. Horner shifted to follow his gaze and Colonel Bloor made direct eye contact with me for the first time since my promotion to corporal.

His demeanor had remained steady throughout the intense pressure and chaos of the battles we faced. He had done everything he could for his men, and was the only colonel in the 36th Division who remained in command of his organization throughout the war. We were proud to have him as our commander. But it wasn't easy to stand under his attention now, not until he gave me a long, respectful nod. I slowly returned it with the realization that a successful military career was well within my reach if I wanted it.

CHAPTER FORTY-ONE

"I cannot forget the brilliant services which the valorous Indian soldiers of the American armies have rendered to the common cause and the energy, as well as the courage which they have shown to bring about victory— decisive victory—by attack." —Ferdinand Foch, Marshall of France

Louppy-le-Petit Training Area, France
November 1918

After our push to take Forest Ferme and the river loop in the final days of October, they pulled the 36th Division back for a rest at Louppy-le-Petit training area. I didn't get much rest. They detailed Choctaws in Company E and the other companies for special training in transmitting messages over the telephone.

Our commanding officers had recognized the value of using Indian languages and dialects to confound the enemy. Befuddled, some German officers suspected the Allies had invented a new technology that made the speaker sound as if he were underwater. We got a chuckle out of that.

Still, there was the issue of not having words in our native tongue for modern warfare. During the first part of November, we worked on our code with liaison officer Lieutenant Black and Lieutenant Ben Cloud, a Northern Cheyenne, and an Osage, Private George BaconRind, to determine words to use in place of modern terms. I noted some of the words in my journal to memorize before burning the page.

Okla: Tribe (Regiment)
Tanch nihi tuklo: Two grains of corn (2nd Battalion)
Tanampo chino: Big gun (Artillery)
Ittibbi: Fight (Attack)
Tikba pisa lawa: Many scouts (Patrol)
Tikba pisa: Scalps (Casualty)

Our trainers called us the Choctaw Telephone Squad. We were like the legendary *biskinik*, a messenger bird God blessed after the Great Flood to be a special friend to His people, the Choctaws. The little messenger bird would warn warriors of the approach of an enemy. If there was a coming night attack, *Biskinik* would tap out messages on trees all around the camp to alert the warriors.

After we had a solid list of terms, Lieutenant Colonel Morrissey came by to get a copy of it for his report. He also made Colonel Bloor a copy. Bloor said he would put in for commendations from the U.S. government for our special work.

On break between drills, a group of us Choctaws gathered in a loose circle, some sitting cross-legged, others laying flat out. Conversation drifted to talk of the future. The war couldn't last forever, and our thoughts were of home.

"Well, we're back at the barn and still on our horses," Jim said, leaning back on his elbows in the drying mud on the unusually sunshiny day. He had a piece of straw dangling from his lips. "What you all doing when you get home?"

"Got my wife and kids waiting on me. The farm'll need a lot of work."

"I'm going to college."

Noel coughed the whole time. He hadn't looked good since that last fight at Forest Ferme.

Solomon was pretty quiet until Mitchell nudged him. "What about you, now that you're an old married man and all?"

We chuckled, but as usual, Solomon was five thoughts ahead of us.

"I'm going to settle on my allotment in Bennington, get into farming, but mostly, help our people when I can, and preach the gospel."

He had everyone's attention. Jim nodded. "I want to become a pastor for our people."

A surge of joyful expectation went through me at that and I smiled, but didn't say anything. Not yet.

Albert didn't have his blasted bugle with him, but he had another noise maker he'd bought from a doughboy in camp—a harmonica. When things got too quiet, he pulled it out of his pocket.

Jim flicked away his piece of straw. "Hey Albert, play that one tune you're good at."

We chuckled and Ben jabbed his elbow at Albert. But Albert just grinned and played his harmonica. Even his bugle would have sounded good that day as we lay spread out on French soil in the autumn sunshine, free from whizzbangs and scout planes and snipers and machine guns.

Rat-a-tat-tat.

We talked about getting up a stickball game if only we had *kapucha*, our sticks. Playing the game wasn't outlawed in France like back in Oklahoma. Ben joked that we should challenge Jerry to a match. Stickball was known as 'the little brother of war,' and it was how our ancestors sought to settle disputes back in our Mississippi homelands.

If only the world could settle their conflicts with a game.

◆◆◆

Somewhere in France

Dear Ida,

Thank you for the prayers. I came through okay. Samson would have, too, if he had been here. Things are quiet for me right now.

I wrote my mother about my uncle Matthew. I hope to see him when I can get leave.

There are rumors of an Armistice being signed soon, but no one believes it. Still, I hope I get to come home soon and see you.

Your friend,
B.B.

◆ ◆ ◆

Over the next several days, Lieutenants Black and Cloud, along with Private BaconRind, didn't ease up with us working on the code. The American General Headquarters was making plans to train large numbers of Indians as telephone operators and disperse them throughout the AEF on the Western Front. They wanted us ready for when the war restarted in earnest come spring.

But the first rumblings of an armistice being agreed on had spread through the 36th. The rumors were disregarded at first. Then the rumblings grew louder and before long, I stood among thousands of other doughboys on the morning of November 11, 1918 at Louppy-le-Petit, holding a collective breath in the cold. Surely it couldn't really be coming to an end? No more buddies being blown up or shot down? They wouldn't need us for any more code talking.

It felt like what we'd done helped this day arrive sooner.

At 11 a.m., a bell rang out from a church not far away. The clanging, a sign of the official announcement, brought a collective sigh throughout the training camp. I swore I could hear boys all the way from the front line whooping and hollering louder than any shell explosion. Next to me, Albert blasted away on his bugle. Jim gave a whoop and threw his overseas cap in the air. Tobias danced on one foot, his other leg still sore from the sniper bullet.

Surrounded by the hubbub, I sank to my knees and rubbed my palms up and down my thighs.

We were going home. Home, where I could visit Samson's grave. Home, where I could remember the buddies I'd lost and write about each one of them in my journal. Home, where I could finally release pent up grief.

Somehow, I'd thought holding it all in was a part of having courage. With the war officially over, I found I wasn't afraid to cry.

Amid the wild celebrations, someone knelt beside me and spoke in Choctaw.

"I do not hate you."

My eyes burned. I gripped Isaac's shoulder and said something ten years overdue. *"Sv nukhaklo."* *I am sorry.*

"You could not...stop it." He struggled with his own tears, ten years overdue. "The whipping. Darkness."

"But I should have suffered with you instead of lying. That would have been the right thing."

"You showed courage here. You are an *anumpa* warrior."

CHAPTER FORTY-TWO

"Shades of Prince Bismarck! Everything else had the Kaiser taken into consideration when he sprinted into the late unpleasantness, but he had failed to teach his soldiers or officers Choctaw." —The Stars and Stripes, Official Newspaper of the American Expeditionary Forces

Paris, France
December 1918

My head bumped hard against the wood plank of the 8-40 box car. I raised my head until the car stopped swaying on the curve, then leaned back again.

When they said a train would take us to Paris for leave, I thought they meant we'd get to ride in a passenger car. But even riding in the box car built for 8 horses or 40 men with 49 other doughboys packed in still beat marching.

I'd received leave not long after the armistice and hopped right on a train to Paris. Solomon had been ahead of me in getting leave, but he offered his spot to me. My buddies knew I had something urgent to do.

After the armistice, I learned more details from a nurse in the 142nd about what had happened with my uncle. At St. Etienne, Private Joseph Oklahombi had come by to talk and found him unconscious inside his tent. The field doctor, worried he wouldn't pull through, sent him to Paris for treatment. I found Joseph and thanked him for helping my uncle.

My head bumped the box car wall again, but I kept my eyes closed, thinking back on the past few weeks following the armistice. I had been called to translate for Isaac during the court martial of the soldier accused of murdering the French farmer. Captain Horner told me that I saved my friend that morning after the stabbing when I got to the truth of where Isaac had been. Instead of being tried, Isaac was a key witness and the soldier was found guilty.

Everyone was ashamed of what had happened. We'd come to help the French, and I hated to think of American soldiers doing them harm.

After the hearing, Isaac and I ate a meal together, just the two of us. We talked in our native tongue about the war, home, and what it meant to be Choctaw.

I'd shared about my great-grandmother crossing the trail of tears, singing hymns and praying. She hadn't known if she would live or die, just as I hadn't known if I would return to my people after the war. What courage I had came from my ancestors and the legacy they left me, the legacy of trusting in God.

We finished eating, then sang a hymn.

Klaist a auet is sɵm ihissashke;
Keyukmɷno, sɵlla he banoshke.

Give me Christ, or else I die.

When I had spoken the Choctaw language in front of white men, it had sewn the rips in my heart. When Isaac watched me using our language proudly, it had sewn the rip between us. Our war was finally over. We were brothers again.

What a good, good day it was.

Someone hollered from the front of the box car, "Next stop, Paris!"

All the doughboys cheered. Smiling, I reached into my coat pocket, withdrew my Choctaw Bible and flipped through it, thinking of my uncle Matthew and his unwavering dedication to truth. I would honor God and my ancestors as he had commissioned me to back by the lake on Uncle Preston's ranch. He had shown me what it meant to be Choctaw no matter where I was. And I would speak our language wherever in the world I went.

In France, I had learned that every star, every miracle has a genealogy.

My family was mine.

◆ ◆ ◆

This being my first visit to Paris, I found it was still grand, mostly untouched by the devastation of war. But the World War had demolished entire cities and villages in France. One out of three young men like me were dead. I doubted there was one family in Paris untouched by intimate loss. I moved respectfully through the celebrating, grieving people as I made my way through the city.

Not long before the 36th Division arrived, the doughboys were helping Parisians celebrate Bastille Day on July 14th when an emergency recall came for them to hurry back to the front. The German forces had made a final push to end the war in their favor that summer. Paris was in danger, but the enemy was stopped by the Allies at places like the Second Battle of the Marne, Château Thierry, and Soissons. My uncle had been right in the middle of it all.

I found myself on the street rechristened Avenue du President Wilson in honor of the American president. On July 4th, 1918, a year after the 1st Division had arrived, a fresh set of American doughboys paraded down the street. They marched right under the shadow of George Washington's sword like he was inspecting the troops from his stone chiseled horse. I stopped to look at his statue awhile, thinking about American and Choctaw history and how the two couldn't be separated.

I planned to come back to Paris to explore when I had more time so I could tell Mama all about it, but at the moment, I was only there for one reason.

"*Parlez-vous anglais?*" After three tries, I found someone who spoke English and could direct me to the American Red Cross Military Hospital No. 35.

On the second floor, it wasn't hard to spot my uncle among the wounded soldiers, most of whom chatted with one another, flirted with nurses, or played card games on their beds.

My uncle, meanwhile, was propped up in his bed, writing, his face intense as always when he wrote, even when it was about victory. I was sure he had a unique take on the armistice and I couldn't help but smile. That was Matthew Teller, all right.

"*Halito, vmoshi.*" Hello, my uncle.

His head jerked up and he blinked a few seconds while his mind came back from wherever it had been. He hadn't seen me in 3 years, and never in my uniform. His eyes finally lit up with recognition.

"*Sv baiyi!*" My nephew!

Uncle Matthew dropped his tablet and reached out with both hands to take my right hand. He shook it firmly, then pulled me down into a strong hug. I wouldn't have guessed he was recovering from a near-fatal heart attack.

I disengaged from my uncle's strong grip. "You look well."

His sharp eye took me in. What did he see? How I'd filled out my uniform, how straight and respectful I stood? Would he see strength in my eyes, or perhaps homesickness?

I saw both of those things in him. He'd been overseas for

most of four years. I had thought it was because of his intense interest in the war. But I knew from my days growing up in a family fighting for truth in a changing nation, it was much more, going back to centuries of culture and pride brushed aside by government and politics. He needed to get away from a lifetime of prejudices that had plagued him, needed to know a different suffering, and needed so many more things I couldn't understand at my age. I was wise enough to know I had a lot of learning yet to do.

Uncle Matthew indicated a wooden stool nearby. "Sit."

I drew the stool close to his side. He didn't look as bad as I thought he would. "How are you feeling?"

"I'm fine." He acted as if a heart attack was no more than a head cold. "Do you have your journal?"

I winced. As if realizing he had leaped to his reporter instinct too quickly, Uncle Matthew changed the subject.

"Half the soldiers in the hospital have no physical wounds. They're calling it shell shock. The horror of it all…"

His gaze drifted. He'd been through more than I had, except he hadn't killed anyone. Not in this war, leastways. His gaze snapped back to me.

"Are you all right?"

I wanted to ask him the same thing. But I didn't need to. The strength and stubbornness in his eyes couldn't be mistaken. He was one tough, tough Choctaw.

"I'm all right, *umoshi*. Ready for us all to go home. And about the journal…"

I didn't quite know how to tell him that I'd only written one sentence in it.

My soul is safe in Chihowa.

But I didn't have to tell him. He chuckled and I joined in. Nothing more needed to be said.

There was something else, and I tried to say it. "I have a story for you about something really important that happened…"

I couldn't finish. What we'd done, how we'd used our language on the battlefield…a sense of sacredness came over me. It was a story I needed to write myself. Uncle Matthew and all our people would know the story then.

I recalled the feeling I'd had when Kent Powell took an interest in us, wanting to write a book about Choctaws and our language. Like a weapon, we'd used our language. Like our ancestors, we'd fought as warriors. Our language would be on my tongue forever. That was enough.

"B.B.?" Uncle Matthew was studying me again.

I focused on him and smiled to let him know I wasn't shell shocked.

"I'll fill up that journal, and it'll have a good story for you to read."

He nodded. "I'll publish it in the *Choctaw Tribune* as soon as it's ready."

Uncle Matthew's eyes were full of fire and determination. *"There's nothing more powerful than the press, except God Almighty,"* he'd always said. He was a language warrior. Always had been.

We quieted awhile. I sensed it was time to give him what I brought in my heart, to express how he had showed me what it took to live the Choctaw spirit.

I pulled out my Bible. "I read a verse on the train coming here that made me think of you, of all you've done in your life and how much it means for young fellows like me." I read aloud, *"Chihowa hvt achukma hosh, isht i̱ hullo vt abilliakmvt, isht ai a̱hli ai unchululi poiyutta kak kia ma̱ha̱ya hoka̱."* For the LORD is good; his mercy is everlasting; and his truth endureth to all generations.

I kept my eyes on the page. *"Yakoke, ʋmoshi.* Thank you for spending your life preserving truth for me. You're a warrior for our people."

I heard a deep sigh and looked up. Uncle Matthew's eyes were red.

"What is going on here!"

The tone was scolding, but I also heard teasing in it. I stood and let Victoria smother me. She was still pristine in her Red Cross uniform and I let her take over.

She held me at arm's length. "It is about time you came, Bertram. I received a response from my friend in New York."

Uh-oh.

"She passed along your school history, and the potential sponsor showed great interest. When not in school, you would work summers at his department store in New York. It's a marvelous opportunity, and you only need to…"

Her eyes flickered to her father. Her chin was set as stubborn as his. I wished they were on the same side.

She squeezed my arms. "You need to be more like me."

That was the crossroads in my future, to be white or Indian. Though with a full scholarship, I could play football *and* become a lawyer for the tribe like my father. Or I could accept Captain Horner's offer to write a letter of recommendation for military school. But neither of these were the path God had for me. He guided my heart when I transmitted those first messages in Choctaw. He had used the whole mess with the war and Isaac and our language to build my courage to do what no one could have forced me to do before.

"Victoria, there's something I want to tell you. Being Choctaw did some good over here. In the war."

She stared at me. She knew she'd already lost the battle. "Perhaps here. But not in the States. It will always bring pain."

"Not always, especially not in church."

"Bertram, you cannot be considering…"

"Chihowa is doing something special and He has me being part of it. I've learned I don't have to be white with whites and Choctaw with Choctaws. I can be myself, a bridge between cultures, and bring light to them through the love and kindness of Christ."

"Bertram…"

"I'm going to school to be a preacher, and you can come hear me preach someday." I could hardly believe I was saying it out loud. "You will, won't you?"

Her expression softened. I was winning her over. She never could resist her little cousin.

"I have my first sermon thought out on how my cousin taught me to make the stars dance and how I did it on a battlefield on the Western Front. You'll come?"

"Bertram." I knew she would.

A doctor called for her and she left with final hugs—one for me and one for her father. After she left, I heard my uncle take in a deep breath. We would travel home separately, but that was okay. Family was always together in spirit.

And someday I would tell the story of how we used the Choctaw language to fool the Germans. I would write the story and share it with my people.

I talked with my uncle a good while. He advised me to buy my mama a miniature replica of the Eiffel Tower. The wrought iron structure had been built for the Paris Exposition Universelle in 1889. In response to the magnificent achievement, Chicago strived to top it with an enormous contraption—the Ferris Wheel that held 2,000 riders at a time. Mama had ridden the wheel at the Chicago World's Fair in 1893.

My uncle always knew the right ways to make her smile.

When our conversation lulled, Uncle Matthew gave me a poem to read. It was written by one of his buddies who was also in the hospital. I recognized the name and my uncle said he'd introduce me to him later.

I was at Bathelémont
A cool November morn
I met a chap all down and out.
Disconsolate and forlorn
He didn't know a word of ours,
Nor I a word of French.
So, there we sat, both he and I
Each smiling in the trench
I looked at him a moment.
He grinned from ear to ear.
And says "Bonjour," Sammie
And I say, "Souvenir."
He took my only cigarette,
I took his cheap cigar,
And then the fire works started
And lasted for an hour.

Showed him next my kiddies,
And then he showed me his.
The funny little Frenchies
With hair all in a frizz:
Annette and petit Louise, he says
And the tears begin to fall
We were comrades then, we knew.
Though we hardly spoke at all
Soon after we were parted
Each to follow his own star.
And have never seen each other.
But that's the way of war.
Since the World War closed
I've often wondered
If God had spared him long enough
To see Annette and Louise.

Otis Leader
1st Division
American Expeditionary Forces

We were quiet awhile before I said, "We helped end this war, *vmoshi*. We can all go home now."

CHAPTER FORTY-THREE

"All Texas and Oklahoma rejoices over the valiant work of the 36th Division. This is particularly true of the people of Fort Worth who came to know and regard the boys so highly while here. On behalf of all our people permit the Star-Telegram to congratulate you and every one of the brave men of your command and to transmit to them the following from the Governors of the two states."—Fort Worth Star-Telegram

"All Texas is proud of her brave sons and rejoices over their wonderful achievements. On their behalf permit me to congratulate you."
—Governor Hobby

"As Governor of Oklahoma I join in congratulations to the 36th Division. We are proud of them and glory in the account they have given of themselves and appreciate every one of them. To every Oklahoman we send greeting."—Governor Williams

Bar-sur-Aube and Paris, France
Winter 1918-19

The waiting was torture, worse than the war itself many men said. The timetable for demobilization dragged on.

Agonizing months passed while the AEF troops attempted to keep themselves occupied.

In the 36th Division, we finally got our shoulder patch insignia. The blue arrowhead had a large khaki T over it, representing Oklahoma and Texas merged into one division. I sewed mine onto my coat sleeve.

Second Lieutenant Ray H. Duncan of Alba, Texas, was asked by a reporter in our new 36th Division newspaper, the *Arrow Head*, for his opinion about Indian soldiers who had served under him. He said, "They were fearless under fire and volunteered for hazardous duty generally shunned by whites."

They also quoted Lieutenant Colonel William Morrissey who said if he had to fight the war over again, "I would make every effort to fill my regiment with Indians. I was in a position to closely observe the Indians during all the fighting, and found them absolutely fearless and loyal in every respect. Their ability as fighters is beyond a question of doubt.

"As to his initiative in battle, I have this to say, he absolutely set out to lick Germany alone. My company of Indians were in the assault battalion, Meuse-Argonne, Champagne, and received the heartiest commendation of our divisional commander, Colonel Alfred W. Bloor. All officers have the very highest regard for the fighting qualities of the Indians."

I clipped out what Captain Elijah Horner said and saved it in my journal.

The Indian was always the equal of the white man, sometimes his superior.

In censoring their mail I got a glimpse of their inside life. They would write home: "George Good Eagle is no more. Like a good American, he has gone on."

At the battle of St. Etienne, the Marines had been in the forefront of the fight, and they were relieved. None of the 36th Division had ever been on the firing line before. We were now to be ushered into the hardest fighting of the war. Being fresh troops, the Marines remained in support to watch as we entered the engagement.

The Marines never got through talking about how those Indians fought.

The divisional newspaper had other stories to cover, namely football. Like Armstrong Academy and Camp Bowie, we distracted ourselves with sports much of winter with football teams organized throughout the AEF. Our team made me proud to be in the 36th Division. We stomped the competition, especially with what the *Arrow Head* called the "brilliant defense" of Indian right guard and former Haskell Indian Nations University player Charles Choate.

After we won the First American Army Championship in a tie-breaker at Bar-sur-Aube against the undefeated 29th Division, it was on to Paris for the AEF championship game.

Thousands of football-mad soldiers and civilians came out to watch, clogging traffic around Paris. Even Commander-in-Chief General John J. Pershing was there, brought in by motorcade with the king and queen of Belgium. The 142nd Infantry band played the Belgian national anthem for King Albert and Queen Elizabeth in the pre-game parade.

It was a close game. We only lost to the 89th Division because Charles Choate had already shipped home.

After the game, despite the weather, the queen wanted to take pictures of the two championship teams. One wise-guy voiced our sentiments.

"Hurry up, kid, it's cold out here!"

She smiled graciously and snapped a picture.

Another soldier shouted out the real complaint of every doughboy. "When do we get to go home?"

General Pershing turned his head toward us. That silenced everyone.

With sicknesses and cramped quarters, the waiting was miserable. Noel Johnson beat us all in going home. He was sent out in March on the tuberculous ship. I had a bad feeling about his sickness. Made me think of Samson.

I did enjoy seeing more of France. Jim, Solomon, Tobias, Albert, and I took leave together and went on a tour. So many cathedrals to visit, art to see, and food to eat despite the destruction and the country stalled by war. I visited Uncle Matthew again at the hospital and introduced him to my buddies.

Throughout the waiting, several of the Choctaws were awarded service medals, including me. But we didn't talk about them much. The best times during the waiting were just sitting around a fire and singing hymns, swapping battle stories and talking about what we'd done as anumpa warriors.

We wouldn't be talking about it much when we got home. No one wanted to take the war back to their families, and though the French and the AEF *Stars and Stripes* had written stories about our code talking, some of us were told not to talk about it in case the military ever needed to use us in another war.

But I clung to what others said: this was the war to end all wars. Though my uncle was skeptical about that, I just wanted to think about getting home and the world never going to war again.

CHAPTER FORTY-FOUR

"The war game has shown us how to make a stand for truth in the face of death. The American Indian has proven himself a worthy citizen. With a broader mind and a larger heart, we are coming home." —Philip Frazier, 355ᵗʰ Infantry Regiment

France and America
May 1919

In late spring of 1919, my turn finally came. Some of the men in the 142ⁿᵈ I'd never see again, but I would never forget them. Our experiences together were written in blood.

It was a full six months after the armistice when I sailed home on the USS Pueblo. There would be a lot of fanfare and celebration when I landed in New York, traveled across the country, and in Oklahoma. I knew things wouldn't have changed much as far as prejudices. But that was okay. God's grace hadn't changed either.

Lee Hoade had shocked everyone in Company E the month before with the announcement that he'd married a

German refugee girl in France, and that she was meeting him in America. I guessed that meant he wouldn't be blowing his new German brother-in-law sky high when he got home.

Well, if Lee Hoade could overcome prejudices, anyone could.

Several days on a rough sea led to a final tragic casualty in Company E. Corporal Harry S. Hovey and a private from another company were washed overboard. We couldn't rescue them in time.

After it happened, we were put below deck with the hatchways covered for several days until the funeral services.

While banished from the deck, I pulled out letters from home. I had bought a wooden box with an intricate seaside scene carved on the top from a little store in Paris where Tobias had gotten one. He was going to put all his important papers and letters in it to keep safe and, someday, pass on to his children and grandchildren.

My box held photos, letters, a replica of the Eiffel Tower, and my journal. I'd had more time to write during the agonizingly slow demobilization, and tried to record my war experiences as best as I could.

I reread my letters from home where folks had read stories of how well the 36th conducted ourselves as a division. They had also read my uncle Matthew's special story about the all-Indian Company E. He asked me several questions for it, and ended up putting a lot of my words in the story. I had more to say than I thought I did. I just might make a good preacher like Pastor Turner someday.

Rat-a-tat-tat.

My parents wrote of how proud they were of me—a Choctaw warrior, an American soldier, and a fine young man who honored our ancestors in the traditions instilled in me from birth.

I couldn't wait to see my mama and daddy and siblings and Pokni and—well, everyone.

Jim tried to get a peek at my letters one time. I socked him in the arm. From then on, I double secured the box by wrapping it like a package, using the last of Samson's ball of string from the otherwise empty bag of useful stuff. Sergeant Chill said I'd finished my duty with it.

Dear B.B.,

I am excited at the news that you are coming home soon. Mrs. Holmes keeps gossiping about all the doughboys and what they will do when they get home. She wrote Mrs. Veach to ask if there was any word from "Big Chief" about when the boys were shipping home.

I am including a recent photograph from school so you will recognize me when you get home. I would like a photograph of you in your uniform to include in my scrapbook please.

Your friend,
Ida

On May 31st, hearts pounding for home, we gathered on the deck to watch for the unmistakable landmark in New York, a gift from France that held more meaning than ever before. It stood tall as a reminder of the long Franco-American relationship.

On the crowded deck, I squeezed into a spot on the rail next to Isaac. Lee Hoade was on my other side, and he wasn't smoking. Spread down the rail was most of my Choctaw buddies from Company E, and our commanding officer, Captain Horner.

When the landmark came into sight, we all whistled and cheered.

Isaac reached into his breast pocket and withdrew a neatly folded piece of paper which he handed to me. I unfolded it to discover an artfully drawn map of the old Choctaw Nation with all the places important to our people shown by diamond symbols. Near Durant, Isaac had marked Samson's grave.

From our conversations over the past few months, he'd drawn this map straight from my heart. I nodded my thanks, the ocean mist stinging my eyes.

I met Isaac's steady gaze and asked in Choctaw, "Why did you join the army, my brother?"

"To defend my home. I am a warrior."

When it came down to it, that was at the heart of every doughboy on the ship, in the whole AEF, of every race and nationality. Our hearts beat the same.

Lee Hoade whacked me with his elbow when he took out his tobacco bag filled with cigarettes and threw them overboard, something he'd promised his bride.

He lightly saluted the Statue of Liberty as she watched our approach. "Honey, if you ever want to see my face again, you'll have to turn around."

I thought of what I'd written in my journal that morning.

It was a long way from Durant and the Choctaw Nation to Forest Ferme in France and back to the Statue of Liberty, but the more I learn about the countries of the world and its peoples, the more I am convinced we can live together as brothers if we try.

This war has changed me. I have a renewed faith and confidence. As the fading sound of shells exploding and the rapid blast of machine gun fire echo no more in my mind, I am returning forever to the split-rail fences and open country ready to welcome me home.

I am a new person with new direction and new meaning to my life. I am no longer just a young, mixed-blood Indian.

I am Bertram Robert Dunn of the Choctaw Nation and the United States of America. I am who I was created to be.

My body trembled as we drew close to American soil, a land once populated only with Indian people like my ancestors. A land that now held every nation in the world, including the resilient Choctaw Nation. Before me lay America and the history and future we all shared.

Like the rest of the doughboys, American Indians had gone over there and fought with every weapon we had. I was returning home a *tvshka anumpa*. A language warrior.

It was a good, good day to be Choctaw and American.

THE GREAT WAR'S END

Forest Ferme, France
August 1919

The Aisne River flowed peacefully around the horseshoe bend, sliding through stubble of what was once pasture-land, of what would be pastureland once again someday. The banks of the river had little definition left for the thousands of boots and armament that had scaled them, for the artillery shells that had slammed into them, for the rivulets of blood tracing down them. No cows in the pastures struggling to yield vegetation.

No signs of life.

Standing at an overlook on the outskirts of the tattered village of Voncq, Matthew viewed the river loop, the last bat-tle site where his nephew had fought and—mercifully—survived. On both sides of Matthew, deep scars cut the dirt where a German 15cm schwere Feldhaubitze 13 had been dragged back and forth and finally away for good when Americans in the 36th Division had taken the river loop. From there, the Allies had picked up the pursuit across the river and liberated the village. Forest Ferme was one of the final battles of the war, a turning point, a way of bringing an end to four years of carnage and destruction.

Matthew stood still, feeling the memories of millions throughout the world crying out in pain and fear and praying for the end.

The end had come at last and most everyone had gone home. Except Matthew, and the familiar man driving up the winding road to the top of the high hill where he stood.

He went to the pair of horses he had rented and tucked his tablet in the brown suitcase strapped to the back of one. His photographer friend would have to figure out how to attach his equipment to the other saddle. An automobile couldn't go to the places they wanted to see on this last venture into the former No Man's Land.

The driver eased the automobile into the turnaround as Matthew walked back to the edge of the overlook.

The door of the automobile opened and shut—loud for this day on the quiet outskirts of the village where no one moved about. The war had been over for nine months and many attempted to reclaim their farmland. Even with anticipating a fall harvest of this first crop, heavy loss kept the French people in a daze.

The village's grief was made worse when a young farm boy who had survived the war died in a field while removing unexploded shells. Even after the armistice, the high cost of the war continued.

Tom Alders came up next to Matthew. He'd left his photography gear in the automobile. Like Matthew, he must have felt their reunion after four years of war deserved a sense of solitude and privacy.

They shook hands in greeting but the silence stretched on. Tom would make a good Choctaw. He had a sense for time, for knowing that only when things were ready, should things begin.

A farmer's cart, pulled by a skeletal milk cow led by a young boy, rattled up the incline, giving release to the moment.

"It's not over." Tom reached inside his coat pocket and withdrew a pipe.

He and Matthew had exchanged letters in which they agreed that the Treaty of Versailles only delayed the inevitable. Germany faced poverty and chaos. Bitter roots grew deep for all the countries involved. Europe would face war again someday.

Tom lit his pipe. "Many of those boys will never recover."

Matthew thought of B.B.'s buddy, Noel Johnson. Last he'd heard, the young Choctaw was still in a veteran's hospital in South Carolina, dying of tuberculosis he'd contracted right in the vicinity where Matthew stood. Tom was right. The war wasn't over for all.

But Matthew had looked toward going home for too long to let the uncertain future overcome the bittersweet beauty of the present.

He continued to watch the river for signs of life, for anything to indicate that the land would be restored someday, that nature and people would find their way home.

Matthew sighed. "It's over for now."

Feeling Tom studying him, likely concerned about his physical condition, Matthew turned to him. From a heart that had grown strong again thanks to his daughter, he smiled. "I've recovered from the heart attack. How have you been?"

Tom tapped the burnt tobacco out of his pipe and ground the smoldering ashes with his heel. "I'm coming along. Not sure where in the world I belong now, though."

Matthew shrugged. "Oklahoma's a fresh state."

"Those words you always ended your letters with—what do they mean?"

"*Chi pisa la chike.* I will see you again. We don't say goodbye in my first language."

"You're an Indian?"

Matthew turned fully to Tom and didn't take his eyes off the man's face. Tom had aged considerably in the years of war and too much drink. His crow's feet dove deeper but his eyes still shone with an honesty that masked nothing.

"Choctaw."

"Right. Choctaw. One of the Five Civilized Tribes." Tom flipped his coat back and put one hand on his hip, still facing the sweeping view of the once beautiful countryside. "The world could stand to learn something from your people."

Matthew thought of the hundreds of Indian soldiers he'd met. Only one face came to mind and he smiled. "My nephew did his part." He nodded at the battlefield.

Now B.B. was at seminary, readying himself to preach the gospel. To bring healing to a world torn apart by war and prejudices. He'd already helped by doing his part to end the war so his uncle could go home.

Tom pulled a flask out of his back pocket and offered it to Matthew.

He shook his head. "I don't drink."

"I know. That's why I'm giving it to you. Your letters helped end that war for me."

Matthew took the flask with a nod. He reached inside his coat pocket, hesitated, then withdrew an envelope that held a letter. It offered a small fortune to him if he would make a four hundred mile trip from the North Sea down to Switzerland, tracing the Western Front and writing an epic series for one of the largest newspapers in America.

He handed the envelope to Tom. "Get in touch with Frank Palmer. He'll be happy to partner with you for the trip."

"But…that's why you dragged me back here, to do the story."

"Maybe next time. Though I hope and pray there will never be a next time."

While laid up in the hospital, Matthew had thought the trip was something he needed for healing, to come full circle by joining up with Tom again like those first months of the war, slipping behind German lines in a brazen quest to report the truth. But there was nothing left for Matthew to do in

Europe. It was time to go home, to return to his people and their ongoing struggles. He was ready. But Tom wasn't. He needed to take this journey for healing.

Tom shrugged and coughed. Matthew detected extra vibration in his throat.

No one was immune to the horrific effects of war.

He turned to Tom. "I'll be praying for you, too."

Tom blinked, then squatted, hands on his knees as he squinted at the river loop below them. Matthew spotted them, too, former German concrete bunkers. "I need to photograph those."

"Yes. You do."

That was all Matthew could say. His chest was too tight for anything else.

"Well, look there." Tom straightened and pointed at the river that flowed below where they stood on the high hill.

A single duck waddled down the crumbling bank. Four ducklings followed her, creatures returning to their home.

"I need to get a picture of that." Tom's voice trembled. He didn't move.

Matthew nodded and put a hand over his eyes as the tears flowed. He recalled the feeling of Victoria's soft hand stroking his forehead while he lay in the hospital bed, her murmuring so tenderly in Choctaw, assuring him she would come home often and see him, love him, and make sure he was taking care of himself.

"*Chi pisa la chike*," she'd whispered when they parted. *I will see you again.*

Matthew had thought all his tears were spent, but once Tom let his fall there on the overlook, Matthew couldn't hold back.

"Sirs? Are you all right?"

The two men turned toward the French farm boy standing behind them, hesitantly watching them as he clung to the halter on his skeletal milk cow pulling the empty cart.

Matthew and Tom chuckled. Tom replied in French, "We are well. Go along home now."

Matthew looked back over the river loop, the section where Company E of the 142nd Infantry, 36th Division of cowboys and Indians—Americans—had charged and won their final victory. He planned to write a story just about this battle when he got back to Oklahoma and reopened his *Choctaw Tribune* newspaper. There was power in words.

"*Ome*. We can all go home now."

"The North American Indian took his place beside every other American in offering his life in the great cause, where as a splendid soldier, he fought with the courage and valor of his ancestors."

—General John J. Pershing
September 1920

SHARE THE STORY

Did you know about Choctaw Code Talkers of World War I before you read this book? If not, would you tell someone about their special service? It is my sincere desire that their story be shared with as many people as possible.

One way to share the story is by leaving a review on Goodreads and your favorite online retail store.

It's up to us to tell their story.

Yakoke!

EXCLUSIVE SHORT STORY

Want to experience the sinking of the Lusitania with Matthew Teller? Get onboard the doomed cruise ship and see how he survives in an exclusive short story available only to my newsletter subscribers: www.NativeCodeTalkers.com

THE UNKNOWN CODE TALKER

Mighty Warrior
You served your country
Protected your family
You fought the good fight

Mighty warrior
You did not let fear
Stop your tongue
You were the answer
To your ancestors' prayers

Mighty warrior
We do not know your name
But God knows you are an
Anumpa Warrior

AUTHOR NOTES

Numerous sources mention there were eight Choctaws who were used to transmit messages at Forest Ferme. There are at least three lists that name these men, however, the lists do not match and total 11 men. I chose to use the five photographed at Camp Merritt after the war, plus Ben Carterby and Noel Johnson. For the eighth one, I used B.B. to represent the unknown code talkers. Based on my research, I believe there may have been more used in the combat area.

A great deal of background information on life for Choctaws growing up in the new state of Oklahoma came from *Touched by Greatness: Based on the true story of Charles Watson McGilberry* by Carolee and Wayne Maxwell. They graciously allowed me to use information and actual quotes from Carolee's grandfather, Charles McGilberry, a full-blood Choctaw who attended Mercersburg Academy and went on to be commissioned as a second lieutenant during the war. B.B.'s journal entry in the last chapter was a real piece Charles wrote, combined with a few changes I made to personalize it to B.B. The truck ride from the Newkirk football game was based on Charles' story, though I changed the school from Chilocco Indian School to Armstrong Academy.

My research for this work included the Choctaw Nation Historic Preservation, Genealogy, School of Language, and Historic Projects departments; the Choctaw Code Talkers Association; Dr. William Meadows of Missouri State University; Sequoyah Research Center in Little Rock, Arkansas; National Archives in D.C. and College Park, Maryland; Texas Military Forces Museum; homes of code talker descendants, and hundreds of miles covered in the French countryside, including St. Etienne and Forest Ferme battle sites.

The following characters were fictional: B.B., Matthew, and their family, Isaac Hotinlubbi, Lee Hoade, Samson Coxwell, Sergeant Chill, Ida Claire Jessop, Kent Powell, Tom Alders, and Mr. Watson. There are other minor fictional character sprinkled in, but the remainder of the characters were actual men who served in WWI. Also real was the staff at Armstrong Academy (with the exception of Mr. Watson)—C.E. Fair and Peru Farver. Fans of the *Choctaw Tribune* series, set in 1890s old Choctaw Nation, likely recognized Matthew and Ruth Ann Teller. I was careful to avoid as many spoilers as possible with having them in this story.

Some of the incidents in the story may seem outlandish, however, the vast majority are based on actual stories and quotes from WWI veterans.

Censorship was harsh during WWI with both side barely permitting war correspondents at the front. However, there were a few renegades who broke through at their own risk and did face being arrested or shot.

The food account featuring *tanchi labona*, relayed fictitiously by Ben Carterby, dates back to the 1810s or earlier, and was related by Choctaw elder Dixon Tuckalumbee of Winston County in 1880. The translation is by the recorder, Henry Halbert, as included in *Choctaw Food: Remembering the Land, Rekindling Ancient Knowledge* by Dr. Ian Thompson. Used with permission of the author.

The adventures of Otis Leader—accused of being a spy to chosen as the "ideal American soldier" to his heroism on the battlefield—were based on his journal and newspaper accounts.

Among the tribes credited with Code Talkers in WWI are Cherokee, Eastern Band Cherokee, Cheyenne, Choctaw, Comanche, Osage, Yankton Sioux, and Standing Rock Sioux (Lakota). There were four Choctaws credited with using their language in World War II.

I took a few liberties with the historical timeline in a few instances. The First Oklahoma Infantry actually moved from Fort Sill to Camp Bowie at the end of August. I compressed the timeline and had the move in October. The message B.B. receives from Noel was an actual message I discovered at the National Archives in College Park, Maryland. I moved it to October 26 from the 27 for the purposes of that scene. Based on primary source documentation, I determined the evacuation took place over those two days.

For more extras, including bios, medals, and other recognitions of the Choctaw Code Talkers, and the blog post series of my research trip in France, please visit www.NativeCodeTalkers.com.

You'll also find images of the original memo written by Colonel Alfred Bloor, Captain Elijah W. Horner and James Edwards' reports, newspaper articles, historical photos, and more.

SOURCES

Though this is a work of fiction, I wanted to include a short list of sources:

The Horrors of the Western Front, Original Journal by Otis Leader (Journal of Chickasaw History and Culture)

"Educate or We Perish": The Armstrong Academy's History as Part of the Choctaw Educational System by Dennis Miles (The Chronicles Of Oklahoma)

Story of the 36th: The Experiences of the 36th Division by Capt. Ben H. Chastaine, 142nd Infantry

Panthers to Arrowheads: The 36th (Texas-Oklahoma) Division In World War I by Lonnie J. White

History of the 142nd Infantry of the 36th Division by Chaplain C.H. Barnes

Selected Writings of Capt. Ben D. Locke, Choctaw Humorist, Naturalist, and Soldier of the First World War edited by Cody Lynn Berry and Francine Locke Bray

Touched by Greatness: Based on the true story of Charles Watson McGilberry by Carolee and Wayne Maxwell

Circuits of Victory by Captain A. Lincoln Lavine, Air Service, formerly of the American Telephone and Telegraph Company

American Indians in WWI by Thomas A. Britten

Choctaw Food: Remembering the Land, Rekindling Ancient Knowledge by Dr. Ian Thompson

Choctaw Code Talkers directed and produced by Valerie Red-Horse

Back Over There and *The Last of the Doughboys* by Richard Rubin

…And dozens of primary source documents, military reports, books, newspapers, online history sites, descendant interviews, and more.

FINAL THOUGHTS

The record of Company E and the estimated 12,000 American Indians who served in WWI played a role in granting full United States citizenship to Indians with a congressional act that passed in 1924.

American Indians still volunteer for the armed forces at the highest ratio today.

Glossary of Choctaw Words

Akana: My friend

Chahta sia hoke: I am Choctaw!

Chihowa: God

Chi hullo li: I love you

Chi pisa la chike: I will be seeing you / I will see you again

Chim achukma: How are you?

Chishnato? And you?

Halito: A friendly greeting

Mahli okpulo: bad air or wind

Ome: Expressing a ready assent, agreement or acknowledgment

Peh makachi: Just say it / that

Pokni: Grandmother

Vm achukma: I'm doing well

Vmoshi: my uncle, my mother's brother

Yakoke: Thank you

YAKOKE

This project is the greatest undertaking of my writing career to-date, and there is no possible way I could have made it without an army of support. That said, any errors remaining in the book are my own.

First, I cannot pen a word without staying in prayer and receiving inspiration from my heavenly Father through a personal relationship with Jesus Christ.

Second, I'm thankful for every miracle, every person on this journey. Here's my heartiest "yakoke," thank you for sticking with me:

My bestest friend, mentor, editor, and the one who lifted me off the floor when I couldn't bear to think of the black hole of research I'd fallen into with this project. She listened to me ramble for hours at the breakfast table or in the van about random plot points, exciting discoveries in research, embarrassing mistakes, and heart-rending decisions. She hammered character issues, cultural points, and realistic portrayals while keeping me encouraged throughout the hard editing process. This book would not be what it is or even be in your hands without her— my mama, Lynda Kay Sawyer. *Chi hullo li.*

People do judge a book by its cover, and this one turned out epic thanks to the heart effort of these folks: photograph by Lynda Kay Sawyer of my brother, Jon (Johnny) Sawyer, a handsome Choctaw to represent the original code talkers. He wore 100% authentic WWI uniform and gear generously loaned by Paul Porter, WWI collector and living history presenter—wool winter uniform coat, breeches, puttees, cartridge belt, trench knife, canteen, gas mask case, steel Brody helmet, and rare U.S. 1917 field phone. Most, if not all, of the gear was worn in France by real doughboys. Kelly and Matthew Dale provided lighting assistance and the use of the family's photo studio. The cover was dynamically brought to life by Kirk DouPonce (DogEaredDesign.com). I'm thrilled to pieces with every detail Kirk put into the design.

God brought Mollie Reeder (www.writeratops.com) into my life as a close friend—a sister—at the moment I needed. She prayed over and talked me through plot and character problems, discouragement, fatigue, and was the greatest cheerleader. She was the first reader on the project and helped me re-structure the story from the beginning, and did one of the final edits on the book.

Catherine Frappier, a talented young writer, gave me a tremendously detailed edit that helped this story sing to life. And make sense!

Judy Allen, Choctaw Nation Historic Projects Officer, provided her database of Choctaw Code Talker history with photos, newspaper clippings, personal stories, military reports, and descendant names. We worked through misreported information as I tried to piece together the story as best as possible with scant and contradictory records from 100 years ago.

Dr. Ian Thompson, director of the Choctaw Nation Historic Preservation Department and author of *Choctaw Food: Remembering the Land, Rekindling Ancient Knowledge* allowed me to read his manuscript before publication, which inspired the traditional foods I included in the novel. He also directed me to *Touched by Greatness: Based on the true story of Charles Watson McGilberry* which provided background information I needed. I met the authors, Carolee and Wayne Maxwell, and I am so grateful for their permission to use Charles' writings.

Choctaw historian Francine Locke Bray and her husband Michael have supported my work for years. Francine shared early drafts of the book she is editing about her uncle, Ben D. Locke. Mr. Michael helped dig out Major Morrissey's military record and reports on the NARA I hadn't found.

Elizabeth M. B. Bass, Director of Publications at the Oklahoma Historical Society, sent me an article previously published by The Chronicles of Oklahoma about Armstrong Academy.

Suzanne Heard and Melissa Shelton at Jones Academy answered questions about early boarding school history.

Overhearing Eric Reed (Choctaw) telling a story of hunting with a rabbit stick inspired me to include the rabbit stick hunt in the novel, especially when I read about Armstrong boys doing the same.

Regina Green, director at the Choctaw Nation Museum, supported the project with resources and made room near Otis Leader's service cap for the replica painting we brought back from France. (More on NativeCodeTalkers.com)

Much appreciation to the Choctaw Nation School of Choctaw Language: Translation Specialist and first speaker Dora Wickson took the time to translate an actual military message I found at the National Archives and Records Administration at College Park, Maryland, from English to Choctaw. She also provided the sentence translations and wrote the prayer in English and Choctaw in the opening scene of the book. Language Instructor and code talker descendant Chantelle Standefer read an early draft of the manuscript and helped resolve language issues. Teri Billy, Assistant Director, answered last minute questions on the language.

I had tremendous help and support from members and officers within the Choctaw Code Talkers Association:

Nuchi Nashoba, Ben Carterby's granddaughter and current president of the association, spent time sharing an overview of the code talker experience and encouraged me with her desire to see the story brought to life.

Chester Cowen shared historical details and helped me connect with descendants.

Lee Hester gave me military background and an inside look at what the Choctaws experienced in training.

Beth Lawless, granddaughter of Tobias Frazier, brought me into her world of family and historical preservation. Her humility is inspiring.

Evangeline Wilson founded the association. Her father, Johnson Wilson Bobb—cousins with Mitchell Bobb—served in WWI, and James Edwards was her uncle Jim. I named the fictional main character in the book Bertram Robert (B.B.) in honor of Evangeline's brother and our former chaplain of the Choctaw Nation, Brother Bertram Bobb. He advocated for the recognition of the Choctaw Code Talkers in the halls of congress. Yakoke to her daughter, Cynthia Wilson, for hosting my interview with Evangeline.

The Choctaw Code Talkers Association has worked tirelessly in gaining recognition nationally and internationally for the special work these men performed. From monuments to renaming bridges in Oklahoma for each code talker, the association isn't slowing down. You can support their work through membership and donations.

At the Sequoyah Research Center in Little Rock, Arkansas, Dr. Daniel Littlefield and Erin Fehr were a wealth of resources for Indian soldiers in WWI and generously shared information about Captain Elijah W. Horner. Erin arranged for me to join her in interviewing Horner's daughter, Kathryn Widder, where we collected yet more information on him and the Choctaw Code Talkers. Kathryn, at 91 years old, also shared precious memories of her father.

Dr. William C. Meadows, Missouri State University and Code Talker scholar, was one of my first contacts in this project and shared background information on the 36th Division and his findings about the Choctaw Code Talkers based on his previous articles and testimony given before congress. We continued sharing resources and information throughout our book projects.

Deputy Director of The Texas Military Forces Museum Lisa Sharik went over details of 36th history and shared digital copies of rare books and records that I lacked.

Andrew Woods, Research Historian at the First Division Museum at Cantigny Park, shared colorful details through articles and photos of the 1st Division and helped with the actual route Otis Leader took through Paris in the July 4th 1917 parade.

My cousin and fellow Choctaw writer, Stacy Wells, connected me with the WWI centennial commission in Fort Worth which led to a wealth of assistance through Anita Robeson. Stacy also provided valuable feedback on early manuscript drafts.

Rudy Bowling and Jon M. Poort of the No. 1 British Flying Training School Museum supported the project with historical details.

I appreciate long-time family friend Elaine Alvarado for supporting the search for gear when we were doing the photo shoot, and for sharing her box full of WWI books!

Kenny Sivard with the Oklahoma Historical Society shared research on Choctaw and early Oklahoma history that I used in the book.

Lisa Reed at Choctaw Nation invited me to write an article about my research trip to France, and directed me to Stacy Hutto, current editor of the *Biskinik*, our tribal newspaper. I appreciated her willingness to work with my robust word count.

Author Travis Perry helped clear up military rank and other details.

Vicki Prough in the Choctaw Nation Membership Department shared her collection of Choctaw Code Talkers research with me, including Noel Johnson's death certificate from South Carolina, which cleared up misunderstandings about his death.

Christopher Zellner at the Chickasaw Holisso Research Center sent me a digital copy of Otis Leader's journal, which I used to recreate his phenomenal story.

Tia Carter and her father, Charles DeWeese, inherited many of Otis Leader's papers, including his discharge papers. I appreciate them allowing us to photograph them, and that they decided to donate them to the Choctaw Nation Museum.

Brett J. Derbes, Managing Editor of the Handbook of Texas, sent me military reports with valuable details.

One of the greatest honors I had in this project was talking with descendants of the code talkers themselves. In addition to ones mentioned previously, I appreciate those who took time to share with me over the phone or by email:

Michael Louis, grandson of Solomon Bond Louis.
Alicia Dickerson, niece of Mary Louis, Solomon's wife.
Bruce Barnes, grandson of Benjamin (Bennie) Hampton.
Deloris Marshall, granddaughter of Bennie Hampton.

LeRoy Billy, grandson of Albert Billy.

Lila Swink, relative of Walter Veach.

Tewanna Edwards shared a boxful of papers she collected about her great-uncle Otis Leader, and a heart-full of stories from when she knew him like a grandfather.

Denny and Bridgett Huebshman have supported me from my first published flash fiction, and I was honored when Denny shared about his beloved grandfather, who was also in WWI. Ernst Gustav Hubschmann was a German soldier who survived the war, and later moved to America with his wife and son.

The research/realness for this project exploded when I traveled to France. My heartiest appreciation to all those who made it possible:

I assisted Tiajuana Cochnauer during her presentation of the Choctaw Code Talkers of World War I story at the National Association for Interpretation's international conference in Reims, France. Then we hit the road for research to the battlefields where the Choctaws fought and became language warriors. Though I'd met Tiajuana before, it was her cousin, Janice Dyer Whaling, who put us in touch for the trip.

Linda Teel was the first to give me travel tips and soothe my mama's concerns about my first overseas trip. She got me started with a contribution and a lesson in euros! Shelia Kirven and Verree Shaw armed me with extra flags and lapel pins in the Choctaw Nation Marketing Department for me to gift in France. Lorie Carmichael (Chickasaw Nation) gave me invaluable travel tips that helped keep me healthy and rested. Crystal Bully at the Choctaw Nation graciously helped with my application for support from the Choctaw Nation. Donna and Patrick Jackson of North Augusta, South Carolina, offered travel tips and an excellent recommendation for lodging safely and centrally in Paris. Dennis Harkins recommended Richard Rubin's *Back Over There* which became my guidebook for the trip.

James S. Bertelson, assistant superintendent at the Meuse-Argonne American Cemetery, sent me a list of local guides. We connected with two of them: Jean-Paul de Vries welcomed us into his private museum in Romagne and invited us on a hike into the woods with a visiting class of Dutch students. Roger Cook—Meuse-Argonne historian, author, translator and tour guide—took us on a grand WWI adventure in his blue cabriolet for an incredible three days. I do not think we would have located and obtained permission to set foot on Forest Ferme (still in operation) nor made it up to the overlook at Voncq without his dedicated research, connections, and navigation.

Bruce Malone, superintendent of the Meuse-Argonne American

Cemetery, spent time with us discussing WWI history and little known battle stories. He also reviewed an early draft of the manuscript for Army accuracy.

Jeffrey Hays, superintendent of the Saint-Mihiel American Cemetery, gave us a tour of the cemetery, stunning chapel, and created a highlight moment when he asked if we wanted to help fold the American flags at the end of the day.

Without Jeffrey Aarnio's (formerly with the American Battle Monuments Commission) connections, I highly doubt we could have viewed and obtained permission to replicate the portrait of Otis Leader located in Musée de l'Armée in Hôtel national des Invalides. Jeffrey also offered much needed travel and navigation advice which helped the process go smoothly. He had told the story of the Choctaw Code Talkers of World War I for many years in France, making their service a part of the ABMC narrative. He also read an early draft of the manuscript and offered invaluable input.

Laëtitia Desserrieres of the Musée de l'Armée made us welcome as she showed us the original portrait by Raymond Desvarreux. She also shared details about the painter. Sylvie Le Ray-Burimi helped arrange the meeting, and authorized the use of the digital copy for a replica.

After our return, Tiajuana and I presented the replica to the Choctaw Nation, a long-time dream come true for me. Connie Rule (Connie's Framing) had graciously donated the framing work on the canvas replica.

Though I missed connecting with Vincent Hazard, who was doing a radio program on Joseph Oklahombi the week before our trip, he later connected me with French author Thomas Grillot. He shared some history I've not seen anywhere else.

Randy Gaulke—WWI historian, France battlefield tour guide, and re-enactor—helped with historical photos of Forest Ferme and St. Etienne.

Recalling the miracles on this journey, I want to thank the prayer warriors who uplifted me throughout this draining process:

The Reeder family—James, Karla, and Mollie—prayed for me throughout this process. They also braved a late-night drive through Dallas to pick me up at the airport after I landed from the France trip. Some of James' spiritual messages found their way into the book.

Early in this journey, Pollie Labor called me a "warrior" for my people. You have no idea how those few words inspired me.

Being avid fans of the *Choctaw Tribune* series, Mark and Deborah Potts share my books with others and encourage me continually. I felt so blessed when they came to my house right before the trip and prayed over me.

I would like to recognize dedicated staff at the Chahta Foundation for their support:

Executive director Seth Fairchild arranged for me to view and photograph the Walter Veach letters that had recently been donated to the Foundation's care. Seth also connected me with funding options for my France research trip.

Scholarship specialist Scott Wesley sent me videos of Ruth Frazier's interview about her father, Tobias Frazier. I'm so grateful Scott recorded the stories before her passing.

Program specialist Martha Lowery helped with travel advice and made me realize the importance of including French food details in the story!

Employees at the Choctaw Store work hard to promote Choctaw artists, and I'm honored every time they recommend my books or feature me in the store. Special thanks to Carolyn, Randall, Jeannie, and Steve.

Writing mentors Scott and Sandi Tompkins recorded and saved a WWI special for me to watch that featured the Choctaw Code Talkers.

I appreciate illustrator Nola Song jumping in and getting the map done. Superb!

Choctaw artist Paul King's work inspires me with the grit and heart of the Choctaw soldiers shown through his incredible paintings and illustrations. I appreciate him allowing me to use one on the title page.

I had over 15 dedicated readers who checked early drafts of the manuscript for historical, cultural, and military accuracy. Those I haven't recognized yet:

Jennifer Wingard, Choctaw friend and fellow writer, has an eye for details and caught things that made it through many previous edits.

Constant Lebastard, of the ABMC, graciously agreed to review the manuscript and provide feedback from a French perspective.

Ryan Spring and Jennifer Byram in the Choctaw Nation Historic Preservation department were both huge supports during this process, and I especially appreciated Jennifer's feedback on the manuscript.

Finally, I want to thank each of you who financially supported my France research trip. I'm not exaggerating when I say it would not have happened without you! I didn't have a research trip to France budgeted, but my brother, Doug Davis, encouraged me to do a crowdfunding campaign. Wonderful friends and readers came together to help. Here are my extraordinary Go Fund Me donors:

FAN
Howard Schneider
Maria Arcara
Sue Schooler

HISTORY LOVER
Linda Teel
Karen Ross
Dan Hunt
Patricia Wilson
Scotta Petmecky
Elaine Alvarado
Barbara Vandever
Carolyn Fowler
Margo Williams
Laura Ferris

HISTORY NUT
Elizabeth Pietzsch
Robbie Farley
Jennifer Hickman
Michael Cathey
Mark Smith
Scott & Sandi Tompkins

PRESERVATIONIST
Bryan Varney
Tewanna Edwards
Brenda Williams
Beverly Allen
Mark and Deborah Potts
Linda Whale
Robert Brooks

Some donors marked their contributions as private. To respect that, they are not listed. But you know who you are, and this is my thanks to you!

I tried to keep track of every person who helped with this epic project, but I'm bound to have missed someone.

This is for you. Yakoke.

SARAH ELISABETH SAWYER is an award-winning inspirational author, speaker and Choctaw storyteller of traditional and fictional tales based on the lives of her people. The Smithsonian's National Museum of the American Indian has honored her as a literary artist through their Artist Leadership Program for her work in preserving Trail of Tears stories. In 2015, First Peoples Fund awarded her an Artist in Business Leadership Fellowship. She writes from her hometown in Texas, partnering with her mother, Lynda Kay Sawyer, in continued research for future novels. Learn more about their work in preserving Choctaw history:

SarahElisabethWrites.com

Facebook.com/SarahElisabethSawyer

Also by Sarah Elisabeth Sawyer

CHOCTAW TRIBUNE SERIES:

THE EXECUTIONS (Book 1)

TRAITORS (Book 2)

Other works:

TOUCH MY TEARS:
TALES FROM THE TRAIL OF TEARS

TUSHPA'S STORY
(Touch My Tears Collection)

THIRD SIDE OF THE COIN
(A Short Story Collection)

CPSIA information can be obtained
at www.ICGtesting.com
Printed in the USA
LVHW031604130521
687356LV00001B/131